Philip K. Dick was born in Chicago in 1928 and lived most of his life in California. He attended college for a year at Berkeley. Apart from writing, his main interest was music: at one time he ran a record shop and also a classical music programme for a local radio station. He won the Hugo Award for his classic novel of alternative history, *The Man in the High Castle* (1962). He was married five times and had three children. He died in March 1982.

'Dick quietly produced serious fiction in a popular form and there can be no greater praise'
Michael Moorcock

'One of the most original practitioners writing any kind of fiction, Philip K. Dick made most of the European avant-garde seem navel-gazers in a cul-de-sac'
Sunday Times

'No other writer of his generation had such a powerful intellectual presence. He has stamped himself not only on our memories but in our imaginations'
Brian Aldiss

PHILIP K. DICK

In Milton Lumky Territory

PALADIN
GRAFTON BOOKS
A Division of the Collins Publishing Group

LONDON GLASGOW
TORONTO SYDNEY AUCKLAND

Paladin
Grafton Books
A Division of the Collins Publishing Group
8 Grafton Street, London W1X 3LA

Published in Paladin Books 1987

First published in Great Britain by
Victor Gollancz Ltd 1985

ISBN 0-586-08602-1

Printed and bound in Great Britain by
Collins, Glasgow

Set in Times

Author's Foreword:

This is actually a very funny book, and a good one, too, in that the funny things that happen happen to real people who come alive. The ending is a happy one. What more can an author say? What more can he give?

In Milton Lumky Territory

1

AT SUNSET, acrid-smelling air from the lake puffed along the empty streets of Montario, Idaho. With the air appeared clouds of sharp-winged yellow flies; they smashed against the windshields of cars in motion. The drivers strove to clear them away with their wipers. As the street lights lit up Hill Street, stores began to close until only the drugstores — one at each end of town — remained open. The Luxor movie theater did not open until six-thirty. The several cafes did not count as parts of the town; open or shut, they belonged to the highway, US 95, which made use of Hill Street.

Hooting and clacking and sliding along the northernmost of fourteen parallel tracks, the Union Pacific sleeper appeared, passing from Portland to Boise. It did not stop, but at the Hill Street crossing it slowed until the mail car appeared to be a dingy-green metal building among the brick warehouses along the track, scarcely in motion, with its doors open and two trainmen in striped suits hanging out with their hands dangling down. A middle-aged woman, wrapped up in quilted wool to keep warm, stepped forward at the sidewalk and deftly handed several letters up to one of the trainmen.

The wig-wag signal bonged and the red light flashed for a considerable period after the last car of the train had gone off out of sight.

At the lunch counter in his drugstore, Mr. Hagopian ate a small fried hamburger steak and canned string beans while he read a copy of *Confidential* taken from the rack by the front door. Now, at six, no customers bothered him. He sat so that he could see the street outside. If anyone came along he intended to stop eating and wipe his mouth and hands with a paper napkin.

Far off, running and whirling about to run backwards with his head up, came a boy wearing a Davy Crockett cap with tail. The boy circled his way across the street, and Mr. Hagopian realized that he was coming into the drugstore.

The boy, hands in his pockets, his motions stiff and jerky, stepped into the store and to the candy bars all intermingled under the sign, 3 for 25¢. Mr. Hagopian continued eating and reading. The boy at last picked out a box of Milk Duds, a package of M & M chocolates, and a Hershey bar.

"Fred," Mr. Hagopian called.

His son Fred pushed the curtains aside, from the back room, and came out to wait on the boy.

At seven o'clock Mr. Hagopian said to his son Fred, "You might as well go on home. There won't be enough more tonight to make it worth both our time." He felt irritable, thinking about it. "Nobody of consequence is going to show up and buy anything the rest of tonight."

"I'll stick around awhile longer," Fred said. "I don't have anything to do anyhow."

The telephone rang. It was Mrs. de Rouge, on Pine Street, wanting a prescription filled and delivered. Mr. Hagopian got out the book, and when he looked up the number he found that it was for Mrs. de Rouge's pain pills. So he told her that Fred would bring them by eight o'clock.

While he was making up the pills — capsules of codeine — the door of the drugstore opened and a young man, well-dressed in a single-breasted suit and tie, stepped in. He had a sandy, bony nose and short-cropped hair; by that, Mr. Hagopian recognized him, and also by his smile. He had good strong white teeth.

"Can I help you, sir?" Fred said.

"Just looking right now," the man said. Hands in his pockets he moved over to the magazine racks.

I wonder why he hasn't been in here for awhile, Mr. Hagopian thought to himself. He used to come in here all the time. Since he was a kid. Has he been taking his business up to Wickley's? At that, the old man felt growing indignation. He finished up Mrs. de Rouge's pills, dropped them into a bottle, and walked to the counter.

The young man, Skip Stevens, had brought a copy of *Life* up to Fred, and was rummaging in his trouser pocket for change.

"Anything else, sir?" Fred said.

Mr. Hagopian started to speak to Skip Stevens, but at that moment Skip leaned toward Fred and said in a low voice, "Yes, I wanted to pick up a package of Trojans." So Mr. Hagopian delicately turned away and busied himself until Fred had wrapped the package of contraceptives and rung up the sale on the register.

"Thank you sir," Fred said, in the business-like tone he always took when somebody bought contraceptives. As he left the counter he winked at his father.

His magazine under his arm, Skip started toward the door, very slowly, eyeing the magazines and shelves to show that he did not feel intimidated. Mr. Hagopian caught up with him and said, "Long time no see." His indignation made his voice rattle. "I hope you and your family have been well."

"Everybody's fine," Skip said. "I haven't seen them for a couple of months. I'm living down in Reno. I have a job there."

"Oh," Mr. Hagopian said, not believing him. "I see."

Fred tilted his head, listening.

"You remember Skip Stevens," Mr. Hagopian said to his son.

"Oh yeah," Fred said. "I didn't recognize you." He nodded at Skip. "Haven't seen you in months."

"I'm located down in Reno now," Skip explained. "This is the first time I've been up here to Montario since April."

"I wondered why we hadn't seen you," Fred said.

Mr. Hagopian asked Skip, "Your brother still off back east at school?"

"No," Skip said. "He's out of school now, and married."

This boy isn't living down in Reno, Mr. Hagopian thought. He's just ashamed to admit why he hasn't been in. Skip shifted about from one foot to the other, obviously ill-at-ease. He obviously wanted to leave.

"What line of work are you in?" Fred said.

Skip said, "I'm a buyer."

"What kind of buyer?"

"For C.B.B.," he said.

"Television?" Mr. Hagopian said.

"For Consumers' Buying Bureau," Skip said.

"What's that?"

Skip said, "Something like a department store. It's a new place down on Highway 40, between Reno and Sparks."

With a strange look on his face, Fred said, "I know what that is. Some guy was up here telling me about it." To his father, he said, "It's one of those discount houses."

At first, the old man did not understand. And then he remembered what he had heard about discount houses. "Do you want to drive the retailers out of business?" he said loudly to Skip.

Skip, turning red, said, "It's no different from a supermarket. It buys in volume and passes the savings on to the consumer. That's how Henry Ford operated, producing in volume."

"It's not the American way," Mr. Hagopian said.

"Sure it is," Skip said. "It means a higher standard of living because it eliminates overhead and the middleman's costs."

Mr. Hagopian returned to the counter. To his son he said, "Mrs. de Rouge wants some more pain pills." He held out the bottle, and Fred accepted it. "I told her before eight."

He did not care to talk to Skip Stevens any further. Competing with Chinese and Japs was bad enough. To him, the big new discount houses seemed worse; they pretended to be American — they had neon signs and they advertised and they had parking lots, and unless you knew what they were they did look like supermarkets. He did not know who ran them. Nobody ever saw the owners of discount houses. In fact, he himself had never even seen a discount house.

"It doesn't cut into your business," Skip said, following after Fred as he wrapped Mrs. de Rouge's package. "Nobody drives five hundred miles to shop, even for major items like furniture."

Mr. Hagopian made out a tag while his son wrapped.

Skip said, "It's only in big cities anyhow. This town isn't large enough. Boise might be."

Neither Fred nor his father said anything. Fred put on his coat, got the tag from his father, and left the drugstore.

The old man busied himself with sorting different articles that had been delivered during the day. Presently the door closed after Skip Stevens.

* * * * *

As he drove along the unlighted residential streets of Montario, over the gravel that served as pavement, Bruce Stevens thought about old Hagopian, whom he had encountered now and again all his life. Years ago, the old man had chased him away from the comic books and out the front door of the drugstore. For months Hagopian had simmered in silence as the children, scrunched down behind the shelf of mineral oil bottles, had read Tip Top Comics and King Comics and seldom if ever bought anything. Then he had made up his mind and gone at the first child who next put in an appearance. It had been Bruce Stevens; Skip Stevens in those days, because of his bright round freckled face and reddish hair. The old man still called him "Skip." What a heck of a world, Bruce thought, as he watched the houses. I made him sore then, and he's still sore. It's a wonder he didn't call the police when I bought the box of Trojans.

But the old man's outrage toward the idea of him working for a discount house in Reno did not bother him, because he knew how the little retailers felt; they had felt that way when the first supermarkets had opened just after World War Two. And in some respects their animosity delighted him. It proved that people were beginning to buy from discount houses, or at least were beginning to be aware of them.

It's the coming thing, he told himself once again. Another ten years and nobody'll think to pick up razor blades one day and soap the next; they'll shop for everything one day of the week, in a place where they can get any kind of thing there is, from phonograph records to autos.

But then it occurred to him that he hadn't bought his package of contraceptives back in Reno, but here in a small drugstore, at full retail price. In fact he did not even know if the discount people for whom he worked stocked contraceptives.

And a magazine, too, he realized. To hide his actual intentions. Whenever he had bought contraceptives he felt embarrassed. The clerk behind the counter always gave him a bad time. Dropping the little metal tin so people would glance over to see. Or calling from the length of the store, "Which did you ask for, Trojans or —" whatever the other brand was. Sheiks or something. Since his nineteenth year, the first year he had started carrying contraceptives around with him, he had stuck to Trojans. That's America, he said to himself. Buy by brand. Know your product.

His trip up from Reno was to end in Boise, but passing through his home town he had decided to stop off and perhaps drop in on a girl he had gone around with, the year before. He could easily get back on the road the next morning; Boise was only fifteen miles northeast, on US Highway 95, up from Nevada. Or, if things didn't work out, he could continue on tonight.

He was twenty-four years old. He liked his job at C.B.B., which did not pay too much — about three hundred a month — but which gave him a chance to get out on the road in his '55 Merc, and to meet people and bargain with them, to snoop into different establishments with the keen inner urge for discovery. And he liked his boss, Ed von Scharf, who had a big black Ronald Colman mustache and who had been a sergeant in the Marine Corps in World War Two, when Bruce had been eight years old.

And he liked living by himself in an apartment in Reno, away from his parents and away from an essentially farming-town in a potato-growing state that had lettered on its highways: DON'T BE A GUBERIF, which meant "don't be a firebug," and which always infuriated him when he drove onto one of them. From Reno he could get easily over the Sierras into California, or the other direction to Salt Lake City for whatever that was worth. The air in Nevada was cleaner, lacking the heavy brackish fog that rolled into Montario carrying the flies that he had stepped on and inhaled all his life.

Now, on the hood, bumpers, fenders, and windshield of his car, hundreds of those same flies lay squashed and dead. They had fouled the radiator. Their thin hairy bodies dotted his field of vision and made the finding of Peg's house that much harder.

At last he recognized it, by the wide lawn and porch and tree. There were lights on inside. And several cars were parked nearby.

When he had parked, and was stepping up onto the porch to ring the bell, he heard unmistakable sounds of music and people from inside the house. There goes that, he said to himself as he rang.

The door flew open. Peg recognized him, gasped, raised her hands and then slid aside and drew him into the house. "What a surprise! Of all people!"

In the living room a number of persons sat about with drinks, listening to the phonograph playing Johnny Ray records. Three or four men and as many women.

"I guess I should have phoned," he said.

"No," she said. "You know you're welcome." Her face sparkled, small and round and smooth. She had on an orange blouse and a dark skirt, and her hair was fluffed up and soft-looking. To him, she seemed quite pretty, and he longed to kiss her. But several of the people had craned their necks, smiling tentatively in welcome, so he did not.

"Did you just drive in right now?" she asked.

"Yes," he said. "I got on the road about seven this morning. Made good time. Around seventy, mostly."

"You must be real tired. Have you had dinner?"

"I pulled off for awhile around five," he said. "I never feel too hungry when I'm on the road.

"Don't you want something now?" She led him down the hall, past the living room and into the kitchen. Spread out on the tile drainboard were a bowl of ice cubes, bottles of ginger ale and bitters, lemon rind, a full bottle of cheap bourbon. Opening the refrigerator she said, "Let me fix you something hot to eat; I know you only get a sandwich and a shake when you're driving. I remember." She began carrying dishes of food to the table.

"Honestly," he said. "Listen." He stopped her. "I'll just shove along. I have to make Boise. There's some business I have to conduct there, tomorrow."

Halting, she said, "How's your job?"

"Not bad," he said.

Peg said, "Come on in the other room and let me introduce you to people."

"I'm too tired," he said.

"Just for a few minutes. They saw you come in. They're just friends who stopped over. We ate in Boise. We had a Chinese dinner. Noodles and duck, and pork chow mein. They drove me home."

"I don't want to intrude."

"You're just being a martyr. You should have called me." Shutting the refrigerator she came toward him with her arms out, allowing him to take hold of her and kiss her. "You know how long it's been since we had time to be together. Maybe I can get rid of them. They'll probably leave soon anyhow. Stay for a little while, and I'll sort of start talking about work tomorrow."

"No," he said. But he let her lead him down the hall and back to the living room. She was right; it had been a long time since last time, and in his eight or nine months in Reno he had not yet met a girl and gotten to know her well enough. That well. So in that eight or nine months he hadn't had any. Now, after kissing her, and feeling her small damp warm fingers wrapped about his wrist, he began to require. It was one thing merely to be without it, and another thing to have it before him, available.

At a glance he recognized the people as clerkish types from the office building at which Peg worked. They had that thin, indoor look, and at the same time what he thought of as the Idaho Look. By that he meant a kind of slowness. A lapse of time between hearing and understanding, a measurable interval. Watching them, he could see the gradual course of response. They just plain did not get with it. Even the simplest things had to be mulled over, and the hard things — well, the hard things had never gotten up into Idaho and never would. So it was no problem.

"This is Bruce Stevens," Peg said, to them in general. "He just got in from Reno; he's been on the road all day long."

By the time she had introduced him to the last person he had already forgotten the name of the first one. And by the time she had fixed him a drink, bourbon and ice, he had forgotten all their names. They had gone back to listening to the phonograph, so it made no difference. A conversation went on, too, something that had to do with Russian attempts to reach the moon, and were the planets inhabited. He seated himself with his drink, as near Peg as possible.

The thin, indoor clerks chatted and ignored him. He kept his eyes fixed on Peg, wondering if and drinking his drink. And, while he did that, the door to the bathroom opened at the far end of the house, and a woman came along the hall and into the living room. He had not seen her before; evidently she had been in there since his arrival. Looking up, he saw a dark-haired older woman, very attractive, wearing a white scarf around her neck and great ring-like earrings. With a swirl of skirts she seated herself on the arm of the couch, and he saw that she had on sandals. Her legs were bare. She smiled at him.

"I just got here," he said.

"Oh, Susan," Peg said, coming to life. "Susan, this is Bruce Stevens. Bruce, I want you to meet Susan Faine."

He said hello.

"Hello," Susan Faine said. That was all she said. Ducking her head, she joined with the others in their conversation, as if it had been going on when she had left the room. Probably it had been. He watched the way her hair, tied back in a pony-tail, swung from side to side. Besides a long skirt she wore a leather belt, very wide, with a coppery-looking buckle, and a black sweater. On her right shoulder a silver pin had been pinned. Studying it he decided that it was Mexican. And the sandals, too, perhaps. The more he looked at her, the more attractive she seemed.

In his ear, Peg said, "Susan just got back from Mexico City. She got a divorce down there."

"Oh yeah," he said, nodding. "I'll be darned."

He kept on watching her, holding his drink glass up so that he appeared — or hoped he appeared — to be inspecting it. Her hands had a strong, competent manner, and he guessed that she did something manual. Beneath her black sweater he could see the straps of her bra, and, when she bent over, a bit of bare back between the top of her skirt and the sweater.

Suddenly she turned her head, conscious that he was watching her. She looked at him so intently that he could not stand it; he ceased to watch her and let his gaze wander off blankly, feeling his cheeks flush at the same time. Then she went back to talking with those on the couch.

To Peg, he said, "Miss or Mrs.?"

"Who?"

"Her," he said, indicating Susan Faine with his glass.

"I just said she got a divorce," Peg said.

"That's right," he said. "I remember now that you did. What's she do? What line is she in?"

"She runs a typewriter rental service," Peg said. "And she does typing and mimeographing. She does work for us." By that she meant the firm of lawyers that employed her as a secretary.

Susan Faine said, "Talking about me?"

"Yes," Peg said. "Bruce asked what you do."

"I understand you just got back from Mexico," Bruce said.

"Yes," Susan Faine said, "but that's not what I do." The people took that as funny and laughed. "Not exactly," she added. "In spite of what you may possibly hear."

She hopped down from the arm of the couch, then, and went off into the kitchen with her empty glass. One of the thin clerkish-looking men arose and followed her.

As he sipped his drink, Bruce thought, I know her. I've seen her before.

He tried to remember where.

"Don't you want me to hang your coat up?" Peg said to him.

"Thanks," he said. Preoccupied, he set his drink down, got up, and unbuttoned his coat. As she took it and carried it to the hall closet he followed after her. "I think I know that woman," he said.

"Do you?" Peg said. She fixed the coat around a hanger, and while she was doing that one of those things happened that no man can anticipate and few can live through. From the pocket of the coat the box of Trojans, in its Hagopian's Drug and Pharmacy bag, fell out and onto the carpet.

"What's this?" Peg said, stooping to pick it up. "So small."

Of course Fred Hagopian had wrapped the tin so that it came easily out of the bag, visible to all. Seeing it, Peg got a weird, frigid expression on her face. Without a word she returned the tin to the bag and the bag to the coat pocket. Closing the closet door she said, "Well, I see you came prepared."

He wished he had driven on through to Boise.

"You always were so optimistic," Peg said. "But they last, don't they? I mean, they're good any time." Returning to the living room she said over her shoulder, "I don't want you to have wasted your investment."

"What investment is that?" one of the dull figures on the couch asked.

Neither he nor Peg said anything. And this time he did not trouble to sit near her. Certainly, it was hopeless now. He sat drinking his drink and wondering how to leave.

2

AN OPPORTUNITY to leave occurred almost at once. Across from him a small bald-headed clerk arose from the couch and declared that he had to get started home, by bus.

Bruce, also standing, said, "I'll give you a lift. I'm going on to Boise anyhow."

Nobody protested. Peg nodded good-bye and disappeared into the kitchen as he and Mr. Muir started from the house.

It took some time, after they had gotten to Boise, to locate Mr. Muir's street. The man, not being a motorist himself, had little idea of direction. After he had let him off at last, Bruce started back onto the highway, searching for a motel. And then, just as he made out a fair-looking motel, he realized that he had left his coat hanging in the hall closet back at Peg's. His shame had caused him to strike it from his mind.

Should I go back for it? he asked himself.

Should I not?

Stopping at the side of the road, he looked at his watch. After nine o'clock. It would be nine-thirty by the time he got back to Montario. Better to wait until tomorrow? He had to have it; he couldn't show up for his business appointment without it.

Tomorrow, he decided, Peg would start off early for work. If he missed her, he would not see his coat again.

Starting up the car, he made a U-turn and drove back in the direction that he had come.

THE CARS that had been parked near her house had gone. And the lights had been shut off. The house, dark and shut-up, had a deserted look. He hurried up the path to the porch and rang the bell.

No one answered.

He rang again. Experience told him, first, that no one even in Montario went to bed at nine-thirty, and second, that the party could not have broken up so fast. They might have all gone off somewhere else, to another house. Or to Hill Street for something or other, a second dinner, or beer at one of the bars, or God knew.

But in any case his coat was in the house. Trying the door, he found it locked. So he went around the familiar path, through the gate, to the back. The laundry room window had been propped open; he remembered it. Setting a box against the house he managed to get the window open, and then himself through it, hands-first, to sprawl onto the floor of the laundry room.

One light guided him, the bathroom light. He made his way down the hall, to the closet, opened it and found his coat. Thank God, he thought. He put it on and then entered the living room.

A smell of cigarettes hung over the living room. An odd lonely empty place, with the people gone . . . the warmth and reminders of them, crumpled cigarette package in an ashtray, glasses, even an earring on the end-table. As if they had gone up in smoke, like elves. Ready to return as soon as mortals − himself, for instance − had turned their back. Standing, listening, he heard a hum.

The phonograph has been left on. Its tiny red light shone as he lifted the lid to shut it off. So evidently they hadn't intended to be gone very long, or they had rushed out on the spur of the moment.

The mystery of the abandoned sailing ship, he thought, as he wandered into the kitchen. Food on the table . . . on the drainboard the bottle of bourbon, now only half-full, remained. The bowl of now-melted ice cubes. Lemon rind. More empty glasses. And, in the sink, dishes.

What am I waiting for? he asked himself. I have my coat. Why don't I just go?

Damn it, he thought. If that accident hadn't happened regarding my purchase at Hagopian's, I might be staying here tonight.

As he stood there, partly in the kitchen and partly in the hall, his hands down deep in his pockets, he heard someone sigh. Far off, in another room of the house, someone rustled and sighed.

It frightened him.

I better be careful, he thought. Making no noise at all, he walked back down the hall, to the living room and the front door. At the door he paused, his hand on the knob, feeling a little more secure, listening.

No sound.

Now it seemed less menacing. He opened the door, hesitated, and then, leaving it slightly open, walked back. The house was so dark that he knew he could not be seen; at least, not very well. An outline, at most, his shape, too vague to be identified. There was something exciting in this, almost a child's game. Memory of earlier days . . . Again stopping, he raised his head, put his hand behind his ear, and holding his breath, listened.

Distinct breathing from what he knew to be a bedroom. The door had not been shut. Trembling, anticipating, he approached it one step at a time and stuck his head past the door to look into the room. There was just enough light for him to make out the bed, the dresser, a lamp.

On the bed lay Susan Faine, smoking a cigarette, one arm under her head, gazing up at the ceiling. She had kicked off her sandals. At the foot of the bed various coats and purses had been piled up, those of the other guests. At once she became aware of him; sitting up she said, "Back already?"

"No," he mumbled.

She gazed at him. Then she said, "I thought you left a long time ago."

"I forgot my coat," he said, foolishly.

"You have it on."

"Now I've got it," he said. Presently he said, "Where did they all go?"

"Off to buy some more mixer," she said.

"I got back in through the window," he said. "The front door was locked."

"That's what that noise was," she said. "I thought it was them on the porch opening the door. I wondered why I didn't hear anyone talking. I must have dozed off. Apparently I have some virus infection. What I'm afraid of is that it's something I picked up in Mexico. Since I got back I've been continually nauseated. I can't drink anything and keep it down; it comes right back up. And every now and then I feel so darn weak and dizzy. I just have to lie down."

"Oh," he said.

Susan Faine said, "Down there we were warned not to eat any of the leafy vegetables or any fruits or even unboiled water. But when you go into a restaurant you can't ask them to boil your glass of water. Can you? You can't boil the dishes they give you."

"Could it be just Asiatic Flu?" he asked.

"That's possible," she said. "I have these recurrent pains in my stomach." She had unbuckled her belt and now she rubbed her flat waist. Then she sat up, put out her cigarette, and arose from the bed. "They should be right back," she said, as she put her feet into her sandals. "Unless they stopped off somewhere. I think I'll fix myself some coffee. Would you like some?" She passed by him — her motions were agile, but obviously weary — and out of the room. When next he caught sight of her, she had switched on the kitchen light and was standing on tiptoe to peer into a cupboard above the sink. There, she found a jar of instant coffee.

"None for me," he said, hanging around in the general region of the kitchen table.

"Walt, my husband, I mean my former husband, lived in dread that one of us would get amoebic dysentery when we were down in Mazatlan one summer. That's supposed to be quite serious. Sometimes fatal. Have you ever been down there?"

"No," he said.

"You ought to go sometime."

In his mind he had a notion of Mexico; he had talked with a couple of fellows who had driven down from Los Angeles, across the border at Tiajuana. Their tale built up in him a picture of girls in bathing suits, T-bone steaks at fancy restaurants for 40¢, the best hotel rooms for $2.00 a night, maid service, no tax on whiskey, and any sort of pleasure wanted, picked up then and there on the street. Gas cost only 20¢ a gallon and that appealed to him particularly, because he used so much on his trips for his job. And there were top-quality English woolens in clothing stores, at dirt-cheap prices.

Of course, it was true as she said; you had to watch what you ate, but if you kept off the native foods you were okay.

At the stove, Susan Faine put on a pot of water to boil for the coffee. So he said, "Better late than never."

"What?" she said.

"Boiling the water," he said.

"This is for the coffee," she said, in a serious voice.

"I know that," he said. "I was just kidding. I guess I shouldn't kid anybody who doesn't feel well."

She seated herself at the table, rested her arms on the table, and then laid her head on her arms. "Do you live here in town?" she asked.

"No," he said. "I'm up from Reno."

"You know what I'm going to do?" she said. "I'm going to put some cognac in the coffee. I saw a bottle up in the upper shelf of the cupboard. Would you get it down for me? It's pushed back so nobody'll find it who just happens to be wandering through."

Obligingly, he got the cognac bottle down for her. It had not been opened. She examined it at great length, reading the label, holding the bottle up to the light. On the stove the water boiled.

"It looks good," she said. "Peg won't care. Somebody probably gave it to her. Anyhow I'll probably throw it up." She handed it back to him, and he understood that he was expected to open it.

The bottle had a cork for a stopper, and it gave him trouble. He had to clasp the bottle between his knees, stoop down like an animal, and, running a knife through the opener, get grip enough to pull with all his might. The cork traveled up by degrees, and at last out of the bottle entirely, expanding at once. To him it seemed offensive, and he stood holding the opener only, not touching the cork.

All the time, Susan watched critically. Then, when he had gotten the cork out, she poured the boiling water into the cup, stirred the instant coffee in, and added some of the cognac.

"Please have some," she said.

"No thanks." He did not care for brandy, especially French brandy. Standing to one side, he rearranged his sleeves, which had become wrinkled; the tugging and straining had done it.

"Aren't you old enough?"

"Sure," he grumbled. "It's just too sweet for me. Scotch is my drink."

Nodding, she sat down her café royal. At the first taste she pushed it aside and shuddered. "I can't drink it," she said.

"You ought to see a doctor," he said. "Find out if it's serious."

"I hate doctors," she said. "I know it's not serious. It's just psycho-somatic. Because I'm worried and full of anxiety, because of my marriage breaking up. I got so dependent on Walt. That was part of the trouble. I was just like a child with him; I let him make all the decisions and that wasn't right. If anything went wrong I blamed him. It was a vicious circle. Then finally we both realized I had to get free and try living on my own again. I don't think I was ready for marriage. You have to be able to reach a certain stage before you're ready for it. I wasn't. I just thought I was."

"How long were you married?" he asked.

"Two years."

"That's a long time."

"Not long enough," she said. "We were still getting acquainted. Are you married, Mr. −" His name did not materialize.

"Stevens," he said. "Bruce."

"Mr. Stevens?" she finished.

"No," he said. "I've given it some thought, but I'd like to wait until I'm absolutely positive. I don't want to make any mistakes on something that serious."

"Weren't you going steady with Peg Googer?"

"For awhile," he said. "Last year or so."

"Did you live up here?"

"Yes," he said vaguely, not wishing to spoil the deception that he came from Reno.

"Did you drive up to see Peg?"

"No," he said. "I came up this way on business." He told her, then, about Consumers' Buying Bureau, what he did and what it did. He told her that it sold goods at an average of twenty-five percent off, that it didn't have to advertise, that its overhead was low because it had no windows to dress and few fixtures to maintain, only one vast long single-story building, like a factory, with counters, and with clerks who did not even need to wear ties. He explained that a discount house never stocked complete lines of anything, only those items that it could get hold of cheaply enough. The items came and went, according to what the buyers could lay their hands on.

Right now, he told her, he had driven up here to Boise to scout out a warehouse of car wax.

That seemed to intrigue her. "Car wax," she said. "Really? Five hundred miles for *car wax*?"

"It's good stuff," he said. "A paste wax." The thing was, he explained, that paste wax did not sell well any more because it was so much work to apply. Now there were new silicates that could be dabbed on and then wiped without rubbing. But nothing gave a finish like good old paste wax, out of a can and not a bottle or spout, and every car owner deep down inside knew that, or thought he knew that. And at a discount sale-price of about ninety cents a can, the wax would move. A man would spend an entire Saturday rubbing it on his car to save a dollar off what he knew to be the retail price.

She listened intently. "And how much will you have to pay?"

"We'll make an offer on the lot," he said. His boss had authorized him to start at forty cents a can, and to go up to sixty at most. There was some doubt as to how many cans there were. And of course, if the wax was too old, if it had gotten dry, then the deal was off.

"And you go all over looking for buys like that?" Susan said.

"Everywhere. As far east as Denver and all the way out to the Coast. Down to L.A." He basked in his grandeur.

"How fascinating," she said. "And nobody knows where you get the things you sell. I imagine regular retailers come to you very angry and wanting to know if their suppliers sold to you at more of a discount than they get."

"That's right," he said. "But we never disclose our sources of supply." Now he found himself passing out information ordinarily kept quiet. "Sometimes naturally we do get hold of stuff directly from the local jobbers, at a price. And a really good deal is to drive to the manufacturer — we have our own big trucks — and pick it up direct, at what the wholesaler pays or even less. And then sometimes when a retail outlet goes bust, we get stuff that way. Or overstock that doesn't move. Or even old stock."

At the table, Susan Faine stirred her cup of coffee and brandy at so slow and depressed a tempo that he realized his talk had adversely affected her. "And these deals go on all the time?" she murmured. "No wonder I can't get anywhere."

"You're not in retail selling," he said. "Are you?"

"Oh," she said listlessly, "I sell a couple of typewriter ribbons and a few sheets of carbon paper now and then."

She got to her feet and wandered off to stand facing him, her arms folded just beneath her breasts. Her belt, still undone, allowed the top of her skirt to separate where it was intended to fit together, two edges of fabric unconnected and hanging loose. She had narrow, modern-looking hips, and he got the impression that unless she fastened her belt something would presently slip gradually off. But she remained unconscious of herself; she had a frowning, introverted expression on her face. He noticed that she had rubbed off her lipstick; it left her lips straw-colored, with countless radiating lines, a dry mouth. Her skin, too, had a dryness, but it was stretched smooth. In spite of her stark black hair, her skin was light. And her eyes, he saw, were blue. Looking more intently at her hair, he discovered that at the roots it became reddish brown. So evidently she had dyed it. That explained its lack of luster.

And once again he thought, I know her. I've seen her before, talked to her; she's familiar to me, her voice, mannerisms, choice of words. Especially her choice of words. I'm accustomed to listening to her talk. It is a voice as well-known to me as anybody in the world's.

While he was pondering that, a great wave of sound rolled in from the front of the house. The door burst open, people pushed indoors, turning on lights and chattering. Peg and her clerkish pals had returned home with the ginger ale.

Without batting an eye — as if she didn't hear the people — Susan said, "I'm very interested in all this. I suppose I really have to be. It's the new trend in selling, more or less. In fact —" She turned her head as Peg appeared with a paper bag at her shoulder.

"What are you doing back?" Peg said, amazed to see him. "I thought you left." Sweeping past him she set down the bag on the drainboard. The bag clinked.

"I forgot my coat," he said.

"How did you get in? The door was locked."

Susan said, "I let him in."

"You're supposed to be lying down sick," Peg said to her. She left the kitchen and returned to the living room, leaving them.

"Is she angry with you?" Susan said. "She acted strangely after you left. You left so hurriedly. How long will you be up here, before you drive back to Reno?"

"It depends on how I make out," he said. "A day at the most."

"I'd like to talk to you again sometime," Susan said, leaning back against the edge of the sink.

"So would I," he said. "You know, I have the feeling I know you. But I can't place you."

"I have the feeling I know you, too," she said.

"Of course," he said, "people always say that."

"A 'Some Enchanted Evening' sort of thing." She smiled. "instantaneous identification of the beloved."

That quickened his pulse, hearing that.

"You know," Susan said, "listening to you talk about selling and buying made me feel better. My stomach's stopped growling."

"Good," he said, shelving such statements off to the back of his mind; they did not go with his image of her, the rest of their discussion and all.

"Maybe that's what I need," she said. "Everything's been so mixed up since I got back from Mexico City. That was only a month or so ago, actually. I can't seem to get back in with things . . . why don't you drop by and visit us one day? Here, I'll give you our official card." She trailed past him, out of the kitchen. He remained. When she returned she carried a business card which she presented to him with a formal flourish. "Drop by," she said, "and you can take me out and buy me lunch."

"I'd love to do that," he said, already considering how and when he would be up at Boise again. Was it worth making the drive, over a thousand miles round trip, on his own time? If he waited for company business, it might be another six months, and then, as now, it would permit him only a day or so. While he battled it out in his mind, Susan left him and went into the living room with the others.

I could really go for her, he thought. In a big way.

A FEW MINUTES LATER he had said good-bye to everyone and had left the house, for a second time.

As he drove along in his car, back toward the highway, he thought to himself how much better-groomed an older woman was. If they looked good they do so on purpose, not because of chance. Not because nature had flung them a nice build and teeth and legs. They had a cultivated beauty.

And in addition to that, he was positive — without having tried it — that they knew what to do.

He had gotten almost to the highway when, all at once, he remembered who Susan Faine was. Slowing, he drove by reflex, letting the car roll.

Back in those days she had lived in Montario. None of them had known her first name, and of course "Faine" was her married name. Naturally, she had not had that name, then. They all thought of her as Miss Reuben. The last time he had seen her had been in 1949, when he was in high school, still a student, and of course he had thought of himself that way, and so had she. It had been natural for both of them to think of him as a student from the beginning.

Susan Faine had been his fifth grade teacher. At the Garret A. Hobart Grammar School, in Montario. Back in 1944, when he had been eleven years old.

3

HE SPENT THE NIGHT at a motel on the outskirts of Boise. The next morning he met with the auto supply people and negotiated successfully for the lot of car wax.

At eleven in the morning he had rented a trailer and had begun loading as many cartons as possible onto the trailer and into his car. The auto supply people had meantime confirmed his check. They signed the tag, arranged for delivery of the balance of the cartons, and off he drove, the load and trailer keeping his speed down.

With such a load he could not make the drive back to Reno during the heat of day. Were he to get out on the desert now, the engine of the Merc would overheat, boil off its water, and possibly warp the head. Usually, in circumstances of this kind, he paid a dollar or so and got use of a motel room for the day; he could nap, take it easy, read, and then, at sunset, get back out on the road.

He drove along the motel strip for a time, but then he changed his mind, made a U-turn, and returned to downtown Boise.

At one in the afternoon he parked his car and trailer in front of a shoe store, got out, made certain that the cartons in the trailer could not be pried loose by passing thieves, and then he walked along the sidewalk, with the midday shoppers, until he saw ahead of him a small office with a sign above it reading: R & J Mimeographing Service.

Perspiring with nervousness, he entered the office noticing that the counter and fixtures were modern and that directly across from the doorway another modern office, a real estate and notary public firm, did business. A fan, on the counter, cooled the place. Several dark-shiny waiting room chairs had been set out for customers.

A friendly-looking middle-aged woman wearing a smock approached him. "Hello," she said.

Bruce said, "Is Miss Reuben around?" Then he wished he had asked for Mrs. Faine; he had given it all away right off the bat. If she heard him she knew he had known her in the past.

But the middle-aged woman said, "Susan didn't come in today. She phoned about nine this morning and said she wasn't feeling well."

"That's too bad," he said, relieved. Now he became calmer. "I'll drop by again some other time," he said.

"Is there anything I can do for you?" the woman asked, standing with her hands clasped together, into the sleeves of her smock. She wore tortoise-shell glasses, and her hair was done up in a braided ring. She had a sympathetic, wrinkled face, round, heavy at the jowls, and when she smiled she showed a variety of gold and silver dental work.

"No," she said. "I'm a friend of hers. I'm up from Reno and I thought I'd drop by and say hello."

"What a pity you missed her."

"Well," he said, "I saw her last night."

"Oh, over at Peg Googer's?"

"Yes," he said.

"How was she feeling then?"

"Not too well," he said. "She was lying down for awhile. She said something about being afraid she had picked up a bug in Mexico. It sounded more to me like Asiatic Flu."

"Listen," the woman said, with agitation. "Why don't you drive up to the house? You have a car, don't you?" She hurried away from him, back behind the counter. Gathering together piles of papers, she said, "I have these things she has to see, today. I was going to close up at four and take a cab out there." She returned to the counter with an armload. "Checks she has to sign, mail, a manuscript a student brought in that has math symbols in it; we can't type the symbols,

but Susan can draw them in — she's the one who does that, not me."
She held out the armload to him.

"I don't know if I can,"he muttered, but the armload was dropped
into his hands and he found himself holding it. "I've never been there."

"It's not hard to find." She took hold of the sleeve of his coat and
led him over to a large lacquered wall map of the city. "Here," she
said, pointing to a red x on the map. "This is where we are. You
drive out this way." She explained the route in detail and wrote down
the address, obviously relieved that she had found someone to deliver
the things to her partner. "I really appreciate it," she finished up.
"I have so much to do here, with Susan away. She's been away, you
know, out of the country. I've had it all to do," she called, as she
went back behind the counter and seated herself at a big old-fashioned
electric typewriter. Smiling at him over her glasses, she began to
type. "I hope you'll excuse me," she said.

"Thanks for telling me how to get there," he said, disturbed that
she would give the firm's checkbook to a stranger simply because
he mentioned the other owner's name. What a guileless soul, he
thought. And what a haphazard way to run a business. "Do you think
there's any medicine or anything I can pick up for her?" he said. "As
long as I'm going out there?"

"No," she said cheerfully. "The mail and the checkbooks are the
important thing. And don't forget to remind her that she or I have
to call that student — his name's on the manuscript — before we start
on it, so he'll know how much it'll be. He only has fifty dollars."

Saying good-bye, he left the office. A moment later he had opened
his car door and was depositing the heap of papers, envelopes, and
the heavy board check ledger on the car seat.

Now I have to go out there, he realized.

He started up the car, drove out into traffic, and in the direction
of Susan Faine's house.

YEARS AGO, when he had been in high school, he had been a paper
boy. He had delivered papers after school, in Montario, and Miss
Reuben had lived along his route. For the first few months he had
had no contact with her, because she had not subscribed to the paper.
But one day, when he had picked up his bundle, he found a notice
of a new subscriber on route 36, plus one additional newspaper to
add to his pack. So he walked up the wide cement steps, past the

trees and flower beds, until he stood below the second-story balcony, and from there he had lobbed a folded-up paper over the railing and onto the porch of the house. And six times a week he did the same after that, for almost a year.

This house now did not resemble that fine stone mansion with its trees, fountain, fish pool and bird bath, its outdoor sprinkling system. In those days, she had been single and she had shared the house with three other women. They did not own it; they only rented it. This house, smaller, stuck up square and regular, wood, not stone. The windows were small. The yard, in front, had no trees in it, only a few bushes, flowers, no grass at all. The steps were brick. But it was a modern house, in good condition, and he saw that behind it a long grassy yard stretched out, flat and well-kept, with what appeared to be a ping pong table in the middle of it, and roses growing up into an arbor . . . The house had recently been painted a pleasant off-white. Dried drops of paint on the leaves of the shrubs suggested that the job had been done during the last month or so.

He closed and locked the car door, crossed the sidewalk, and then stepped up to the porch and rang the bell before he could have time to suffer any further doubts.

Nobody answered the ring. He rang again.

Off somewhere within the house a radio could be heard, tuned to a program of dance music. After waiting and ringing, he walked back down to the path and around the side of the house, through an open gate and into the back yard.

At first the garden seemed empty. He started back toward the front again, and then he saw Susan Faine; motionless, she blended with the garden. She sat on the back step, with a lap of brightly-colored clothes; apparently she had been darning or sewing, because on the step beside her lay a pair of scissors and a number of spools of thread. What she had were children's socks. And now he noticed toys strewn about the yard, a rusted metal horse, blocks, parts of games. Susan had on a white frilly blouse, short-sleeved, and a great long unpressed wrinkled green skirt of some thin material that whipped about her legs each time a breeze moved through the yard. Her legs and arms seemed unusually white. Her feet were bare, but he saw a pair of canvas shoes that had been kicked off, nearby.

If she had been darning socks she certainly had stopped, now. She sat bent over, with one red sock across her right wrist and hand, her fingers inside it. A thimble sparkled from the second finger of her left hand. But he saw no sign of needle or thread.

"Where's your needle and thread?" he said.

She lifted her head. "What?" she said slowly, squinting at him to see who it was. Her movements were retarded, as if she had been almost asleep. "Oh," she said. "It's you." Reaching down, she brushed her fingers across the ground at her feet. "I dropped it," she said.

As he approached, she found her needle, held it up and inspected it, and then resumed her darning. The bright midday sunlight made her frown; lines scoured her forehead, and her eyes, fixed on the dazzling sock, became almost shut.

"I have a lot of stuff for you," he said, balancing his armload. Again she raised her head.

"From your office." He held out the armload.

"Did Mrs. de Lima give them to you?" Susan said.

"That woman who was there," he said. "Middle-aged, brown hair."

"I told her I wasn't feeling well," Susan said. "I really ought to be down there. I haven't been down there more than one day in the last month."

"Don't go down if you're not feeling well," he said.

"I feel okay," she said. "I just can't bring myself to go down there. It's so depressing. I'm just not cut out to be a businesswoman. I used to teach school."

He nodded at that.

Susan sighed. "Put them inside. The checks and the mail. What's that big packet?"

"A manuscript." He related to her the details that Mrs. de Lima had asked him to pass on.

Susan put down her lap of socks and got to her feet. "I know what she wants; she wants me to type it here at home. She knows I have an Underwood electric here. I suppose I should. What's the matter with me? I shouldn't make her do all the work . . . she's really been very good about it, the last month. Come on in. Excuse me for being so slow . . . I can't seem to focus on anything today." She disappeared on inside the house, and he followed.

The back porch, with its laundry tubs and shelves, was cool. Susan had gone on into a yellow, brightly-decorated kitchen, and then on along a hall and into a front room. When he arrived there he found her collapsed in a deep, old-fashioned easy chair, her arms resting on its fuzzy, black-fabric arms, her head back, eyes fixed on the ceiling.

Setting his armload down on a table he said, "I was surprised when she gave me this stuff."

"Why?" Susan said, her eyes shut.

"She doesn't know me."

"Poor Zoe," Susan said. "She's a nut. She trusts everybody. She's as bad as I am. Neither of us have any business sense. I don't know how we ever got started."

"Anyhow you're making a living," he said.

"No," she said. "We're not making a living — Bruce? Is that your first name? The thing that depresses me is that now is when I really can use a source of income. And that's what it isn't."

He asked, "Who owns the toys I saw out back?"

"Taffy," she said. "My daughter. She's in school. Second grade."

He had an impulse, at that moment, to tell her that she had been his teacher. The message almost came out of him; he stammered a few words and then said instead, "If you were a teacher, why don't you educate her at home? That seems ideal to me."

"The group," Susan said. "A child needs training to prepare him to live with a group. Would you like some coffee?" Arising from her chair she started out of the room.

"No, thanks," he mumbled. The impulse passed, and, strangely, no intention to tell her remained, no desire at all. Probably he would never get around to telling her; the subject had closed itself for good, leaving nothing behind. Except that he knew. He remembered her, the young woman teacher of those days, who had been there, one morning when they arrived.

In those days, he thought, she probably was twenty-three or -four. Good God, he thought. The age I am now.

Thinking that, he tried to picture her as she had actually been in those days, not as she had looked to him a fifth grade student eleven years old. The image was unclear as it could possibly be. He could shut his eyes and imagine various cronies of the times: Nigger Lips Tate, Bud McVae, Earl Smith, Louis Selkirk, the kid in the apartment house across the street who had pantsed him one afternoon in plain sight of everyone, the girl who sat across from him in class and who had the long black hair and whom Gene Scanlan had written the note to, for him, which old Mrs. Jaffey, their former teacher, had happened on and – thank God – been unable to read. All that was still visible to him, but when he thought about her, about Miss Reuben, he saw only a tight-faced woman, with angry eyes and pale, twitching lips, who stood very tall with her arms folded, at the front of the room, wearing a blue suit with huge buttons like campaign badges, only white. And the carrying-power of her voice, especially on the playground during recess; she had stood up on the ramp by the door to the building supervising them, wearing a heavy coat over her shoulders. She had come out to Idaho from Florida, and she was not accustomed to the cold. In the winter and first months of spring she had shivered and complained, even to them, and her face had been drawn and pinched, her lips tucked in almost out of sight. In class she talked constantly about Florida and how wonderful the climate there was, the oranges and lemons, the beaches. They had all listened. They were obliged to.

From the first day, he had been frightened of her. All of them had seen that she was a mean, intense young woman, simmering with strength, quite different from old Mrs. Jaffey, who had been ill and who had gone downstairs to the nurse one day, in the middle of the afternoon, and who had not come back. For months Mrs. Jaffey had complained of weariness and fever. After she had left the room, the children began screaming and hurling erasers. They had a fine time until the Principal appeared and hushed them up. And then, a few days later, they had arrived at their classroom to find Miss Reuben.

Mrs. Jaffey had been the oldest teacher at the Garret A. Hobart Grammar School, and none of the other teachers had gotten on with her very well. She had intended to retire at the end of the semester anyhow. She was sixty-eight years old. According to Mr. Hillings the Principal she had taught at the school when it first opened up, forty-one years ago, in 1904.

He, Skip Stevens, had gotten along swell with Mrs. Jaffey. In fact, she had supervised his election to Class President, which entitled him to hold forth at assemblies in the name of Fifth Grade, plus honorary powers such as deciding when to water the Fifth Grade Vegetable Garden in back of the school. At that time he had been a beefy, large boy, with red hair and freckles, good at kickball during recess, the first out of the cafeteria at lunch time and onto the playing field.

Now, looking back, he realized that he had been a bully. Since he had outweighed the other boys, it had been a natural role; he did not feel guilt. Somebody had to be the bully, at that age.

As far as Mrs. Jaffey went, during her last months she had become too infirm and inobservant to bother anyone. By the time she had given up and gone downstairs to the nurse, he had had the run of the room. One day he had started a fire in the clockroom. And once, when Mrs. Jaffey had left to go to the teachers' washroom, he had dumped the wastebasket onto her desk.

Susan, re-emerging from the kitchen, holding an aluminum coffee pot, said, "Bruce, do you have your car? There's no milk. I wonder if I could talk you into going down and getting a carton of milk. Here." She sat down the coffee pot and went over to pick up her purse from the living room sofa. Handing him a fifty-cent piece she said, "There's a grocery store down about four blocks, on the corner. What happened about you car wax? Did you get that cleared up?"

"Yes," he said. "I closed the deal." He did not accept the fifty-cent piece. But he started toward the front door.

"And when do you have to go back to Reno?"

"This evening," he said.

"Oh good," she said. "Then you don't have to leave right away."

"I'll be right back," he said, opening the door and going out onto the porch.

As he drove off, away from the house, he wondered to himself why he did not mind doing this. Errands, he thought. But it meant he could do something for her.

That pleased him.

Should it? he asked himself. Should I want to do something for her? A woman I feared . . . a young lady teacher who bawled me out, humiliated me in front of the class. Perhaps, he thought, I am re-entering the pattern. Obedience. Slavery. The inequality of childhood . . .

But he did not feel chained, compulsively following orders from her. He got a kick out of it; driving along in his Merc, searching for the grocery store, he felt important. Useful. To be depended on.

WHEN HE ARRIVED back at the house, with the carton of milk, he found her in the living room. She had a fountain pen out, and was signing checks, grim-faced, with her lips drawn tightly together. That expression was stong in his memory: the tight, fierce resentment on her face. The lines crossing her forehead. She had put a shawl-like sweater over her shoulders, unbuttoned — a loose grandmotherish pink sweater, for warmth. The living room seemed cool to him, too. Dark and quiet and out of the sun. During his absence she had shut off the radio; the dance music no longer played. Without it, the house seemed older, more serious and sturdy. In her sweater she, too, seemed older. She had put shoes on, not the ones he had noticed in the yard, but a pair of saddle shoes. And white cotton bobby socks.

"Does your discount house sell typewriters?" she asked, without looking up. "Or did I ask you that."

He carried the carton of milk into the kitchen. In addition to it he had bought a couple of bottles of Lucky Lager beer and a bag of cheese-flavored crackers. "We carry a few lines of portables," he said. "No office models or electrics."

Pushing a piece of folded-up shiny paper toward him she said, "See what you think of this."

He read it over. It was an ad for a portable that used the new carbon ribbon.

"The salesmen come in," Susan said. "They start giving us all the verbiage . . . honestly, the way they push the retailer around. Loading them up."

"You have to fight back," he said.

"We sell a few used machines. We just don't have enough money to stock portables. If they'd give them to us on consignment . . . does it tell how much they want for this one?"

He saw no price on the ad, either wholesale or retail. "No," he said.

"Thanks for getting the milk," she said. Arising, she shut the checkbook, stuck the fountain pen away, and started past him. But then she halted, directly in front of him and very close to him, so that she breathed up into his face. For the first time he realized that she was much shorter than he. To talk to him while standing so close she had to look almost straight up. It gave her an imploring manner, as if she were begging him for something. "How can we make any profit if we don't have any money to start out with? All we can do is meet the bills that come in for gas and lights. The Idaho Power Company really has us. And the paper and carbon paper we use — of course, we get it at cost. But still." Standing in front of him, petitioning him, she seemed not only small, but bony and cold as well. Under her sweater her shoulders pulled forward, as if she were shivering. And all the time she kept her eyes fixed on his face.

He had never had an opportunity to see her this close up. It broke apart his memory of her. For one thing, he could tell that his life-long impression of her physical strength was erroneous; she had no more than any other woman, and he had always recognized that by and large, most women were delicate and even somewhat frail. And it seemed to him that she recognized it, too. But no doubt she always had. She had appeared mean and strong to them because first of all they had been so small, and, in addition, she had been angry at them, and it has been her job to terrify and badger and impress them. That was why the school board had chosen her; they needed a teacher that could keep the children in hand. Outside of her job, she had probably been like this even then. Yes, he thought, when he had later on delivered the paper to her house he had one day seen inside and noticed tiny china teacups on a table in the dining room. She had been serving tea to lady friends. It had not jibed with his image of her. So his image had always been false.

She padded past him, across the carpet, her shoes making no sound. "Oh," she said, "I'll bet you got homogenized milk. I should have told you to get the regular, so we can pour off the cream." She opened the brown paper bag and saw the beer. "Beer," she said.

"It's a warm day," he said, with nervousness.

"You did get regular milk," she said, lifting out the carton.

"That's right," he said.

"Do you want coffee?"

"I'd rather have beer."

"No beer for me. I can never drink beer." At the drainboard she produced an opener and opened his beer bottle for him. She poured him a glassful and held it out to him. "What did you think of the R & J Mimeographing Service?" she said.

"Seemed very nice at first glance. Modern."

She said, "Would you look over the office and tell me what you think we ought to do? I know you have experience we don't have."

Taken by surprise he could say nothing.

"Do you know what I wish?" she said. "I wish you'd take it over and run it. You could put in a line of portables. Then at Christmas when everybody else is making money we'd have something to sell." With intensity she glared up at him, her eyes small. "I mean it. While you were gone I thought about it. Zoe is no good at all; I have to get rid of her. I'm going to anyhow. Each of us has three thousand dollars in it; that's all. Just six thousand dollars in all. The settlement I reached with Walt gives me just about that. I was going to pay off this house, but what I think I'll do — what I really want to do — is buy out Zoe and run the office myself. Then you can take it over and do what you want. Maybe I can make a deal with the bank and borrow enough so you can put in portables, or if you don't want to do that, you can put in whatever else you want."

He was silent with disbelief.

"I want to wash my hands of it," she said.

"I know you do," he murmured.

"I'm not cut out for cutthroat things like business. I want to stay home and be with Taffy. I only see her for an hour or so in the evenings. I have a woman come in about two and clean up the house and then go pick up Taffy and bring her home and be here with her until I get home at six. She took care of the house and Taffy while I was down in Mexico. Walt's in Utah, in Salt Lake City. He's been there for almost a year."

"I see," he said.

"Couldn't you do that?" she demanded. "Run the office?"

"I guess so," he said.

"Here's what I thought about paying you. Zoe and I draw two salaries out. You can have exactly half the profits. Not a salary but exactly fifty percent of the net. How's that? As much as I make, and you don't have to worry about any investment."

"That's wrong," he said.

"Why?"

"It's not fair to you."

In an agonized voice she said, "I have to have somebody to help me." She moved away from him, her arms folded tightly about her. "I need somebody I can depend on. I don't have Walt — I used to depend on him. He's in the galvanized pipe business. All my time has to be spent with Taffy; that's all there is to it. That has to come first. I don't know how much you're making now . . . you're probably making more. But if you were smart, you could make it pay off. Don't you agree? It's small, but it's a good location."

"Yes it is," he said.

Suddenly she spun around to face him. "Bruce," she said, in a husky, almost tearful voice, "last night I lay awake thinking about you. I knew you'd come by. I was sitting out in the backyard hoping you'd come by. I waited all morning. I knew you had this —" She waved her hand. "This business to finish up. That's why I stayed home from the office. I didn't want to see you down there. Zoe and I don't get along at all; I don't want her to know anything about this until it's all been arranged and there's nothing left but simply to walk up to her and face her squarely and tell her I want to buy her share. It's part of the legal agreement between us. We agreed when we became partners. I dread telling her . . . we've been friends for years. She and I lived together in Montario, when I was teaching at Garret A. Hobart."

He thought: Perhaps she was one of the women in that house.

"Listen, Bruce," she said in a grindingly serious voice. "I'm going to be totally honest with you. I'm really up against it. I didn't get any alimony from Walt. He's out of the state. He will send some money every month, but that's for Taffy. And it won't be much. I have exactly four thousand dollars that was my share of what we had, plus this house. There's about five thousand more in the house. He kept the car. I got some furniture but it isn't much. I really feel desperate. I'm not going to get a job; I've had my fill of that. I gave up teaching when I got married. I'd go to my grave before I'd teach again, or get a job as a secretary or a typist or a clerk somewhere. I won't be degraded. I'd let Walt have Taffy and I'd —" She broke off. Rocking back and forth, her arms wrapped about her, she said, "I'm very lonely. Most of our friends are off me because they think it's my fault Walt and I split up. You saw those people at Peg's. They're just a bunch of —"

"Clerks," he said.

"Yes," she said.

"That's what you get in a small town," he said.

"Maybe that's what I should do. Go down and live in Reno. Or go to the East Coast. But I have this goddamn mimeographing and typing business. Bruce —" Her voice rose. "I have to make it pay." She advanced toward him. "I'll bet with you running it it would pay. I know it would. If you hadn't come by I would have gone down to Reno on the Greyhound and looked you up. I even called them and found out when the buses go. I'll show you." She shot past him, out of the room. Almost at once she was back, waving a folded piece of typing paper on which, in pencil, she had jotted down the bus schedule.

"I'd have to think it over," he said, thinking about his job at C.B.B., his apartment in Reno, his friends there, his boss Ed von Scharf, on whom he depended, everything that he had planned for himself.

But, he thought, I could make it pay. I could run it. A retail outlet of my own, a business of my own. Nobody to tell me what to do. I'd have a free hand. Put my talent and experience to work.

"It does sound good," he admitted.

"Do you know when we have to order merchandise for Christmas?"

"In the Fall," he said.

"In August," she said, with resentment. "I'd want you to be already in and fully organized by then."

He nodded. And then he took the bottle opener, opened the other bottle of beer, found a tall tumbler in the rack on the drainboard, and poured a second glass of beer. Susan watched absently.

"Here," he said, holding it out to her. "As a sort of celebration," he said, feeling clumsy and thick-tongued.

"Oh no thanks," she said. "It's too early in the day. Anyhow i have the darn checks to finish." She started off, and when he followed he found her again seated with the checkbook before her, pen in hand, writing and frowning.

"I guess it's agreed on," he said, bewildered, but aware that unbelievably, in essence, he had said he would do it.

"Thank God," she said with fervor, pausing in her check-writing. "I really need you, Bruce," she said. And then she resumed her work.

He stood sipping his beer, standing in the cool living room.

4

WHEN HE GOT BACK to ... to with the load of car wax he drove directly to the Consumers' Buying Bureau building and searched up his boss, Ed von Scharf. He found him in a stock room in the rear, seated on a carton, with a Popsicle in one hand and an inventory sheet on the floor before him. Wearing his tie, vest, black oxfords and herring-bone trousers, his boss had been making an inventory and flinging around cartons of electric mixers. His black hair was speckled with the dust of the brown cardboard cartons; it made his look distinguished.

Bruce said, "I ran into an emergency up in Montario. I have to go back. If I can't get an indefinite leave of absence, then I guess I'm quitting my job." On the drive he had worked out his story. "My Dad's ill," he said, knowing how little his employers could complain against that reason. "I want to be up there indefinitely."

They argued for an hour and a half. Then they went upstairs and discussed it with two of the Pareti brothers who owned C.B.B. At last the Paretis wrote out a two-weeks' paycheck, shook hands with him, and told him he was free to go. He left with the assurance that his job would be there if and when he wanted it again.

His boss walked out to his car with him, grave and discouraged.

"It's a hell of a surprise," he said, as Bruce unhitched the trailer load of car wax. "Keep in touch. Will you?"

He clapped Bruce on the back, wished him and his family luck, and then returned to the C.B.B. building.

With a strong sense of guilt, Bruce drove away in the direction of his apartment. But, at least, he had made sure of his job, if things did not work out. It was only practical.

After he had told the landlady, he went upstairs and got out a suitcase and began packing his things. By sundown he had carried all his things down to the Merc, loaded them where the boxes of wax had been only a few hours earlier, and then had given Mrs. O'Neill back the apartment key. She wished him luck, too, getting up from the dinner table to follow him down the hall.

At eight-thirty he began the drive back to Idaho.

THE NEXT MORNING he blearily entered Boise. He stopped at a motel and rented a room. Without unloading any of his things he undressed, got into bed, and slept through the day. At five-thirty in the evening he arose, took a shower, shaved, put on clean clothes, and then drove over to downtown Boise and the R & J Mimeographing Service.

As he was parking, Susan Faine appeared at the office doorway, half a block away, waved to him, and disappeared back inside. He finished parking, got out of the car, and walked down.

Inside the office, Zoe de Lima greeted him with a frigid nod and at once turned her back. He said hello to her but she did not answer; she busied herself at her typewriter.

She knows, he said to himself.

With her coat and purse, Susan approached him from the back of the office. "Let's go," she said.

Together, they walked down the sidewalk and got into the car. "I told her," Susan said. "We screamed at each other all day. Did you do it?" She craned her neck and saw all his clothes, suitcases, boxes of personal articles crammed into the back. "You did."

"I quit my job," he said, "And gave up my apartment."

"Let's go eat," she said. "I'm starved."

"Should you leave her?" he said.

"Why not?" Susan said. "Oh, I see what you mean. But she's still a partner. She has a key. I can't make her leave. It'll take a week or so to have the legal business finished. Anyhow I don't think she'd do anything vindictive. She's hurt, and she's mad at me, but she's a reputable person. I've known her for years. We still expect to be friends."

He said, "Well, you know her; I don't."

They sat for an interval in the car. The late-afternoon glare from the sidewalks was intolerable, and Susan shifted about uncomfortably. "Maybe I'll go back inside and tell her we might as well close up for the day," she said. She got out of the car and hurried back down the sidewalk. Time passed. Bruce put on the radio and listened to the news. Then, at last, he saw Mrs. de Lima leave the office, walking off briskly in the opposite direction. Susan locked up the office and came toward him, smiling.

"That's that," she said, getting in beside him.

"Where do you want to eat?" he asked, starting up the car.

"I have to go home," Susan said. "Mrs. Poppinjay has to leave exactly at six forty-five on the dot, hail or rain or snow. And I really have to have dinner with Taffy; it's something I need, as well as her. Mrs. Poppinjay starts a roast usually and then I take over when I get home and finish up and serve the meal, and Taffy and I eat together. It works out pretty well. Have you had dinner? I don't know why I didn't ask . . . I just took it for granted that you'd eat with us."

"Okay," he said.

When they got to her house Susan introduced him to Mrs. Poppinjay, a white-haired plump short old lady who obviously wanted to leave and get home to her own family. Taffy was off in her own room, coloring with crayons and listening to a children's program on TV, her back to the set. She barely noticed him as Susan brought him into the room and told her what his name was and that he'd be working at the office.

"Nice-looking little girl," he said, although he had not been able to see much more than that there was a little girl there, and that she was busy on the floor, and that she had light, almost blond hair. "Does she take after you or Walt?"

Susan, with a laugh, said, "She's not Walt's child. God forbid. I've been married twice."

"Oh," he said.

"Taffy was born during the Korean War. I didn't meet Walt until early in 1955. I remember he had a brand new '55 Chevrolet V8 and he was always telling me that it was the first V8 Chevy built and there was something wrong with the rings. It used oil."

"Yes," he said. "That's a fact."

"Walt's on the road a lot, too, like you. Over to Salt Lake City and over to the Coast, to L.A. in particular. That's strange, isn't it . . . to think of you both driving around. He's a factory representative. Conferences and sales meetings." She hung up her coat and put on an apron.

"There's plenty of money in galvanized iron," he said.

"Yes," she said, "and look how much I got out of it."

AFTER DINNNER they sat smoking and relaxing. Taffy had gone off by herself, probably back to her room. She seemed to be a quiet child, resourceful, not minding having to be by herself. The house was warm and peaceful. It smelled of pot roast.

"Am I enough of a cook for you?" Susan said.

"You certainly are," he said. What a pleasure it had been, compared with the restaurant and roadside cafe meals he had endured for the last two years. None of the fried greasiness. The overcooked vegetables, watery and tasteless.

"I'm excited," Susan said.

"So am I."

"I know we're going to be successful. And I've told Zoe; that's a terrible load off my mind. As soon as you left yesterday I began preparing myself for it. And this morning when we opened the office I said, 'Zoe, I want to talk to you.' And I told her."

"Good," he murmured, feeling sleepy.

"Is it heartless?" Susan said.

"No," he murmured. "That goes on all the time."

"Now I'm having misgivings."

That roused him. "It's done," he said. "I'm up here; I quit my job and gave up my apartment."

She nodded in agreement. "And it's going to be wonderful. We'll go in together tomorrow, and I'll start showing you around. Or actually we could drive over tonight. No, we can wait." And then a thought struck her. "Bruce, maybe we should wait until Zoe is out. I don't think it would be a good idea for you to have to bump into her; we'll wait. How are you fixed for money?"

"How do you mean?" he said. "I have a two weeks' paycheck they gave me. And I have some cash." He did not know what she was driving at.

Considering at length, Susan said, "Where are you staying?"

"At the Jack Rabbit Inn Motel," he said.

"How much is it?"

"Six bucks a day."

She winced. "That's forty-two dollars a week."

"I'll start looking for a room," he said. "I don't intend to be there as long as a week. If I'm not coming into the office right away I can start looking."

Susan said, "But I want you to come in right away. I want to get started." She fooled irritably with her cigarette. "I don't want to wait — what do you think? Would it bother you to have to be there while Zoe's there?"

"I don't care," he said. He doubted if it would bother him. After all, he did not know the woman; he had nothing to lose by her animosity.

"I want to start paying you," Susan said, "but I can't until the legal papers are signed and she's officially not connected with the business. That means not until she's received the money from me, for her share. So you won't get paid anything for at least a week."

That jolted him. "Okay," he said, hoping he would be able to get by.

"That puts you in a bad spot," she said. "I can see it does. I'm sorry, Bruce; I didn't think of it until after we'd decided and you'd already started back to Reno."

They both were silent.

Suddenly she said, "Listen, why don't you stay here?"

He felt as if the top of his head had come loose.

"Of course," she said, reaching out and tapping him urgently on the hand. "you can sleep here and eat here; there's two spare bedrooms, and plenty of closet space. Why not?"

Struggling, he said, "If nobody minds."

"The neighbors, you mean? I don't think they'll even notice. I hope not. Why should they? Anyhow, we have a lot to get settled. I want you to start working right now; we can go down together to the office at night, after dinner. After Taffy goes to bed. And I'll have a key made for you. And the weekend's coming up." She put out her cigarette and leaped up. "Let's go carry your things in from the car. Do you have everything you need?"

"Yes," he said. He hadn't left anything at the motel. "But are you sure you want to do this?" To him it seemed a big step.

"I know I do," she said, opening the front door. "It's perfectly natural; I'm surprised we didn't think of it earlier." Pausing, she said over her shoulder, "Unless you feel squeamish about it."

"Squeamish," he echoed. "How?"

"I guess you don't. Embarrassed, maybe I mean. We're going to be together all the time anyhow. In a small business with just two people — you're used to a big outfit, aren't you? A small business is much more personal, almost like a family."

At one time he had worked for a drugstore that employed only one clerk, in addition to himself as stockboy. So he knew.

"I'm pretty easy to get along with," he said.

"I hope so," she said, "because I'm not. I have moods. I get depressed. When you came here yesterday I was having one of my depressed periods. But you snapped me out of it." In a spontaneous flurry, she caught hold of his sleeve and tugged him along with her, down the path to the car. "You're good therapy for me," she told him over her shoulder.

Within the hour he found himself installed in a high-ceilinged bedroom, his suitcases and boxes piled up on the floor off to one side and his clothes hanging in the closet. His shaving gear was put away in the medicine cabinet in the bathroom, along with his squeeze bottle of deodorant, hairbrush, toothbrush, and all the rest of the little bottles and tubes and tins.

By now Susan's child had gone to bed. The TV set was off. The house, with just him and Susan up and about, had become informal to a degree new to him; he had never known such an absence of pressure on him.

The two of them sat in the living room, relaxing. Presently Susan started hearkening back to her days as a school teacher. It seemed always in the back of her mind.

"I was still teaching when I met Pete," she said. "Taffy's Dad. That was in 1949. He wanted me to quit, and I did when Taffy came along. And we moved from Montario to Boise." From a bureau drawer she brought forth a huge scrapbook. Seated beside him she turned pages, showing him snapshots and documents from the near past. "My sixth grade class at Garret A. Hobart in 1948," she said, pointing to a print.

At last he got to see the class picture for the fifth grade of 1945, his class. Sure enough, his fat round face peered from the second row. There he was, one of a number of grumpy, stodgy-looking small boys, lost among his peers and certainly so different in appearance from now that no one would make the connection. In fact, had he not known this print, he would have failed to recognize himself or even be aware that he was somewhere among the faces. Both he and Susan studied the class picture. There she was, quite easy to spot; she stood to one side, rigid and formal, with a smile, her eyes partly shut because of the bright sun. Wearing her suit with the big buttons . . . astonishing, he thought, to see this picture again. A copy had belonged to him but his mother had gotten it years ago; he had not seen it since that time.

And, in the photograph, Miss Reuben as she was then, in 1945, but not as he remembered her. He saw only a very pretty, muscular young woman, smartly-dressed, somewhat thin, with anxious lines around her eyes and mouth. A worrier, he thought. Tense, ferociously conscious of the responsibility of managing a class. Perhaps too tense. Too concerned. He remembered that one day a boy had been cut badly on a broken pop bottle during recess; Miss Reuben had run for the nurse, and although she had brought the nurse at once, and managed to get the other children to return to their business, she had been forced to go off by herself for awhile, and even then, even as fifth graders, they had been aware of her near-hysteria. She had stood gripping her handkerchief, her back to everybody, poking at her eyes and nose. At that time, of course, it had made them all giggle. They had barely been able to restrain their mirth.

While he sat studying the picture he saw beneath it, in microscopic print, the names of the students. Sure enough, there was his name: Bruce Stevens. However, Susan did not notice. She had started recalling other events and was no longer interested in the page.

"I never should have given up teaching," she said. "But I just wasn't suited for it. I used to come home shaking from head to foot. The noise and confusion. It always gave me a headache. Children running in all directions. Pete said I had no aptitude for dealing with children. He said I was too neurotic. Maybe he was right. That's one of the reasons why we split up. We couldn't agree on how to raise Taffy."

"What's he doing now?" he asked, turning the page to obscure his name.

Susan said, "He's in Chicago. I don't have any idea what he's doing. He was an engineering student when I met him. I was twenty-six and he as twenty-five."

"How old were you when you started teaching?" he said.

"Let's see," she said. "I started in Tampa, Florida. In 1943. I remember, because the Battle of Stalingrad was going on the month I first had a class of my own. I was nineteen."

"What about when you first started at Garret A. Hobart?"

She said, "It was 1945, so I was twenty-one."

So she was exactly ten years older than he. She was thirty-four, now. About what he had thought.

"I've never seen any of those little people since," Susan said. "They just vanished. Thirteen years ago . . . they must be almost grown up by now. My lord, they would be grown up; they were eleven or so then, so they'd be twenty-four years old now. Married, and some of them with children." She got a pensive expression on her face. "Some of them could have children starting to school. That would be stretching it, though. But it makes you stop and think."

"It's a long thirteen years between eleven and twenty-four," he said.

"Very important. But when I look back it doesn't seem to have made very much difference as far as I'm concerned. Twenty-one to thirty-four. But I shouldn't say that. Here I have Taffy, and I've been married and divorced twice! So I don't mean that. But I feel the same. I don't feel I've changed much inside during that period. I suppose I look different." She turned back to re-examine the picture of herself taken in 1945.

"I don't think you look much different," he said. And certainly she did not.

"Thank you," she said. "That's a very nice compliment."

"I mean it," he said.

She closed the scrapbook. "I feel so discouraged," she said. "I don't mean right now; I mean in general, these last few years. When two marriages have failed . . . you always wonder if it's you. I know it was me. Pete said I did nothing but brood and worry, and Walt didn't tell me that, but he might as well have; he said I treated everything as a crisis. He said I have a crisis mentality. I fear calamity any moment. Like Henny Penny. The sky is falling . . . do you recall?"

"Yes," he said.

"And they both feel I'm imparting it to Taffy." Turning toward him she said urgently, "That's why I need somebody around me who's cheerful and easy-going and takes things in his stride. Like you."

"I don't think necessarily you're imparting anything like that to Taffy," he said, thinking that after all she had terrorized him for a year, left a permanent impression in his mind, and yet he had emerged, survived it, arrived at adulthood in an optimistic mood. Was that not proof that she had done no real harm? Of course, he thought, maybe I'm just lucky. And he also thought, Maybe there is damage to me, down under the surface. I just don't know it. I haven't seen it.

AT ELEVEN-THIRTY Susan said good-night and went off to the bathroom to take a bath and go to bed.

Alone, he sat in the living room, watching an old movie on the TV set.

I have moved back to Montario, he thought. No, not exactly to Montario. This is actually Boise. But to him it was the same; it was the place he had come from.

However, it did not discourage him. It was so different. Nothing could be further from the old days, his life as a high school student folding up newspapers and flinging them onto porches . . . or, before that, playing marbles after school, watching "Howdy Doody" on the ten-inch TV screen in the family living room, while his older brother Frank messed about on the back porch with pond water for his microscope.

That made him meditate about Frank.

His older brother Frank now worked in Cincinnati for a chemical company, as a research chemist. He had gone through Wayne University, in Detroit, on a scholarship granted by a soap company. Frank was married and he had a child three years old. How old would Frank be? Twenty-six or so. And he owned — or was paying on — a house and car. So Frank was a success, by any standards; he held a professional job, doing what he had enjoyed all his life . . . he was talented, alert, skilled, and one day he would be publishing in scientific journals. He had a great future; in fact, he had a great present. In school Frank had been popular. Bruce remembered him striding about in his tennis shoes and slacks, his hair combed back and oiled, his skin shining and blemish-free, waving at everyone, being good at school dances, being elected to this and that. Going steady with Ludmilla Meadowland, the blonde whom the senior class had elected Miss Montario for the JC pageant of 1948. In the parade, on June tenth, she had coasted down Hill Street on a float made of potatoes, carrying a banner reading WIN MONTARIO HIGH WIN WIN. The Principal of Montario High had shaken hands with both her and Frank, and the picture of the three of them had appeared in the *Gazette*, the newspaper which Bruce had trudged along with, folding and tossing, folding and tossing day after day, for two whole years.

All his life everyone had dropped it in his ear that his brother Frank was the bright one.

Evidently, he thought, it was true. Look where Frank is. Look where I am.

But, try as he might, he could not drum up a feeling of discouragement. I like this, he thought. I'm getting a deep charge out of this . . . it really appeals to me. There is something satisfying about it, a kind of order. A unity. That someone from his early life could have the power to pull him over backward this way made him feel that all those years had not after all added up to nothing. In those days he had naturally been powerless to help himself. He had done what everyone else did. They shot marbles after school, so he did so, too. They went and stood in line for the kiddies' matinee at the Luxor Theater on Saturday afternoon, so he did so, too, whatever crummy film might be showing. Those repetitive and futile years had been so tiresome that, now and then, he had despaired. What was it all about? What did he get out of it? Nothing, apparently.

Practically the only moment in his first fifteen years that had meant anything to him at the time had shown up by accident. The *Gazette* had run an offer to mail out phonograph records of great symphonic masterpieces for coupons clipped from the daily paper. Since he was a carrier, he had access to the coupons, and he had gathered a batch and sent them off to Illinois, and after a month or so he had received in the mail a flat package wrapped with brown paper and tape. Opening it, he had found three twelve-inch records bundled up in cardboard. The labels on the records were blue and read only "World's Greatest Symphonies." The names of the orchestra and the conductor were not given. This particular set of records − it had no album, only paper sleeves — turned out to be the Haydn Symphony Number 99. He played it on his table-model phonograph, which he had gotten as a Christmas present during junior high. Up to then his musical taste had run to Spike Jones, and after that it more or less still did. But that particular symphony had had an enormous impact on him; it had affected him to the soles of his feet. He played the three records until they turned white and wore away into noisy hissing.

His rabid interest in the music proved that if given a choice he would have swapped his life as he was living it for a different town, other people. It proved that he was not happy. Of course, he knew that. He moped continually about, from home to school and back. What a contrast to his brother Frank, who sailed out daily in the best grade of sweater, slacks, and hair oil.

At fifteen he had lain by himself in the darkness of his room, listening to the music on the phonograph. Sharpening the cactus needles with the little machine that he had bought for a dollar and a half that spun the needle around a disc of sandpaper . . . collecting a Band-Aid box of sharpened needles ready to be stuck in, half way through a record side, if the needle in the arm began to wear too much.

He could have lived entirely in that room, if someone had thought to push food through the keyhole. Piped in by means of a tube, he thought. Perhaps that had been the defect. Outside the room he had suffered. He could not keep the thing with him. And he did like to get out once in awhile and stir around and see what was doing. Eventually he had wound up in Reno working for C.B.B. And in the same manner he had wound up back here, intrigued by things that had fallen in his direction, unable to turn down a chance at something that promised to be new.

When the old movie ended he shut off the TV set, made certain that the front door of the house was locked, turned off the living room light as Susan had at great pains instructed him to do, and then eyed the bathroom to be sure Susan was out. It looked good and dark, so he went into his room, got a towel from his suitcase, and crossed the hall to it. Soon he was washing and brushing, preparing for bed.

In his room he lay tossing restlessly, unable to sleep. Insomnia had plagued him in his childhood and here it was back, probably because this was Boise once more and because he was so reminded, in the last day or so, of the old days.

What pill did he have that he could take? Somewhere he owned a bottle of antihistamine pills, supposedly for allergies and colds, but he had found that antihistamines put him into a relaxed doze and he kept the bottle for that. No doubt it was in the glove compartment of the Merc. For another hour he lay, but still he did not sleep. So at last he got up, put on his blue wool bathrobe and his leather slippers, and set out through the dark house toward the front door.

He successfully reached the car, but he did not find the bottle in the glove compartment. So he had to return to the house, up the dark path and onto the porch and into the living room, without it. Maybe it had been stuck in his suitcase and had filtered down out of sight, among the shoes. Thinking that, he started along the hall to his room, back where he had begun.

Before he could open his door another door opened and Susan looked out into the hall. "Oh," she said. "I thought possibly it was Taffy."

"I left something in the car," he said.

He opened the door to his room.

"I don't want you to worry," she said, from behind him.

"About what?" he said.

"About anything. You seem distraught."

"I just can't get to sleep," he said. "All the excitement." He entered his room and took a look at the clock.

Susan followed after him into the room. She wore a long pink quilt-like robe, with a narrow ropy sash. Her hair floated down in a great number of loose, light strands, without apparent weight. It came to rest on her shoulders, much longer than he had seen it to be before. "I have some phenobarbital," she said.

"That would be fine," he said, with gratitude.

After going off somewhere in the house and rummaging about, she returned with a yellow-plastic drinking cup, and, on the palm of her outstretched hand, a tiny tubular pill.

"Thanks," he said, rolling the pill from her palm and into his own. She passed him the tumbler and he managed to get the pill down, even with her watching. It had always bothered him to have someone watching him when he swallowed a pill.

Suddenly she put up her hand and pressed it against his forehead, startling him as much as if he had been kicked. "You're sunburned," she said. "From driving. I think you have a little sunstroke; you're probably running a fever."

"No," he mumbled.

She glided around the room to the window, lifted the curtains and shade aside to see if the window was closed. "I could hear you tossing around," she said. "Is it because it's a strange house? You know, I was thinking that maybe I'll just put it squarely to Zoe that I want you to start coming in. Tomorrow you come down to the office with me, when I go in at nine. Okay? So go to bed and go to sleep, so you'll be fresh in the morning. I want to show you all the invoices for the past six months, the things I've ordered."

The times that he had spent the night with Peg had been marred by Peg's need of keeping her hair up in metal curlers. And her hair, beneath the curlers, was plastered to her scalp in a hard knobby pad. But here stood Susan, with her hair free and soft, and it surprised him. How limited his experience with women during the night hours was. His mother had gone about the house at night with her hair up in a bag that tied like the tails of a Negro mammy's cap. That ended his experience.

Below her robe, he saw, her feet were bare.

"I'm always fresh," he said.

"Oh how nice," she said. "Good night, Bruce." She swept out of the room and shut the door after her.

The phenobarbital had started to affect him; his senses dulled, he put away his bathrobe and slippers and crept into bed. Presently he began to drift off.

The next he knew, the door was open again and Susan was coming back into the room. She came closer and closer to him, to the bed, and then she bent down so that she was directly over him. her hair brushed across his face, making him want to sneeze. Then the quilt collar of her robe pressed against his shoulder. "Can I get in?" she said. And, sliding and twisting, she was in, beside him in his bed, wrapped up in her quilt robe.

Sighing, she made herself comfortable. She pulled the blankets up over her and then she squirmed over on her side, facing him. And then she sat up, flinging the covers away, and began unfastening her robe. When it was off up over her arms and shoulders she wadded it up and pushed it from the bed, onto the floor. In the darkness he could hear the exertion of her breathing. The bed swayed as she dropped back down beside him, now in a nightgown of some sort; he could not see it but a portion of it rested on his neck.

Now, lying back, she waited. But she did not wait long. All at once she scrambled around, poking her sharp, hard elbows into his chest, to lean over him and peer at him remorselessly. As if, he thought, she could, by staring intently enough, make the room light enough to see. Make him, too, light enough to see. He felt as if she were lighting him up, making him shine everywhere, from head to foot. And still her inspecting gaze traveled over him, making him shine brighter and brighter. The glow of himself made him hurt and he gasped and reached up to move away one of her elbows.

"Hello," she said.

He said, "I can see you're not worrying."

"That's because of you. You keep me from it."

"What do you want me to do?" he said.

She said, "Do what you want." Her voice had a reconciled, obedient quality that was new to him; it was a very small sound, almost a kind of chant. Suddenly her eyelids flew open and she stared at him wildly; her hand rose and she pressed her knuckles into her mouth, as if she were trying not to break out laughing. "This is incredible," she said. Trembling, she rolled away from him and out of the bed, onto her feet; standing with her back to him she became silent, her head down, one hand on her throat, the other stroking rapidly at her hair.

He rose up out of the bed, in his pajamas, and standing directly in front of her, put his hands on her shoulders. Her bones felt hollow, as he pressed his fingers into her; she seemed to give, to become smaller. She let her arms fall to her sides and she remained silent, passive, even somewhat remote. And presently, as he held onto her, the troubled lines left her face. He pressed his hands harder into her, and for her the situation ceased to be a concern. Everything about her smoothed out and became relaxed and at peace.

Letting go of her shoulders he took her by the hand and led her to the bed. She went placidly, stepping in without a complaint, and arranged herself as he unbuttoned his pajamas.

"Cold?" he said.

"Not too much," she said in a detached voice. "I have a little headache, that's all."

As he entered the bed with her he felt her hands reach past him to pull up the covers. She drew them over them both and then she reached up and clasped him.

"I hope Taffy doesn't wake up," she said, all at once becoming concerned and stiff.

"Don't worry about it," he told her.

"But suppose she starts looking for me and comes running in here. Oh the hell with it." With a surge of authority she tugged him down to her.

Her hips were small, and her stomach, beneath him, seemed soft. But she smelled marvelous, from bath salts that she had put on. Her body, all over, was completely smooth, and without fat. She had kept herself in trim, like an athlete or a dancer. Just what he had longed for.

5

AFTER THEY WERE DONE they sat on the back porch in their robes, in the dark chilly night air. Wind blew around them and forced the shrubs and trees in the garden to lean back and forth. They could hear the wind stirring big, invisible trees off somewhere, in another yard.

It all had a world-wide quality.

Neither of them said anything. Susan had put on wool socks, large ski socks that covered her up to her calves. He had on a pair of argyles, but even so he found himself shivering and quaking, on and on, at an orderly rate. An almost mechanical tingling. Probably, he decided, it had to do with muscle fatigue. He felt tired in every part of him, but he did not want to go inside. He enjoyed the sound of the wind off elsewhere, plucking at trees they would never see.

"Scary," Susan whispered.

"I don't agree," he said. He could smell flowers. Once, a moth flapped past, banged against the screen door and departed. Perhaps it had gone inside the house; they had left the door open behind them, to be certain of not being cut off.

Gripping his hand Susan squeezed, and then she knocked her hard head against him.

"You've never been married, have you?" she said.

"No," he said.

"But you've had sex before. Either that or you've read a particularly good book on it. You didn't fumble around. I didn't think you would. I want you to think a long time about this. I'm divorced from Walt. It's a big step for a woman who's been married twice to contimplate a third marriage. But marriages are made and broken. It's better to take a chance and make a mistake than to −" She considered. "Fear isn't a good thing to go by. Holding back for fear of making a mistake. Or is this all so far beyond anything you've been contemplating that it's ridiculous?"

"No," he said. "It isn't." But actually it was. Now he found himself wanting to go back in, go to bed and sleep. "Let's go in," he said to her.

"Fine," she said. "Listen," she said, as she bolted the screen door after them. "You go to your room and I'll go back to mine. Mrs. Poppinjay has a key, and while she's supposed not to come until nine or so, we might oversleep."

"Okay," he said, more interested in sleep. The time was four-thirty and his fatigue had become an ache.

Going off toward her room she paused long enough to blow him a kiss. *Good night*, her mouth declared soundlessly, and then he lost sight of her as each of them opened a door.

What a night, he thought as he climbed into the still warm, damp rumpled, nice-smelling bed.

Marriage, he thought.

And yet the idea did not disturb him. It had a naturalness, as if it could be anticipated in the ordinary course of things.

I guess that would make Taffy my step-daughter, he thought to himself. And what about the office. R & J Mimeographing Service, my job there. Would I inherit part of it . . . become part owner?

It all sounded good to him. He went to sleep pleased, his mind on tomorrow.

THE NEXT MORNING, at ten-thirty, he and Susan drove downtown together in his Merc, to the office.

As they parked across the street, out of the two-hour zone, Susan said, "Listen, I have to run down and see about some dress material. You go on in and I'll see you there in about half an hour." Shading her eyes she peered and said. "The door's unlocked. Zoe must be in there. If she's too obnoxious, just walk out and sit here in the car, or wherever you want. But I don't think she will be. She probably just won't say much to you; she'll probably be busy typing."

"Is there anything you want me to say to her?" he asked, feeling vaguely nettled.

"No," she said, standing on the sidewalk and closing the car door on her side. In her suit she looked quite chic and well-groomed. "Of course," she said, bending down to lean in the car window, "don't mention about your living at the house or anything about last night."

Susan hurried off. He locked up the car, crossed the street, and with a great deal of uneasiness, entered the office.

As Susan had said, Zoe paid no attention to him. In the back at one of the desks she worked determinedly at the old, massive typewriter, turning out one page after another. For a time he hung around in the front, where the customers evidently were supposed to be, and then he took the bull by the horns and passed back of the counter, by the several desks. "Good morning," he said.

"Good morning," Zoe said.

He said, "I'm going to be working here."

"Ah," she said, in a merry, brisk voice. "So Susan tells me." Glancing momentarily in his direction she said, "Of course that has little or no importance to me since I'll be leaving."

"I see," he said, nodding as if it were news to him.

"Probably in the next few days. I've been wanting to get out of this dead-end for at least a year." She ceased typing and swiveled her chair around so that she faced him. More slowly and forcefully she said, "We've lost money steadily, as you probably know. I imagine Susan told you all that. She has as little faith in this business as I have. I don't know why she wants to go on. There's a dime store across the street that sells paper and ribbon and carbon paper; we can't compete with them because they buy so much at once. The big drugstore on the corner sells portables. That doesn't leave anything but renting machines and doing manuscript typing and mimeographing, and there isn't any money in that. Even if she had money to invest it wouldn't do any good, not unless she plans to move to some other location, and if she does that she'll lose almost everything we put into fixing this place up."

He said nothing. It threw him somewhat.

"What, exactly, did she hire you to do?" Zoe said. "Just do general work around here? Can you type? She certainly doesn't plan to do the typing and stencil-cutting herself . . . I've been doing most of it." Refined triumph appeared on her wrinkled, middle-aged face. She had no sympathy for him or Susan; she had become heartless now that she knew she was going to leave.

He asked, "What are your plans after you leave?"

"Oh, I believe I'll open a little place down near Dallas. I have friends living there." She whacked out a few more sentences.

"Well, I wish you luck," he said.

In a firm voice, Zoe said, "I wish you luck, too, working with Susan. Have you known her very long? If you can make a go of this place, it'll be up to you and not to her — she has absolutely no aptitude or concern. She merely wants to be able to draw enough out of it to meet her needs." Abruptly she stopped talking to him and returned to her work. Time passed, and then she said, "Have you had experience in retail selling?" She asked in such a manner as to suggest that it would not surprise her if he had years of it, that Susan had snared someone who could take over and manage the place with utmost efficiency. In spite of her dislike for him she obviously had respect for him, almost an awe. As if, by replacing her, he had already proved himself better equipped for the job. And of course he was a man. He felt, watching her and studying her, that she automatically conceded superiority to men. It would be a failing, a weakness in her. Part of the situation that had retarded them in trying to do business, in dealing with wholesalers and customers.

Two women trying to run a business. A disadvantage.

"I'd like to look over the last few months' invoices," he said.

"They're in the file, in the cabinet. Alphabetically."

Seated at a vacant desk he inspected the invoices, seeing how their costs broke down.

"Are you seeing what our profits have been?" Zoe asked, once.

Almost at once he saw that Susan and Zoe had been buying in the worst possible fashion, little driblets each month at the highest per unit cost. He saw, too, that they never picked their supplies up; they always had things delivered.

"What about returns?" he asked Zoe. "Defective stuff that goes back."

"You'll have to ask Susan about that," Zoe said.

Probably they were missing out on the possibilities of clearing their inventories through periodic returns. He wandered about the office, poking into the supply cupboards, the shelves of reams of typing paper, boxes of ribbon, flat packets of carbon paper, and the weary old typewriters which rented for five dollars or less a month. He could tell at a glance that these ancient machines took up most of the storage space; they lined two entire walls, from ceiling to floor. Most of them had a layer of dust on them. The window space, too, was filled up by machines for sale, all second-hand, nothing new. Like a junk store, he thought morbidly. His experience went entirely against used merchandise; it made him feel queasy even to touch dusty, dirty-looking objects in second-hand shops. He liked things new, in sanitary cellophane packages. Imagine buying a used toothbrush, he thought to himself. Christ.

Lighting a cigarette and meditating, he began to wonder about franchises. If new typewriters were being sold nearby, the manufacturers might be unwilling to open more dealerships. But . . . there were always ways to get hold of merchandise. As long as the buyer had cash, and preferably a means of immediate transportation.

He began to thrill to the notion of it. Transforming this place.

"I think I can do her a lot of good here," he said.

Zoe did not answer.

AT NOON Susan breezed into the office carrying an armload of parcels. She stoped by Zoe and began to show her different items. Bruce, conscious of her, continued working. Eventually she came over to him.

"Hi," she said.

"Hi," he said. "I'm making progress," He had discovered the accounts receivable file and was tabulating the total outstanding.

"You look so busy," Susan said.

From her desk, Zoe said, "If nobody objects I think I'll go and eat." She covered her typewriter and put her smock away.

"Go ahead," Susan said, in a preoccupied voice. As soon as Zoe had left the office, Susan sat down across from him. "How did it go?" she asked urgently. "Did she say much?"

"Very little," he said. He felt a certain amount of coolness at having had to enter the office alone; it seemed to him that she should have accompanied him.

"Good," she said, with relief. "She knows she has to accept your presence here." Leaning toward him she said, "Did she tell you that we tried to get the Underwood franchise and they wouldn't grant it to us?" She studied him anxiously.

"No," he said. "But I was wondering about franchises."

"If we could raise enough money to put in a genuinely big initial order, they'd give it to us. Don't you agree? You know all about that."

"We'll see," he said.

"I'm counting on you to get things for us to sell."

"I know you are," he said. "But I can't scare up the money."

"But you can arrange deals so it doesn't cost us so much. And you can get things on consignment. Don't you suppose?"

"It depends," he said.

"What do you think of the counters? If we get new portables we'll need a place to display them."

He said, "Speaking of money, am I officially at work for you?"

"How . . . I mean," she said, drawing herself up in her chair and frowning in a hectic, worried fashion, "yes, of course, you started to work this morning, as soon as you got here. I consider you an official member of the firm."

With great caution and tact he said, "How are we going to arrange my pay?"

"You get to draw from the receipts, the same as we do. Up to a point, of course. And we always write it down; we have a regular form we fill out, like a receipt, which both of us sign."

"But how much?"

"What — do you think you need?"

He found himself, with her, at this point, up against a blank wall. "It isn't a question of that. It's a question of settling the arrangement so we know where we stand."

That immediately troubled and confused her. "You decide," she said, in an impulsive rush. "Anything you say is all right with me. Especially if —" She broke off and looked behind her. "If we proceed in our plans, which I really hope we do." Her voice sank down. "Bruce, I want you to be free to decide what you want. I'll get out the books and you can see what Zoe and I have been drawing."

After she had shown him the books, and they had discussed it at length, they decided that he could draw up to three-fifty in the thirty-day period.

"Am I robbing you?" she demanded anxiously.

"No," he said, glad to get it settled.

"I want to pay you more. You're worth more. Maybe later on, when we have something to sell." Clenching her fists she said loudly, "God damn it, we have to have something to sell!"

A customer had entered, and Susan got up to wait on him.

LATER IN THE DAY he strolled across the street to the dime store to see for himself what they did and did not sell.

The paper and typewriter supply counter ran along one side, not visible from the street; the next counter sold imitation jewelry and buttons, and the store seemed about evenly committed between typewriter supplies and buttons. Their ribbons were heaped together in two cubbyholes. Each ribbon sold for 89¢, an unfamiliar brand, and he recognized them as inferior extra-short ribbons, good only for typing letters, absolutely unfit for office machines. He saw, too, that the store did not stock ribbons for all model machines. Their typing paper came in 10 and 25¢ packs, not reams. It, too, was cheap second-quality stuff, no rag or linen watermarked bond that typists like for their first copy. That cheered him up. And their carbon paper was blue.

He strolled down to the drugstore.

Sure enough, the drugstore carried four brands of popularly-priced portables, and each was well-displayed. the machines were placed at the end of the photo supplies counter, next to cameras and inexpensive tape recorders. He noticed that the drugstore stocked only the lowest priced portable in each line, and no office model machines.

When the girl meandered over to wait on him he asked about the guarantee on the portables. It was a flat ninety days, she told him.

"And I bring it in here?" he asked. "If something breaks?"

"No," she said, without concern. "You have to take it over to this repair place . . ." She dipped down behind the counter for a much-creased folder. "They don't do any service here. It's out on the highway to Pocatello."

He asked, "Do you know if there's any place around here that I can get professioal typing done?"

"I think there's a place down the street," the girl said.

Thanking her, he left the drugstore.

Obviously they had not gone heavily into typewriters. They aimed mostly at high school students and businessmen who needed some sort of machine around the house for occasional typing. His knowledge of the franchise system came into play; he recalled that often a franchise was let that permitted a dealer to sell only the low-priced items in a line, not the complete line. He could easily find out if the drugstore had a franchise to sell larger machines, were they to want to. Possibly they did not.

He recrossed the street to the office.

Standing in the middle of the office behind the counter was a short, swarthy, round-shouldered man wearing a natty gray single-breasted suit and bow tie. A cloud of cigarette smoke surrounded him as he puffed away. Noticing Bruce he squinted at him through horn-rimmed glasses, grimaced, spat out a bit of cigarette paper, and said in a hoarse but friendly voice, "I can't wait on you. I don't work here."

Near the man Bruce saw a leather briefcase, a satchel with handles. The man evidently was a salesman from some manufacturer. He watched Bruce with an ironic brusqueness, as if he wanted to wait on him but considered himself incompetent and certainly out of place. As if, by being behind the counter but not working there, he was flying false colors. He seemed apologetic.

"That's okay," Bruce said, going past him.

The man's eyes opened wide. "Ha," he groaned. "A slave."

"That's right," Bruce said. He saw no sign of Susan, nor even of Zoe. "Where are they?" he asked the man.

Shrugging, the man said, "Zoe went to the bathroom. Susan isn't here. My name's Milt Lumky." He stuck out his hand, and Bruce saw that the man had short arms, short legs, and a wide, flat hand, gnarled but absolutely spick and span, with the nails professionally manicured. The skin of his face was pocked. But he had well cared for teeth. His shoes, black and imported-looking, were scuffed but polished.

"Who do you represent?" Bruce said, as they shook hands.

"Christian Brothers Brandy," Lumky said in his gravelly voice. And then he ducked his head in a grimace and muttered, "Isn't that a stupid thing to say? This is one of my off-days. It gets me to come in and find nobody around. No wonder there's a recession. I'm from Whalen Paper Supplies. But imagine, a liquor company named 'Christian Brothers.' Sort of like the Jesus Christ Firearms Works. I noticed the display in the grog shop across the street. It had never struck me before."

He told Lumky his name.

"How long have you been working here?" Lumky said. "I don't get in here more than once every second month."

He told him that he had just started.

"Are you going to manage the place?" Lumky said, with resignation if not approval. "That's what they need, someone who can come in and take over. Otherwise they make no decisions. Everything slides. Where were you before?"

He told him that he had been with C.B.B.

"For that you get a kick in the crotch from me," Lumky said.

"Don't you approve of discount houses?"

"Not when they sell stale candy."

That was an argument that he had never heard. It struck him as funny and he laughed, thinking that Lumky was kidding. But the man drew himself up with hauteur and a determination to convince him.

"I got a carton of Mounds at a discount house in Oakland, California," Lumky said, coughing through his cigarette smoke in his insistence to make his point. He waved the smoke aside. "It tasted like soap. They must have found some left-over stock from old World War Two PXs."

"It's not all like that," he said.

"It's your word against mine," Lumky said. He put out his cigarette and extended a pack of Parliaments to Bruce. "I think it's going to fail because you discount people don't do a job of selling. It's a craze, like home freezers. You have to sell people." He said it gloomily, as if it was a fact that he did not necessarily approve of but which he accepted. His hands trembled as he lit a fresh cigarette; the end of the cigarette waggled away from the man's leather-bottomed Ronson lighter and he had to push it back with his thumb. "Anyhow, you stick with your story," he said, out of the side of his mouth. He had gotten smoke in his left eye, and it began to turn red and water. He grinned wryly at Bruce.

Entering the office, Susan said, "Oh, hi, Milt."

Milt Lumky put his lighter away in the pocket of his coat; it made a bulge that destroyed the proper line of his suit. "Where have you been? I helped myself to money from the till, just to teach you a lesson."

Isn't Zoe around?"

"Down using the can," Lumky said. "You want to go out and have a cup of coffee?"

Susan said, "I just ate; that's where I was. I don't think there's anything we want to buy this time. I'm sorry. Unless you have something new you want to show us."

"How about a line of cheap adding machines?"

"No," she said.

"Digital computers."

"No."

"Home-model Univacs for $17.95. That's your cost. Lists for I think $49.95. What a profit. Ideal Easter gift."

She put her arm around him and patted him on the back. "No," she said. "Some other time. We have a lot of reorganization to worry about. Lots of plans."

Twisting his head to look at Bruce, Lumky said to him, "How about you having a cup of coffee with me?"

"That would be a good idea," Susan said. "Milt, this is Bruce Stevens. He's going to do the buying." She lowered her voice. "Zoe is leaving."

"Come on," Lumky said, tilting his head toward the door to wag Bruce along with him. "I'll leave my crud here," he said to Susan, meaning his leather satchel. "You can look through it if you want to be infantile."

He and Bruce soon seated themselves at the counter of the coffee shop a few doors down.

"So Zoe de Lima is leaving," Lumky said, lighting a third cigarette and sitting with his elbows on the counter and his hands in front of his nose, his thumbs hooked into his nostrils. "Susan is doing a smart thing. She should have got out from under that two years ago. Susan is erratic and Zoe is pure chicken about everything. What a combination."

Their coffee arrived.

"You can reason with Susan, at least," Milt said. "But you could never get through to Zoe de Lima. She's rotten clean through, like an old pine plank. All Susan needs is somebody to tell her what to do." He slurped at this coffee, his napkin wadded beneath his chin.

"It's a good location," Bruce said, a little taken aback by Milt Lumky and his outspokenness. He was more accustomed to enthusiastic, sincere-type salesmen who never told the truth.

"I've know Susan for years," Milt said somberly. "She's a fine person. I always wondered about her, though. How she is outside of the business." He picked at one of his teeth, scowling. "Listen," he said. "Don't you agree with me that she's attractive as hell?"

"Yes," Bruce said, in a noncommittal manner.

"I always had it in the back of my mind to try to take her out some evening. For dinner or something. And try to penetrate that efficient pose and find out what she's actually like. Can you believe it that she used to be a school teacher? It's like finding out that the man who delivers your coal is Albert Einstein doing what he likes best. Of course, Einstein is dead. I read *Time*, so I know those things. It pays to keep up with world events. Don't you think so? You never know when it might help you close a big deal."

"Do you live around here?" Bruce said.

Lumky said, "Yes, goddamn it. My territory includes the entire Pacific Northwest, if you can believe it. I've been living up in Oregon, but that means too much driving. So now I'm living here in Idaho. Sort of in the middle. I go from Portland, down to Klamath Falls, then east to Pocatello. This is miserable to live in." He lapsed into silence. "I really hate it here," he said at last. "Idaho oppresses me. Especially the drive between here and Pocatello. Did you ever see such a wretched broken-down pure shit road? In any other state it'd be a county back road for farmers with wagons of melons. Here it's the federal through route. And those bugs down around Montario. Those satanic yellow gossamer flappy silent all-stinger bugs . . . did you ever hold a dead one up close and get a real good look at it? The god damn thing leers. How a bug can leer without teeth or gums or lips I don't know."

"I was born in Montario," Bruce said.

"I'd keep that to myself," Lumky said.

"If you had your choice," Bruce said, "where would you want to live?"

Lumky snorted. "I'd live in L.A."

"Why?"

"Because when you drive into a drive-in and buy a malted milk the girl who brings it has an ass like Marilyn Monroe's."

That answered his question, certainly.

"Don't think I just sit around brooding about women's asses," Lumky droned on in his hoarse voice. "Matter of fact I haven't thought about it for a year. That's what living in Idaho does to you. And there's nothing to do or read or see. There're a couple of good dirty, spitty dark bars here, but that's about all. Maybe it's the cowboy hats that get me. I never trust anybody in a cowboy hat. I always think they're a nut. I wasn't cut out to sell typing paper. Can you see that? Is that obvious? Remember that next time when I come around and show you the summer specials. Just tell me no and I'll go away. I don't give a damn if you buy anything or not. In fact I hope you don't. It means I have to write up an order. I don't even know if I still have my pen." He felt about in his coat. "Look," he said. "The fugging thing leaks all over. What a mess." He buttoned his coat again, morbidly.

"You'd like Reno," Bruce said.

"Maybe so," Milt said. "I'll have to drive down there sometime and see. What do you aim to do working for Susan?"

He said, "Get in something to sell. Get rid of the second-hand junk."

"You're right," Milt said.

"I'd like to carry new portables, but the drugstore's already gone into that."

"I'll tell you what you should go in big for," Milt said. "And I don't handle it so you know I'm not trying to talk you into anything."

"Go ahead and tell me," Bruce said.

Milt said, "Imported portables."

"The Italian thing? The Olivetti?"

"There's a Japanese portable coming on the market. Electric. The first one in the world that I know of."

"Smith-Corona puts out an electric portable," he disagreed.

Milt smiled. "But that has a manual carriage return. This Jap machine is all electric."

"How much?"

"That's the big problem. They were going to have dealers and sell direct. Import them on a direct basis. But a couple of the big U.S. typewriter manufacturers got scared and started negotiating. Meanwhile, the machines have never gotten onto the market. They're holding them up until they work out the franchise basis. There's supposed to be at least one warehouse of them around here some-where."

"I never heard that," Bruce said, his trading blood aroused.

They discussed it awhile, and then they finished their coffee and walked back to the R & J Mimeographing Service.

At the curb, Bruce saw a car unknown to him, a light gray sedan with an old-fashioned but highly classic radiator grill. The car had an archaic quality to it, but its clean lines implied recent concepts in design. Leaving Milt he walked over to inspect the car. A three-pointed star insignia attracted his attention. The car was a Mercedes-Benz. The first he had ever seen.

"There's a car I wouldn't mind having," he said, drinking in the sight with satisfaction. "It's about the only foreign car I can see. Look at the leather inside there." To him, thick leather seats were the last word in elegance.

Milt said, "That's mine."

"It is, is it?" He did not believe him. Surely the short, rumpled paper salesman was kidding again.

Producing a peculiar-looking key, Milt unlocked the right front door of the Mercedes. In the back of the car piles of paper sam-ples had been stacked up; some had slipped down onto the floor. "I've got thirty thousand miles on it," Milt said. "I've had it all over the fourteen Western states and never had a bit of trouble with it."

"Is it an eight?"

"No, no," Milt said sharply. "A six. This is a real road-holding car. It's got swing axles in the back. Synchromesh in low. They cost new about thirty-four hundred."

Bruce opened and shut the door. "Like closing a safe," he said. The door fitted perfectly.

After Milt had locked the car again, they walked on into the office. "I thought if I got a car like that," Milt said, "I'd enjoy all the driving I have to do. But it doesn't make much difference. A little. What I really need is another job."

"You want to come in and work here?" Susan said, overhearing him.

"That's the only thing worse," Milt said. "Retail selling. Of all the degrading occupations in the world."

She gave him a pale, serious look. "Do you feel like that? I wish

I had known. I had no idea. What do you think it does, corrupt?"

"No," he said. "It just corrodes your self-respect. You start looking down on yourself."

"I don't consider that I'm in retail selling," Susan said.

"Sure you are. What are you in, if not?"

"Performing a professional service."

Milt smiled. "That's a laugh. You know better than that. You want to sell something and make money like everybody else. That's what this street is for. That's what I'm for. That's why you hired McFoop here, to make your business pay."

"You're too cynical," Susan said.

"Not quite cynical enough. If I was cynical enough I'd quit this business. I'm just cynical enough not to like what I'm doing. Remember, I'm a great deal older than you, so I know what I say. You just haven't been in business long enough."

Bruce had no doubt that Lumky was kidding. But Susan took it all absolutely seriously; she went around the rest of the day with the grim tense look on her face, and with such preoccupation that at last he asked her if she was all right.

"She's all right," Zoe spoke up. "She just can't stand hearing the facts of life."

"He was just kidding you," Bruce said.

"I think he was," Susan agreed. " But it's so hard to tell with him. He has that ironic way."

Of course, by that time Lumky had driven off in his Mercedes, dour to the last.

"He's a very intelligent person," Susan said to Bruce. "Did he tell you he graduated from Columbia? A B.A. in European history, I think it was."

"How'd he get into the wholesale paper business?" Bruce said.

"His father is one of the partners in Whalen. You saw his car and his clothes. He has quite a bit of money. He's a strange person . . . he's thirty-eight and he's never gotten married. He's about the loneliest person I've ever know, but it's impossible to get close to him; he's so bitter and ironic."

Over at her desk, Zoe de Lima clacked away at her typewriter.

"She doesn't like him," Susan said.

"You bet I don't," Zoe said, without pausing. "He's vulgar and foul-mouthed. He's the worst of the salesmen who come in. I'm afraid to turn my back on him for fear he'll pinch; he's that kind."

"Has he ever?" Susan said.

Zoe said, "He's never had a chance. Not with me, anyhow." She raised her head and said meaningfully, "How about with you?"

"He's not vulgar," Susan said to Bruce, ignoring her. "He has extremely good taste. It's an outside shell, some of the language he uses. I think he's satirizing the men he has to work with. It's his bitterness against the business world and salesmen in general. And many short men are unhappy and lonely. They keep to themselves."

"Do you know him very well?" he asked her.

"We have coffee," Susan said. "When he's through here. One time he asked me to have dinner with him, but I couldn't. Taffy was sick and I had to get right home. I don't think he believed me. He was sure I wouldn't do it anyhow. I just proved he was right."

6

As he and Susan drove home that evening she said, "You didn't mention anything to Milt about your staying at my house, did you? I know you didn't."

"No," he said. He was well aware that salesmen carried tales from one end of the state to the other.

"We have to observe caution," she said. "I'm tired. We really didn't get much sleep. And this tension with Zoe . . . I'll be relieved when she's finally out. I saw you going through the invoices. Did you come across anything important you want to change?"

He outlined different matters he had discovered. Mainly he dealt with the need of buying in quantity. Halfway through, while stopped at a light, he glanced over and saw that she had her mind on something else; the rapt, faraway expression had again appeared on her face and he knew that she had heard little or nothing he had said.

"I'm sorry," she said, when he managed to attract her attention. "But I've just got so much on my mind. I'm worried about Taffy's reaction to not seeing Walt. He had become a father in her mind. I hope you will. That's how it has to be. I really can't interest myself in these little petty business details. I think Milt is right; it corrodes your self-respect."

He said, "I don't feel like that. I enjoy it."

Leaning over she kissed him. "That's why you're no longer living in Reno. You know, we have a wonderful future to look forward to, you and I. Isn't that how you feel? I feel as if I'm coming to life. I know that sounds corny, but that's the way I feel. There's probably a perfectly sound physiological basis for that sort of feeling . . . probably the whole metabolism is affected. The endocrine system, too. New enzymes unlock untouched energy." She clutched his arm with such force that he almost lost control of the car. "Let's stop and pick up something special for dinner. You know what I'd like? A can of crêpe suzettes. When I was getting cigarettes over at the supermarket I noticed that they sell them there."

He stopped the car in the supermarket lot, and while she sat waiting he trudged off and got the can of crêpe suzettes and stood in line, paid, and returned.

"I also have to stop at the drugstore," she informed him, as they drove on. "This one I'll have to get myself; it's not something you can go in and ask for."

While he double-parked, Susan disappeared at a leisurely rate into the drugstore. A car behind him honked until he was forced to drive off and around the block. When he got back again he saw no sign of her, and he drove around once more. This time he found her waiting and pacing on the sidewalk.

"Where did you go?" she demanded, as she hopped in and slammed the door. "I thought you were going to wait."

"I couldn't," he said.

On her lap she held a long square package wrapped with brown paper and white twine. He averted his eyes from it, feeling melancholy. This peculiar frankness of hers bothered him; it had from the start.

"You're so quiet," she said, once later on.

"Tired," he said. He had bought the can of crêpe suzettes with his own money, and he did not have much money. The arrangement about that still made no sense to him, and it remained to plague him.

"When do you feel you'll be able to take over?" Susan said.

"Hard to say."

"In a week?"

"Maybe."

She sighed. "I hope so. Then I can devote all my time to taking care of Taffy." With energy, she said, "You see, as soon as I'm in a position to let Mrs. Poppinjay go, I save two hundred and some dollars a month right there. And that's a lot, even these days. And I'll feel much healthier, too, when I can be home with her, take her to school and pick her up, and be with her after school."

"Does that mean you're not going to be down at the office?" This was the first time he had heard of that. "Two people have to be there. And I can't do any of the typing and stencil-cutting." He had watched Zoe doing it, and beyond any doubt it was a full-time job in itself.

"I can do quite a bit at home," Susan said.

"You'll have to be down at the office," he said.

"I'll be there some."

He let the subject drop.

"You knew I wanted you to take over," she said.

"If you let Zoe go," he said, "you'll have to spend almost as much time down there as you do now. If we can get anything to sell, that will be one job, that plus the general managing, and then the typing and stencil-cutting will be another. Later on we can probably give up the typing and stencil-cutting, but certainly not right away."

"Whatever you say," she said. "You know better than I." But on the rest of the trip to the house she seemed aloof.

After dinner, while he and Susan were doing the dishes, the phone rang. She dried her hands and went off to answer it.

"For you," she said, returning. "It's Milt Lumky."

He went to the phone and said hello, wondering what Milt wanted.

"Hi," Milt growled. "I figured I had a good chance of finding you this way. Finished dinner?"

"Yes," he said, with some resentment.

"How about a beer? I need somebody to talk to. I'll drop by and we'll go down town and have a beer."

"You mean just me? Or me and Susan both?"

Milt said, "Doesn't she have a little daughter?"

"Yes," he admitted.

"If you don't want to just say so," Milt said. "It was just an idea on the spur of the moment. I'll be around town a couple more days and then I take off for Pocatello. And then I'll be back in a week.

All I have here is a room with a bath and private entrance. It's not enough to keep me here. I eat all my meals out."

"Just a second," he said. He re-entered the kitchen.

"What did he want?" Susan said. "All he said to me was hello and were you there."

"He wants me to go downtown and have a beer with him."

"Oh, he must be feeling lonely. Why don't you do that? I'm tired anyhow; I think I'll probably go to bed as soon as Taffy does. I might read awhile in bed or watch TV."

As he returned to the phone he mulled it over. "Thanks anyhow," he said to Lumky. "We have a lot of business to talk over. Maybe some other time, and I'll buy."

"What!" Lumky said.

He said, "I'll have to take a rain check on it."

"What are you, Red or something? Okay, if that's how you feel. Maybe I can find somebody in Pocatello."

"I hope this doesn't mean our relationship is finished," Bruce said.

"No," Lumky said. "Probably not."

They both said good night and hung up.

"I told him no," he said to Susan. He did not especially feel like sitting around in a bar listening to anyone's troubles. "I'm happy where I am," he said, which certainly was true. Down in Reno he had sat around in bars, as lonely as possible; he hoped all that was over. There were, in the world, millions of lonely unattached men drinking beer by themselves. Wanting to tell someone all about it.

"As long as you're not going," Susan said, as she finished up the dishes and put away her apron, "I won't go right to bed. I said that so you'd feel free to come and go as you please. I don't want you to feel tied down, with me. In that connection I have something I picked up for you this afternoon but I forgot to give it to you." She went into the living room for her purse. From it she brought forth a doorkey, which she presented to him. "To the house," she said. "Oh, and also." She fished around in the purse and this time produced a key ring on which hung many keys. "To the office," she said, maneuvering a key from the ring. "See how free and relaxed I feel with you?"

The two keys improved his disposition. They gave him a moment of elation and he said, "I hope you never wish you hadn't."

"I know I won't," she said. "You wouldn't let me down, Bruce.

It isn't so hard to tell one way or another about people. We haven't talked very much about love. Has it been on your mind, though?"

"Somewhat," he said, feeling clumsy.

"It's not so much what you tell me," she said. "Because a person finds himself saying almost anything in a situation where there's so much involved. It's what you feel that you don't say. I've never been very articulate. And I don't demand elaborate expressions of sentiments . . . if I can't give it I don't see that I have any right to ask. I think I can tell what you're thinking. This gives you a lot, doesn't it? I actually know so little about how you used to be, before. I can only guess what you were like before you met me. Were you lonely that night at Peg's?"

"Yes," he admitted. "I had driven up from Reno. It's a lonely trip." He did not want to say that he went around habitually lonely; for some reason he shrank from conceding that. Perhaps because it would seem that he had been drawn to her through sheer loneliness, and that was not true.

Susan said, "I don't even know how many girls you've been in love with. Or how strongly you get to feel, emotionally I mean. Maybe you're not one who gets involved with other people very often or for very long. I guess time will tell. I mean about this."

"Don't sound depressed," he said.

"Oh, I'm not depressed. I've never given anyone the key to the office before. Except of course Zoe has hers."

"What about the key to the house?"

"Mrs. Poppinjay has one. Naturally Walt had his key. I know what you mean. No, Bruce." She said it in a small-girl voice, very low and positive.

At about twelve o'clock they heard something thumping outdoors on the front porch. They had been together in the bedroom, and even though the doorbell did not ring they ceased and returned to the living room, both of them ruffled.

"Somebody's out there," Susan said, smoothing her hair.

He opened the door. Standing on the porch, in the dark, was Milt Lumky. "Is that your Merc out there?" Lumky said. "With the Nevada plates?" Entering the house, he held out a bit of dried, wrinkled, torn paper to Bruce. "I took the liberty of tearing this off it," he said.

It was the remains of the C.B.B. sticker that had been glued to the rear window.

Milt nodded hello to Susan. His face, flushed, radiated heat. He wore a bright yellow short-sleeved sports shirt, a crinkly nylon. And soft gray slacks, without belt. And crepe-soled shoes.

"What's the good word?" Milt said. "You can't kill a guy for dropping by. I drove by and saw your car still here, so I knew you hadn't left yet." He seated himself on the sofa.

"If I don't seem glad to see you," Susan said, "it's because I've got a lot on my mind." Turning her back to him she made a face of lamentation to Bruce. For both of them this could become an ordeal. It depended on how determined Milt was to stay.

"Nice place you have here," Milt said, entrenched in the center of the living room, his hands on his knees. He seemed ill at ease, conscious that he had butted himself into the house against their wishes, but at the same time he intended to stay. He wanted to be there. Obviously he had no other place to go. "I guess you're wondering how to get rid of me," he said in his rough, humbled, but determined growl. "I won't stay long. I'll leave when Bruce does."

What he meant by that, only God knew. It made Bruce uneasy; he had an intuition that the man would crash around until he accidently or deliberately did some damage . . . he wondered if Susan knew any more. She continued to eye Milt with suspicion, but at the same time she seemed amused. Perhaps because he had been drinking. He exasperated and amused her at the same time, and Bruce thought of all the times he had felt like that about friends of his when they had had something to drink. The need to be alert . . . and in this situation, an additional need. But Milt did not have anything against them; that was obvious. He wanted to be around them, as he said. He needed their company, as friends.

But it was not a good time. They had no use for visitors; they were not in the mood to be good company. He had made a mistake. His purposeful manner showed that he recognized that, although possibly he did not understand why it was such a mistake. Now he would begin to ponder that. Why did they seem so displeased to see him? Bruce saw that kind of thought begin to circulate through the man's mind. They had to be friendly to him or he would grasp the nature of the relationship between them. In a second or so he would discover that Bruce was not going to leave. And then they would have to be careful with him.

The sight of Milt Lumky in his yellow nylon sports shirt, all tanked

up with beer, started in Susan a mischievous, heedless quality that
Bruce had never seen before. He had known people who got perpetual
amusement from the sight of drunks. Milt, of course, was not drunk.
But he had lost the capacity to hold his tongue. And that released
Susan from the obligation to be polite. It buoyed her up. She, too,
could say what she wanted; she could shed at least some of her
concern. She could rattle back at him with impunity, and Bruce
thought to himself, If that's something she enjoys then there must
be a lot inside her bottled up that she's either afraid to express or
doesn't know how to express. It's a bad sign, he thought, watching
the two of them. Suppose she takes advantage of him. He hated that.
He could never understand anyone tormenting a person whose reflexes
had slowed down after a few drinks. Cripples, drunks, and animals
had never inspired him. In fact they generally depressed him. He
always felt that he should do something for them, but he never knew
what.

"What about your coat?" Susan said. "Did you leave it somewhere?"

Milt muttered, "It's in the car."

"You must have got cold wandering around outside without it."

"No," he said. "I didn't get cold."

Susan said, "You mean you didn't feel cold."

"Have it your way," Milt said. "Hello little girl," he said, looking
past them toward the hall. "Come on in."

Turning, Bruce saw that Taffy, in her red-striped pajamas, had
come out of her room and was standing at the door of the living room,
staring at them all.

"Doesn't she talk?" Milt said.

Susan said, "She woke up and heard your voice. She probably
thought it was Walt." To the child, Susan said, "You run along back
to bed. I'll go tuck you in. It's not Walt. You can see it isn't."

Milt said, "My name is Milton Lumky and I'm a pipefitter from
Philadelphia, P.A." He held out his hand. "Come over here and sit,
instead of standing there."

Walking cautiously toward him, Taffy said, "Why is your face so
red?"

"I don't know," Milt said, as if it was a riddle. "Why *is* my face
so red?"

Taffy giggled. "I asked you first."

He reached down and lifted her up on the couch. "What was the idea of saying you had chicken pox that night in November 1956 when I wanted to have a big dinner and go dancing?"

Giggling, Taffy said, "I don't know."

To Bruce, Milt said, "Did you ever know a child who wasn't a liar? How old are you?" he asked Taffy.

"Seven and a half," she said.

"You see?" Milt said to Bruce.

"She is," Susan said. "Seven and a half."

"Here," Milt said to Taffy. "I have something for you." He reached into his pocket and hauled out a cylindrical metal object. "Combination bottle opener and ball point pen," he said. The thing, made out of tin and plastic, had stamped on it COMPLIMENTS OF WHALEN INC. SPOKANE WASH. "For writing on the inside of bottles," Milt said, showing her how to scratch blue lines on the back of her hand. "Can't be erased. Good for the rest of your life. I'll tattoo you." He drew a sailing boat on her wrist, with gulls flapping over it. Taffy giggled incessantly, embarrassed.

"What would she do with a bottle opener?" Susan said.

"She could pull off the heads of dolls," Milt said.

Seeing him and the child, Bruce realized that he had never considered her in his relationship with Susan. He and Taffy had no contact, and neither of them expected any to develop. But Taffy had gone directly to Milt Lumky, full of curiosity and friendliness.

It occurred to him, then, that he had never had any contact with children. And certainly he had no experience; he did not know what to do or say, so he did and said nothing.

Susan would want someone who likes children, he thought. Or would she? She had made no attempt to stir up his interest in Taffy. Maybe she did not care. Maybe she intended to be everything herself, fill all roles. If Taffy became dependent on him, then it would be difficult for her if he left as Walt and Pete — and perhaps others — had left.

That isn't what I'm wanted for, he realized. To jiggle Taffy on my lap and tell stories and play games. And, for the first time, he had a deep sinking sensation. Susan had absolutely no idea of an equal relationship. The complete inequality of it confronted him in a sort of revelation, full and undeniable.

But how could he complain? He had made no move to approach the child. No use blaming Susan; he had shown her that he did not notice or care about Taffy. Too late now. But perhaps if he had — as Lumky was busy doing — he would have put an end to his relationship with Susan. He saw her expression as she watched Milt Lumky. There was no sweetness there. No pleasure at his interest in the child. Only a frigidity, a wariness. Almost an outright hostility, as if, at the first pretext, she would snap her fingers and demand Taffy back.

Now, on Taffy's other wrist, Milt had begun to draw a woman's torso. "This is the story of Gina Lollobrigida and the whale," Milt said, sketching in enormous breasts. Taffy giggled witlessly. "Once upon a time Gina Lollobrigida was walking along the seacoast of sunny Italy when a gigantic whale appeared, tipped his hat, and said. 'Lady, have you ever thought of going into show business? Let's face it, with a figure like that you're wasting your time.'"

"That's enough," Susan said.

Milt paused in his sketching. "I'm now drawing the magical sweater on her," he said. "So it's okay; don't worry."

"That's enough," she repeated.

"The magical sweater is important," he said, but he stopped. "The rest of the story," he said to Taffy, "has to do with the wholesale underwear industry and you wouldn't be interested." He released her arm, to her disappointment.

"She can keep the combination bottle opener and pen," Susan said, in a tone that implied she had worked it out as a rational compromise.

"Fine," Milt said, handing the thing over to Taffy.

"What do you say?" Susan said.

Milt said, "I say it's a hell of a cold mean world when you can't do nice things for children."

"I don't mean you," Susan said. "I mean, Taffy, what do you say when somebody gives you something?"

Spluttering and simpering, she managed to say, "Thank you."

"'Thank you, Uncle Lumky,'" Milt said.

"Thank you, Uncle Lumky," she echoed, and then she leaped away and rushed from the room, back up the hall. Susan went with her, into her room, to tuck her into bed.

Milt and Bruce remained.

"That's a pretty nice little girl," Milt said in a subdued voice. "Yes," he said.

"Do you think she looks like Susan?"

Up to now he hadn't thought about it. "Some," he said.

"I never know what to tell kids and what not to tell them," Milt said. "I made a vow once not to moralize with them, but maybe I'm leaning over backward in the other direction."

"There's no use asking me," he said. "That's one topic I know nothing about."

"I like kids," Milt said. "I always feel sorry for a kid. When you're that small you can't take on anybody. Except smaller kids. And that isn't worth much." He rubbed his chin and studied the living room, the furniture and books. "She has a decent place here. Come to think of it, I've never been here before. It's comfortable."

Bruce nodded.

Returning to the room, Susan said, "She asked me why your breath smelled so funny. I told her you had been eating exceptionally strange foods that we don't serve."

"Why did you tell her that?" Milt said.

"I didn't want to tell her that it was beer."

"It wasn't beer. I haven't been drinking beer. I haven't been drinking anything."

"I know you have," Susan said. "I can tell by the way you acted when you first came in. And your face is so flushed."

His face became more flushed. "I'm serious; I haven't had anything to drink." He arose to his feet. "It's my high blood pressure. I have to take reserpine for it." Reaching into his pocket he brought out a pill wrapped in tissue paper. "To keep my blood pressure down."

They both were silent, wondering about him.

"Everybody's so suspicious of everyone else in the world," Milt said. "There's no mutual trust anymore. And they call this a Christian civilization. Kids lie about their age, women accuse you of things you haven't done." He seemed genuinely angry.

"Take it easy," Bruce said.

"I hope when your little girl grows up," Milt said, "she lives in a better society." He moved in the direction of the door. "Well," he said in a morose voice, "I'll see you both when I'm through here again."

As she opened the door for him, Susan said. "Don't leave mad. I was just teasing you."

Facing her calmly he said, "I don't hold it against you." He shook hands with her, and then with Bruce. "It just depresses me; that's all." To Bruce he said, "Where are you staying? I'll look you up when I get back."

Susan said, "He hasn't gotten settled yet."

"That's too bad," Milt said. "It's hard as hell to get settled in a new town. I hope you find a place okay. Anyhow I can always get hold of you at R & J Mimeographing Service."

He said good night, and then the door shut after him. Presently they heard a car start up and leave.

"I thought I should tell him that," Susan said.

"You did right," he said. But it disturbed him.

She said, "I didn't want you to have to take the responsibility of answering. There's no reason why it should fall on your shoulders. Do you think he came over to check and see? Maybe he had a suspicion about us. I don't see that it matters. He's only around here a few times a year. I think he's still interested in me, and it makes him jealous."

"That might be," he said. But in his own mind he believed that Milt had merely been lonely and had wanted company.

"If we went through the legal arrangements," Susan said, "we would be immune to this kind of situation. Otherwise it'll crop up again and again. You'll have your mail to think about . . . and don't you have to give the draft board your permanent address? And your driver's license. A million details like that. Even your withholding statements that I have to fill out, as your employer."

My employer, he thought. That's right.

"That's not enough of a reason to get married," he said.

She gave him a sharp look. "Nobody said it was. But I don't like not telling people the truth. It makes me uncomfortable. I know we're not doing wrong, but if we have to lie then it almost seems like an admission that we're guilty, trying to hide it."

"I'm not adverse to it," he said.

"To marrying me?"

"Yes," he said.

They both considered that.

After they had locked up the house and shut off the lights they closed themselves off in her bedroom, as they had been before Milt Lumky arrived. For a good long time they were free to enjoy each other. But all at once, without sound or warning of any kind, the bedroom door flew open. Susan sprang naked from the bed. There in the doorway stood Taffy.

"I lost it," Taffy sniffled. "It fell down and I can't find it."

Susan, pale and smooth in the darkness, swooped down on her and carried her out of the room. "You can find it tomorrow," her voice carried back to him as he lay in the bed, under the disordered covers, his heart pounding. More murmurs, both Susan's and her daughter's, then a door shutting. Susan padded back and returned to the bed. Against him her body was cold; she shivered and pushed against him.

"God damn that Milt Lumky and his combination bottle opener and ball point pen," she said. "Taffy dropped it down behind the bed; she went to sleep with it. She's got ink or whatever it is — dye, I suppose — all over the pillow."

He said, "She certainly startled me."

The thin, cold body pressed closer and closer. She wrapped her arms around him. "What a night," she said. "Don't worry. She was so sleepy she hardly knew what she was doing. I don't think she realized you were here."

But after that he remained in a state of discomfort.

"I know," Susan said, lying beside him. "It's upsetting. And you're not used to a child around. I am. I taught children. It's second nature to me, to think in terms of them. Don't for God's sake project on an eight-year-old child your own adult feelings. All she could see was me; it's my room and she knows I'm in here. A child is a child."

He tried to imagine himself at that age. Entering his parents' bedroom. The scene remained hazy. "Maybe so," he said.

"I've been married all the time she's been on this earth," Susan said. "Even if she had some notion of you here, it would seem natural. A man is a man. To a child that young."

But he knew that it would have to go one way or the other. Either he would have to move out and find a place of his own, or he would go through with it and marry her. She recognized that, too.

Did he want to marry her?

What can I lose, he thought. I can always get unmarried.

Beside him, Susan had gone to sleep with his hand resting on her breast. She held it there with her own hand. Beneath his fingers he could feel her breathing, the regular, slow breathing of sleep. To go to sleep, he thought, here like this. For myself, my hand resting on her. Doesn't that constitute the important thing in all this? Not the office or figuring out some method of making a lot of money, but times like this, late at night. And having dinner together, and the rest.

This is why I stopped in Montario, he thought. In fact, this is why I stopped at Hagopian's drugstore. Of course he did not have to use his package of Trojans. Susan had something that she owned permanently, refills for which she had picked up on the drive home.

"Are you awake?" he said, waking her up.

"Yes," she said.

He said, "I think I can see going ahead with it."

In the dark she rolled over to him and put her head on his arm. "Bruce," she said, "you know I'm a lot older than you."

"You're ten years older than I am," he said. "But that's okay. But I want to tell you one thing."

"Tell me."

"I was one of your pupils. In the fifth grade, in 1945."

She said, "I don't care whose pupil you were." Her arms closed around him. "Isn't that strange," she said. "That's why I looked familiar to you. I never would have had any reason to be conscious of it." She yawned, settled down until she was comfortable, and then, by degrees, her hands relaxed and released themselves from him. She had again fallen asleep. Her face, against his shoulder, joggled limply.

That's that, he said to himself, a little dazed.

But what a weight it was off his mind

ON THE FOURTH of the month, he and Susan flew down to Reno and were married. They spent three days there and then flew back. That night they told Taffy at dinner. She did not seem surprised. In Reno he had bought her an electric bowling game, and the sight of that did surprise her.

7

HE FOUND SUSAN, during one of the first evenings of their marriage, off by herself in the living room with the big scrapbook on her lap.

"Show me," she said. "Are you sure? Or did you mean you went to Garret A. Hobart." She surrendered the scrapbook to him, and, seated beside her, he turned the pages. Over his shoulder she watched raptly.

"Here," he said. He pointed to himself in the class picture. The round boy-face with its oblique eyes, the shapeless hair. Fat stomach bulging out over his belt. He experienced very little sense of relationship to the picture, but nevertheless it was of him.

"Is that you?" she asked, hanging against him with her hand dangling past his throat, her fingers touching him in a series of nervous digs. Her breath sounded loud and rapid in his ear. "Now don't play coy," she said. She traced the legend under the picture. "Yes," she said. "It does say 'Bruce Stevens.' But I don't remember anybody in that class named Bruce; I'm sure of it." She scrutinized the photograph and then she said in a triumphant, shrill voice, "Your name was Skip!"

"Yes," he said.

"Oh I see," she said, excited. "You were Skip Stevens?" She eyed him minutely, comparing him with the picture. "It's true," she said.

"I remember you. You were the boy the janitor caught downstairs at the nurse's, trying to peep in and see the girls in their underwear."

Coloring, he said, "Yes, that's right."

Her eyes grew large and then tiny. "Why didn't you say?"

He said, "Why should I have said?"

"Skip Stevens," she said. "You were a headache. You were Mrs. Jaffey's special pet; she let you do anything you wanted. I soon put a stop to that. Why —" She gasped with indignation and drew away from him, growing more and more outraged. "You were running riot, all of you. You started a fire in the cloakroom; wasn't that you?"

He nodded.

Her hand reached up toward his face. "I feel like grabbing you by the ear," she said. "And just twisting. You were a bully! Weren't you? Yes, you bullied the little boys; you were overweight."

With a certain amount of bitterness he said, "You can see why I didn't tell you. I waited until I was sure enough of our relationship. I don't see why any of this should be brought into it."

Her attention had returned to the class picture. Jabbing at it she said, "But you were very good in arithmetic. And you made a fine speech in assembly. I was so proud of you that day. But that business about peeping at the girls down at the nurse's. Why did you do that? That was a disgrace. There you were, sneaking around trying to see through the keyhole."

He said, "And you never forgot it."

"No," she agreed.

"You made a lot out of it every time you were sore, after that."

"This is weird," she said. Suddenly she closed the scrapbook. "I agree; we better forget about this. But I want to know one thing. You didn't identify me when you first met me, did you? It was some time."

"Not until after I left Peg's," he said.

"You weren't attracted to me because —" She considered. "Your reaction wasn't predicated on recognizing me. No, I know it wasn't. At least not consciously."

"I don't think subconsciously either," he said.

"Nobody knows what goes on in their subconscious."

He said, "Well, there's no use debating that."

"You're right," she said. She put the scrapbook away. "Let's think about something else. Did I tell you I got the key back from Zoe?"

"No," he said. She had been gone for an hour or so, and she hadn't told him what she had been up to.

"She won't be in tomorrow. We won't give her the money until the end of the month, but I explained to her that you and I were married and we would both be there, and she doesn't really want to come in. So we've seen the last of her. She gets to draw until the end of the month, of course."

"She's still legally part owner?"

"I suppose so. Fancourt would know."

That was a name new to him. "Who's he?" he said.

"My attorney."

"You've had auditors go over the books and make sure of the actual worth of the business?"

At once she became vague. "He had someone come in. They looked at everything. They made an inventory. And I believe they looked at the books and the accounts."

"Weren't you there?" He wondered why he hadn't seen it.

"It was while we were in Reno," she said. "Zoe was there, of course. He's my attorney, not hers. So it's all right. No, I wouldn't let them audit the books while I wasn't there unless it was my attorney doing it. He's a good attorney. I met him when I was doing some political work back in '48. He's a very astute man. As a matter of fact, I met Walt through him."

"What about Zoe? Didn't she have a separate audit made?"

"Yes," Susan said. "I'm sure she must have."

He gave up. In one sense it was none of his concern. But in another it was very much his concern. "I hope you're not overpaying her," he said, "just to get rid of her."

"Oh no," Susan said.

"Let me ask you one thing," he said. "The accounts receivable file. Did you buy it at the full tally?"

"I believe so," she said, hesitating.

"Suppose some of those people never pay. You assume all the risk. Do you remember about how much it came to?" Those were the customers who were billed each month for past purchases or services that they had charged.

"A couple hundred dollars, not much; not enough to worry about."

"How much of this was done since I met you?" he asked. He had an idea that a great deal had been arranged months ago.

Susan, with a smile, said, "Remember, you met me years ago. When you were —" She calculated. "Eleven."

"You know what I mean," he said.

She said, "We worked out most of it last March. We had a terrible scrap. We were going to split up then. But my marriage was breaking up, and frankly I just couldn't endure having everything fall to pieces around me. I patched it up with Zoe, and at least it lasted for a little while. But I knew it couldn't go on much longer. When I came back from Mexico I knew I wanted to buy her out; I told you that. Didn't I? When you first asked me."

She had told him something along those lines; he could not recall the exact words.

"Bruce," she said. "Or should I call you 'Skip'?"

"Not Skip," he said vehemently.

"When you were a little boy in grammar school, in my class, did you have any sex fantasies about me? It's common."

"No," he said.

"How did you feel about me?" She had gotten her dead-serious tone. "Old Mrs. Jaffey was so lenient on all of you . . . did it seem to you as if I was too strict?"

The question could not easily be answered. "Do you want me to say what I thought then?" he said. "Or how it seems to me now? It's not the same."

She leaped up and paced about the room, her arms folded beneath her breasts, pushing them up and forward as if she were carefully carrying them. Lines of worry once more appeared on her forehead, and her lips pinched together. "How did you feel then?"

He said, "I was scared of you."

"Did you feel guilty and you were afraid you'd be — discovered?"

"No," he said with firmness. "I was simply scared."

"Of what?"

"Of what you might do or say. You had complete power over us."

Snorting, she said, "Oh come now. You know that's not true; what about the parents? They terrorize teachers. They get them fired every day — one angry parent in the principal's office throws around more weight than all the teachers' unions in the world. Do you know why I left teaching?" She stopped pacing and intently smoothed and straightened her blouse. "I was asked to quit. I had to. Because of my politics. It was in 1948. During the election. I joined the Progressive Party; I was extremely active for Henry Wallace. So the next time when my contract came up, they didn't renew it. And they asked me to quietly leave and not make a fuss. I naturally asked why." She gestured. "And they told me. So I didn't make a fuss. It was my own fault. And I signed that damn Stockholm Peace Proposal petition, later on. Walt got me to do that. He was very active in the Progressive Party, too. Of course that's all in the past."

"I never knew that," he said.

"Some parents complained because I was teaching what they called 'one-worldism' in the classroom. I had material from the U.N. And then when they did research into me they discovered I had joined the I.P.P. So that was that. It seems like another era, like talking about Hoover and the W.P.A. I was resentful for a while, but anyhow it's over with. I suppose I could teach again. Maybe not in Idaho, but in some other state like California. Now that they're crying for teachers. They destroyed the school system with their witch hunts . . . they made teachers so timid it's no wonder nothing gets taught. A teacher who opened her mouth about sex education or birth control or atomic war got fired. So I didn't have so much power," she wound up, remembering what she had asked. "How do you feel about me now?" She dropped down beside him and placed her hands on his shoulders. "I want you to give me an honest answer."

"I always do," he said, with heat.

"Don't get hot under the collar. But you might imagine you should be polite. Not offend me. Remember, my period as a teacher is over with, so I don't sink or swim according to how good I am as a teacher. I don't conceive of myself in that role, and I haven't in years. But I've always wondered what effect I had. Naturally I tend to think — especially when I'm despondent — that I had no effect. Children are subject to so many outside chaotic forces."

He listened to this set speech, knowing that she was fortifying herself against what he might say.

"Listen," she went on, "I honestly won't be offended."

"That's not the point," he said. Leaning forward he kissed her troubled, rigid mount. It did not respond in the slightest. "To me it's much more important than it is to you; it's not you I'm thinking about."

"Why?" she said.

"You were grown-up. You were formed." He did not want to come out and tell her that she had been one of the great factors affecting his life. "Suppose I had been the worst student you had; what real difference did that make? You had a lot of other students. And it was only a year!" That irked him. Just a year to her, less than that since she had not taught the entire term. But to him at that time — a reality that continued indefinitely. What fifth grader can imagine the end of the fifth grade? It will be with him forever. "Thirty pupils but only one teacher," he pointed out.

"Tell me," she said, becoming upset, now.

He said grudgingly, "You represented a major worry in my life."

"You mean that I made you unhappy several times. I suppose you were unhappy after we marched you down to Mr. Hillings' office, that day we caught you peeping."

"No," he said, "it carried on. Not just an incident. I mean I always was afraid of you. What's so complicated about that? You mean you hadn't even thought of that? Don't you remember the day that Jack Koskoff refused to come to school because he was terrified of you?"

She nodded slowly, trying to understand.

"For years you scared me."

Angrily she said, "I only taught your class for a trifle over a semester!"

"But I remembered you."

"I had no authority, absolutely none, over you, after you got out of Garret A. Hobart. Why, I never even saw you again."

"I delivered your goddamn newspaper," he said, trembling with unhappiness, now that he realized that she did not remember that.

"Did you?" Her face remained blank.

He said, "When you had that big stone house with the other ladies. Don't you remember when you tried to get me to collect just once every three months, and I patiently explained to you that I might not be on that route in three months, and in that case I'd lose the money, and the next carrier would get it for not doing anything?"

"I dimly recall. Was that you?" She laughed nervously. "Did you *tell* me at the time?"

Come to think of it, he did not know for certain if he ever had. She had said hello to him, at the time, as if she had known him, recognized him. But she might merely have realized that she had seen him before, perhaps had him as a student, without identifying him as an individual. Or thought of his name. Or placed him, beyond that general recognition.

"Maybe I only thought you knew it was me," he said. "But you said hello to me every time you saw me. Also, you asked me how my mother was."

"Did I ever call you Skip?"

"No," he said. Not that he could recall.

"I didn't live there long," she said.

He said, "Anyhow, I remembered you."

"That was natural," she said, sighing.

"This really upsets me," he said. "Finding out that maybe you never recognized me, that time."

"Why?"

"I wanted to —" He tried to explain it to her. "Get into the house."

She burst out laughing. "I'm sorry. Like you did at Peg's . . . you mean through a window?"

"I mean I wanted to be admitted and accepted; I used to walk along and see you all inside having tea or something." It was hopeless to try to put across his former anguish to her.

"Not tea," she said. "Do you want to know what that was the four of us used to drink in the afternoon, around five, especially in summer when it was hot? We used to mix ourselves Old Fashioneds, and we drank them out of cups. So if anybody —" She waggled her finger at him. "For just that reason. So if the paperboy looked in he'd say, 'They're drinking tea. How British. How refined.'" She continued to laugh.

At that, he could not help smiling himself.

"Criminals," she said. "We had to be careful. That was 1949, and I was having all that trouble with the Montario school board. You could have come in; in fact you did. I remember. One month I didn't have any change, and I told you to come in. It was winter. And you came in and sat down in the living room while I went all over the damn house searching for change. Nobody was home but me. I finally found a dollar and a half in somebody's drawer."

He remembered sitting there alone in the big empty living room with its piano and fireplace, while somewhere off upstairs Miss Reuben hunted for money. He had heard her cursing with exasperation, and he had felt himself to be nothing more than a nuisance. On the coffee table a book lay open . . . she had been reading. Interrupted by the paper boy, at seven-thirty in the evening. How can I get rid of him? Damn it, where's some change? And, as he sat, he longed to summon up some bright conversation to use when she appeared again, some observation about the books in the bookcase. He examined them feverishly, but none of them were familiar. Just titles, seen through the perspiration and fright that kept him mute and stupid and unable to do anything when she returned but accept the money, mumble thanks and good night, and go out the door once again.

"I remember what you wore," he said, with accusation.

"Do you? How interesting, because I don't."

He said, "You had on black trousers."

"Toreador pants. Yes. Made of black velvet."

"I had never seen anything so exciting."

"That wasn't exciting. I wore them around all the time. I even wore them gardening."

"I tried to think of some way to say something interesting."

"Why didn't you just ask if you could sit around and talk? I would have been glad of company." And then she said, "How old were you then?"

"Fifteen."

"Well," she said, "we could have talked about old times. But I'll bet what you actually wanted to do was tear those tight black exciting toreador pants from me and assault me. Isn't that what fifteen-year-old paperboys secretly want to do all the time? That's just about the age when they read those paperbound books from the drugstore."

He thought, My god. And now this woman is my wife.

BEFORE GOING TO BED that night, Susan filled the tub and took a bath. He accompanied her into the bathroom and sat on the clothes hamper watching her; she did not mind, and he felt a very stong desire to do so. He did not try to explain it or justify it.

The roar of water kept either of them from talking for some time. She had put bubble bath into the water, and it foamed up in massive pink layers as she waited for the tub to fill. At last there was enough water in the tub. He marveled at the amount of water she needed. And she did not want it as hot as it was; she carefully switched on the cold until a good deal of the suds had been damaged. The whole affair struck him as inefficient, but he said nothing. He sat out of her path, a spectator.

In the tub, she lay back resting her head against the porcelain side. Suds covered her.

"Like a French movie," he said.

"Now you see, I never would have thought of that," she said. The suds had begun to depart. She stirred them around and they departed even more quickly. "They don't last," she said.

"You should have gotten in while it was filling."

"Oh really? I always wait. I'm afraid I'll get burned."

"Can't you work the taps with your toes?"

"Oh my god, what a morbid idea. How bizarre. Like a monkey."

All his adult life, while bathing, he had operated the taps with his toes, getting in as soon as there was enough water to cover him. Just enough so that he did not come in contact with the bare porcelain.

"There's one difference between men and women," he said.

"If that's what you do, keep it to yourself." Her hair had been tucked up into a plastic cap, and that, too, was different. And she scrubbed her back with a long-handled brush, and her nails with a small nylon brush. Amazing, he thought. So many differences in such a simple event as bathing.

For half an hour she remained in the tub soaking. He had never stayed in more than a few minutes. When the water got cold, he always hopped out. But she simply sat up, turned the hot water back on, and ran enough of it to rewarm the tub.

"You're not afraid now," he said. "Of getting burned."

She looked at him blankly.

After she had bathed she dried herself and then wrapped herself up in a white towel the size of a rug. Stepping into woven slippers, which she had brought back from Mexico City, she walked from the bathroom to the bedroom, where she had left all her clothes neatly arranged on the bed.

"Maybe I won't dress," she said. "We're about ready to go to bed anyhow, aren't we?" She had him go into the kitchen and see what time it was; the clock in the bedroom had stopped. The time was eleven-thirty, and he reported that to her.

"It's up to you," he said. The trip from Reno had not tired him, much; after making the drive so often he had no complaints about air travel.

"I'm emotionally exhausted," she said, standing in her white robe, still damp from the tub. "But I feel like doing something crazy." She tugged aside the window shade. "It's a dark night. I feel like running out in the backyard with nothing on."

"There's not much in that," he said. "Especially after a bath. And you'd get your Asian Flu back."

"True," she said. "But I do want something. Is there anything to eat? Let's eat something. Can you cook?"

"No," he said.

"I hate to cook. I'm no good at it at all. Fix something to eat," she said coaxingly, but with overtones of firmness.

Finally he went into the kitchen and inspected the canned and frozen food. "How about some shrimp dipped in beer batter?" They still had a can of beer from those he had brought that first day.

"Swell," she said, seating herself at the kitchen table in her robe, her hands folded expectantly. "I'll let you fix it; I'll enjoy the luxury of having someone to do things for me."

So he fried the shrimps in the batter and served them to her, and to himself.

"Bruce," she said, as they ate, "I'm frankly not certain what your legal relationship to the office is. It was mine — I mean, my share of it was mine — before we got married.

"It's still yours," he said, aware of that and having no desire to dispute it.

"But," she said, "as it expands you'll acquire an equity in it. It won't just be as if you worked there as an employee. It'll become joint property. I should have Fancourt tell me the law, for your sake as well as mine. I want you to have an equity in it. In fact, I've been thinking of having him write up the title so that you stand as co-owner. I'd do it like this: I'd *give* you the three thousand as a gift, outright, with no strings, and you'd buy Zoe's half interest, and acquire equal title with me."

"Hell no," he said, horrified.

"Why not?"

"I didn't earn it. All I want to do is build it up into something."

"But that makes you just an employee, who draws a fixed salary each month, for his work."

"That's okay. I'm office manager. In charge." In charge, he thought, of my wife and myself. There aren't very many people to manage. But, he believed, Susan would allow him to make the business decisions: she had already shown that she wanted to lean on him.

"You have complete authority down there," she said, nodding her head slowly up and down. "You'll be able to sign for things, and order things, and sign checks, and write up ads for the newspaper and so on. But you know — it's hard for me to realize it — all our money has to come out of that place. It isn't like it used to be; I could simply live on Walt's earnings when the office lost money. It's got to support two adults and one grammar school child. Two and a half people. That means it's got to net something like five thousand a year minimum, no less."

"That would be only about four hundred a month," he said.

"We've never netted four hundred a month. In all the time we've operated it. You know, all of a sudden I have cold feet." She put down her fork. "It scares me. Real panic."

He sat down next to her and put his arms around her, but she sat as stiffly as she possibly could. "Remember that you hired me because you considered me an expert," he said. That seemed remote, the original business relationship between them in which she had wanted him because he worked as buyer for a large and successful discount house.

"But you've never managed a place," she said.

That chilled him, hearing her talk like that. As if no matter what she said, about anything at all, she could in the next breath take it back, unsay it, force them to start over again at the bottom and therefore perhaps arrive at a different conclusion altogether.

"We settled that," he said. "That's water under the bridge. You presumably made up your mind, so I won't discuss it."

"I'm sorry," she said. "You have to keep me from backtracking; I know it's one of my fundamental weaknesses. Everybody says so. I tell them something, and then next day I get worried and I forget I said it."

"I know I can run the office," he said shortly, "so we can drop the subject."

She appeared genuinely contrite.

While he was putting the dishes into the sink, she said from the table, "Let's go somewhere. To a cocktail lounge or somewhere. I got spoiled down in Reno. I keep wanting to rush right out and have a big time. We do have something to celebrate."

"What about Taffy?"

"If we're only gone a little while she won't wake up," Susan said.

This sort of business being new to him he said, "What if she does?"

"She won't," Susan said.

"I'll take your word for it." He dried his hands. "Better put on something, though."

She disappeared into the bedroom. After some equivocation she decided on a plain dark suit. "Will this do?" she asked.

Putting on a sports coat he told her yes it would do, and then they sneaked out of the house to the Merc. Soon they had parked in the gravel before a highway cocktail lounge and cafe. As they stepped out and up onto the long porch, he said. "Wouldn't it be a typical blow if they asked to see my identification."

"You mean they might think you were too young to buy a drink?"

"Yeah," he said, as lightly as possible. But he wanted to prepare her in advance; it occasionally still happened.

"Then we'd leave," she said.

"No," he said, "I'd show them my identification. I'm not too young." Or don't you grasp that? he thought with some irony.

The waitress served them without comment. The place seemed quiet and warm, with no noisy people. In fact there was virtually no one there except themselves. They seated themselves in a booth at the back, away from the jukebox. Presently, however, a man and woman entered, both of them obviously travel-weary. They seated themselves at the bar, and as they drank their drinks they laid out a map of Idaho and Utah and began arguing in sharp, accusing voices.

"They've been on the road," Bruce said.

"Yes," she said, indifferently.

The couple, middle-aged and well-dressed, could not decide which route to take across Oregon. There were three routes in all. The waitress and the bartender had never driven any of them, so they were no help.

"I'll go talk to them a second." Bruce said. He got up and walked over to the bar. "I've driven the middle one," he said to the couple, who stopped talking and gratefully listened. "Route 26. I've never been on 20, but they tell me it goes over a lot of desert. 26 is mostly through forest. It's fine. Very little traffic, and some nice towns, and the scenery is terrific."

"What about 30?" the man asked.

"The only part of 30 I know is through Idaho," he said. "and it's lousy. But all the roads in Idaho are lousy."

"We found that out," the woman said. "We thought we'd try going across Idaho instead of Nevada this time, and we've lived to regret it. I'd take 40 or 50 across any time, in preference to 30. It's like a goat trail, up the sides of canyons — and all the awful construction work. We're completely worn out."

"It'll be better," he said. "Once you get into Oregon."

The man asked, "Do you live around here?"

He started to answer, No, I live down in Reno. But that was not true, now. "I live here in Boise," he said. "I just moved up here." He added, "I just got married."

The man and woman had noticed Susan, and now they both turned to wave politely at her and say congratulations.

The waitress, overhearing, went to the bartender, conferred with him, and then brought a tray of drinks for Bruce and Susan. "Wedding present," the bartender said, from where he sat on his high stool.

"Thanks," Bruce said. He felt embarrassed.

"What's your wife's name?" the woman asked.

He told her, and the man said that their names were Ralf and Lois McDevitt and that he was in the trout fly game. His company manufactured lures for fishermen.

Bruce invited them to join him and Susan, and they did so. The four of them chatted and joked for a time, although it seemed to him that Susan did not enter in, much; she answered politely, but she volunteered very little and her voice remained low, without luster. And she did not appear to be following the conversation.

Ralf McDevitt asked him what business he was in, and he told him that he and Susan operated a mimeographing and typing service. And then he added that he wanted to change what was now an office doing a service into a store selling merchandise. For a long time he and McDevitt discussed retail buying and selling. He told McDevitt about the chain drugstore across the street, and the dime store, and the Japanese portable that Milt Lumky had talked to him about. Once, he noticed that Susan was frowning at him. Evidently she did not approve of him talking so openly about business, so he switched the conversation back to driving and the various highways. That remained a topic for at least half an hour. In that conversation Susan took no part at all.

"We better get going," he said, deciding that she was tired.

The McDevitts congratulated them again, shook hands with him, gave them their address in California, and then Bruce and Susan said good night and left the cocktail lounge. There, near his Merc, the McDevitts' dirt-stained Buick was parked, with a water bag dangling from the rear bumper, bugs by the thousands dead and dying on the hood, windshield, front bumpers and fenders, and, inside the car, piles of luggage.

It made him conscious of the road. Here they stood, at the edge of the highway that crossed to the coast, into and out of one state after another. Mile after mile of it . . . in the night darkness he could see only a few hundred feet of it. The rest vanished. But he sensed it as he walked by the McDevitts' car.

And he could smell the hot, thinned motor oil that had begun to leak out of the crankcase of the car. It had gone so far, had gotten so hot and been in use so long, that oil now coated the entire underside of the motor.

Years had gone by before he had learned what that smell was. The smell appeared only when the repeated combustions had broken the oil down and nearly destroyed it; carbon had formed on the valves, and scale on the pistons, sediments had sunk down and been expelled from the crankcase through the breather pipe, and the watery crap that remained had been blown out past the oil-seal at the end of the crankshaft, to fly out at the clutch housing in the form of a spray that gradually, hour after hour, became mixed with dust and road grime and bodies of bugs and rock fragments and older oil from previous cars, and the smell of tires, and the smell of the entire car, its metal and rubber and lubrication and fabric, even the smell of the driver and passenger who had been sitting in their seats ever since sunup, getting out only to use the restrooms at gas stations and to eat at roadside diners and to ask instructions in roadside bars and to see what was making the peculiar noise on sharp curves. To Bruce, the smell had a dark nauseating undercurrent. It meant that a motor had been used and overused, and would have to be rebuilt or at least overhauled, given new rings, especially new oil rings, because oil was being forced out under the pressure that built up in the crankcase, but at the same time he thought of that motor wearing itself out on the mountain grades, in the Sierras, and on the long stretches of the desert that got it hotter and hotter; the motor had not broken, it had been worn out doing what it had been built to do. It had worn out over seventy thousand miles of road. Twenty-five times across the country . . .

"What on earth possessed you to rattle on to them about out personal business?" Susan said curtly, as they entered the Merc. "I could hardly believe my ears."

He said, "The man's in the trout fly business. He doesn't even live here in town; they're passing through. What possible harm could it do?" He had prepared himself for her accusation; he saw it coming.

"The first rule of business is that you keep your affairs to yourself," she said, still fuming.

"No harm was done," he said.

"It's the idea of it. What was it, the drinks? Is that why you rattled on and on? I almost got up and walked out; I would have, but I didn't on your account."

They drove in silence for a time.

"Are you going to do that continually?" she asked.

He said, "I'll continue to do what I feel is best."

"I don't see how —" She broke off. "Anyhow, it's done. But I hope you have better sense in the future."

"What's wrong?" he said, aware that something deeper was involved.

"Nothing," she said crossly, stirring about fitfully, unable to get comfortable. "You certainly enjoy talking about cars and driving, don't you? I thought you and he would never stop. It's so late. Don't you realize that Zoe won't be down to open up tomorrow — we have to get there ourselves!"

"Take it easy," he said. "You're tired. Calm down."

Suddenly, with a harsh stricken cry, she blurted out, "Listen, I'm not going to give Zoe the money. I still have it; I'm going to keep it and keep her as half-owner."

He felt as if he had lost control of everything around him; it was all he could do to keep driving the car. The familiar steering wheel felt in his hands as odd as if it were alive. It spun free of him, and he grabbed it back.

"I just don't have what it takes," she said, in a chanting, gasping voice. "I can't do it; I'm sorry. I really am sorry. If I don't give her the money then it's all off. She stays on whether she wants to or not. I know I can back out; as long as I haven't actually turned the money over to her. I asked Fancourt that originally. But that doesn't affect you." She swung around in his direction; in the darkness her eyes gleamed frantically. "You'll still manage the place; I know Zoe won't object."

He could think of nothing to say. He drove.

"It wouldn't keep us alive," she said. "We can't take the chance — don't you see, it would have to start supporting us right away, because we don't have any money. And we would never be able to lay in any stock to sell. Do you have any money?"

"No," he said.

"Can you get any?"

"No," he said.

"We can't do it," she said, with finality so bleak and bitter that he felt more sorrow for her than anything else.

"If Zoe stays on," he said, "you can be sure it won't support us. Isn't that true?"

"But we'd have the three thousand," she said. "That's what keeps preying on my mind. Once I give it to her, it's gone forever. See? We'll keep the three thousand; we'll have that, and then the place won't have to support us."

"Not for awhile, at least," he said.

Susan said, with no warning, "Bruce, let's give up the place. Why not? Zoe can have it. We'll offer to sell it to her, for whatever she wants to pay. Maybe for a monthly payment. How much were you making at that discount house?"

With difficulty, he said, "About three-fifty."

"That wouldn't be enough, but with the three thousand we could get along until you were earning more, and I could do some manuscript typing in the evenings. Can you get your job back?"

For reasons unknown to him he told her the truth. "Yes," he said.

"Let's do that." She had the urgency of a child. "Let's move down to Reno. I thought it was glorious down there. The air is much healthier down there, isn't it? That's why you moved down; I remember, you told me. I forget when. It's an excellent place to bring up a child; it's so clean and modern. Very cosmopolitan."

"That's right," he admitted.

"How would you feel?" Sitting beside him she yearned for him to say he'd like it fine. Her posture, her tension, begged him to agree.

"You change your mind too often," he said.

"Bruce," she said, "I have to be sure of a means of support. I know you're talented, and you know how to buy and sell, but it's too much of a gamble. This has nothing to do with you; it has to do with how much capital we can raise, and the business itself. It's a bad business. I know. I've been in it for several years; you haven't."

He said, "I intend to try."

"But that means buying Zoe out and giving up the three thousand," Her need of retaining the cash stood out as a major factor in her thinking. Evidently now that the time had arrived to surrender it she simply could not do so.

"Buy her out," he told her. "As you were going to."

"No," she said, but her voice wavered.

He repeated, "Buy her out. We'll give it a try. If I can't make it support us, I'll get a job and you can either sell out for what you can get, or you can operate it yourself. We'll see when the time comes."

"Do you genuinely think you could make a profit? Right away?"

"I think so," he said, firmly enough to affect her; he made it clear to her that he had no doubts.

"Suppose you're wrong."

"We won't die. We won't starve. The worst that could happen is that you'd lose your equity. But as soon as I get a job we'd be self-supporting. We'd be like any married couple; we can easily support ourselves and Taffy on what I'd be making. And we have the house. Most people don't have that. Even if it isn't paid off. Don't be so timid. Nobody starves in this country."

"I wish I had your confidence," she said.

"Give her the money," he said again.

"I'll — think about it."

"No," he said. "Don't think about it. Just hand it to her. We can drive over there now and give it to her now. Wake her up and stick it in her face. Where does she live?"

"I'll give it to her tomorrow," she said, falling into obedience to his certitude.

THAT NIGHT, in bed, she scrambled about until she was beneath him, clutching him with her knees and arms, with every part of her thin, smooth body. She wanted to go to sleep that way, but he found himself unable to sleep with her beneath him; she was too hard, too uneven a surface. Then she decided to see if she could spread herself out on top of him. She lay with her head on his chest, her arms around his neck, her legs within his. For a long time her pelvic bones pressed against him, but then at last she relaxed and fell into a doze. Around his neck her arms loosened. She had turned her head on one side, and her breath whistled down into his armpit; it tickled him and he still could not sleep.

Anyhow, he thought, she's asleep.

The next he knew the alarm clock was ringing, and Susan was sliding from him to get up out of bed. She had managed to stay on him all night. As he pushed the covers back and arose from the bed he found himself stiff and aching all over. On his leg a dark bruise had formed. From the bony edge of her knee.

8

THAT MORNING, at the office, he sat down with Susan and kept at her until she telephoned Jack Fancourt and told him to come over. Then he made Zoe de Lima come down from her apartment. When he had the three of them together he prevailed on each of them in turn until at last Fancourt gave Susan the go-ahead. Her face stark with fear, she wrote out a check for three thousand dollars, blotted it, and passed it across to Zoe. The mood of the room was funereal.

As soon as she had the check, Zoe nodded frigidly to them and departed.

Fancourt said a few things, briefly glanced over various legal forms, and then he, too, left.

At the desk, Susan said, "I feel as if some horrible calamity is just about to happen. I don't even want to get up. I just want to sit."

He unlocked the front door, so that they would be in business.

"A ceremony," he said.

"God," she said. "Well, it's done."

An hour or so later the phone rang. When he answered it he found himself talking to Peg Googer.

"I hear you're married," she said.

"That's right," he said.

In the background, muffled voices simpered; no doubt she was phoning from her law office, and the other voices were her secretary pals.

"I just can't believe it," she exclaimed. "It's true, then? Well, congratulations. I'll have to send you two a wedding present."

Her tone of voice did not appeal to him. "You can let it go," he said.

"It's so incredible — you just met her. That night. This must be what you read about in stories." She paused to stifle a giggle; at the other end of the phone a commotion interrupted her. He endured it, having no choice. "Listen now," Peg said, "you two will have to drop by together, and we'll have a party for you, a celebration."

"Okay," he said. "I'll see you."

Again the stifled giggles. He said good-bye and cut her off in the middle of a sentence by hanging up the receiver.

Goddamn stupid individual, he said to himself. It put him in a black mood, but he managed to work himself out of it. That's one thing I don't have to put up with, he decided. The innuendos of ignorant secretaries with their foul minds and their vicious, empty heads. Their dinky claques and foolishness to while away the work-day.

What a difference between them and Susan . . . the contrast that he had been so conscious of that first night. The babbling infantile clerks, and then Susan, self-contained and grave, even a little dire-looking in her black sweater. But completely a woman. Completely remote from them all. Off on her own, brooding, but someone he could respect. Someone worthy of attention. And the deepest possible love.

Now, at this moment, Susan labored away on a manuscript at the best of the several electric typewriters; she was putting something into stencil form.

The time has come to get down to work, he said to himself.

"Can you manage for awhile?" he said to her. "I want to go out."

"Yes," she said, with a forced smile.

He crossed the sidewalk to the Merc and drove off to visit a couple of contacts.

Not much later he was back, with the car loaded full of Underwood and Royal portables and a vast mass of display material, including electric motor operated whirling platforms.

"What I want to do," he said to Susan, "is make this look like a place where a person can buy a typewriter. A new typewriter." He began lugging the stuff into the store.

After that he cleared the second-hand machines from the display window, scrubbed the window clean with Dutch cleanser and hot water, dried it with rags, and then produced cans of quick-drying enamel and began to paint the wood a bright, pastel color.

"Tomorrow morning I'll set up a display," he told Susan.

On the phone he got in touch with a painting outfit and rented a paint sprayer, power-operated paint-removing equipment, ladder, and in addition he contracted to buy paint. He drove over and picked it all up himself. Wearing old clothes he began to scour off the old paint from the ceiling and walls. Flakes of old paint poured down on the floor and desks and second-hand machines. It did not matter, since he intended to modernize with the new plastic surfacing materials.

"Can I help?" Susan asked.

"No," he said. "You keep on mimeographing."

"If I can," she said, retiring to a corner out of sight.

"I want to get hold of a sign," he said.

With nervousness she said, "Did you buy all these portables?"

"No," he said. "They're on consignment. I don't expect to sell very many; I just want to show people that we're in the business of selling typewriters."

While resting up from the paint-removing, he phoned around and got estimates on neon signs. In the end he decided to wait until he had gotten hold of a franchise or two; possibly he could split the cost with a manufacturer. And in that fashion he would get a bigger sign.

After they closed up at six, both he and Susan painted. He drove out to the house and picked up Taffy, and she hung around while the two of them worked. They knocked off at eight o'clock for dinner, and then they resumed. Susan began gradually to gain vigor.

"This is fun," she told him, wearing an old torn smock that had belonged to Zoe. Paint streaked her face; she had tied her hair up in a dishtowel, but paint had gotten onto her arms and neck. "It's very creative."

"It'll make the place newer," he said.

With a small camel's hair brush Taffy did the fine edging. In school she had picked up experience along that line. The idea of staying up late appealed to her; they let her help them until ten o'clock and then Bruce drove her and Susan home and returned, alone, to resume work. He kept at it until two-thirty.

It makes a difference, he said to himself, surveying what he had accomplished.

The next morning he drove down early and began on the display. By nine o'clock, when Susan appeared, he had finished it.

"How does it look?" he said.

"Just wonderful," she said, standing in her coat and gazing around the place, entranced and wide-eyed.

Having finished the window display he set off in the Merc to shop for the counter material. He picked up a synthetic knotty pine; the material came in rolls, like veneer, to be glued on. Then he took a long look at cash registers. Too expensive. But he compromised on a receipt-writer that made three copies. Money would have to continue to be kept in their change-drawer.

All afternoon he glued and tacked away at the counters. When he finished, they had before them a new counter.

"I can't believe it," Susan said.

"These new plastic synthetic wood veneers are great stuff," he said. He then figured out how much it would cost to glue the veneer to the entire interior walls. Too expensive. So he got out his paint brushes and resumed the painting of the walls.

The last item that day consisted of buying and setting up an all-night spotlight for the window. It lit up one gold-colored portable. That, and the whirling platform, remained on all night.

"Costs money to keep it on," he admitted to Susan, "but it acts as a night light. It casts a glow into the store, so if anybody's inside robbing us, the police can see him."

The new colors that he had painted the walls and ceiling made the store much lighter. And they gave the illusion of greater size. The walls and ceiling appeared to recede.

"We just got ourselves some free space," he told Susan.

As they walked out to the car he told her that tomorrow he wanted to lay nylon tile on the floor. He knew where he could pick it up wholesale.

"Isn't that — and all this other — going to set us back a lot?" Susan asked.

"No," he said.

"What else do you intend to do?"

"I want to make changes in the front," he said. "But that'll take professional carpenters. I'll let that go until we're wealthy. Maybe later on this year. And I'm going to dump all the junky old dogs. The used machines. Those damn old Underwood 5 models that you're trying to sell for fifteen dollars. They're not worth the space they occupy. You have to figure the value of the space. In a store this small, space is worth quite a bit. You can plaster and paint and buy new fixtures, but you can't create space." That reminded him that he wanted to see about new overhead lights, the soft fluorescent kind.

"I hope we don't go bankrupt," she said. "Just buying paint."

"We'll go bankrupt buying things to sell," he told her. That was the big thing. Something to sell.

God damn it, he thought, *I've got to get something I can sell!*

ARMED WITH THE STORE'S BOOKS — he affirmed it to be a store, now, and not an office — he showed up at the Idaho Central Bank, Boise Branch, and opened discussions about a loan.

After several hours of discussion the bank informed him that all things considered, they possibly could advance the store a long-term loan of two thousand dollars. It would take at least a week to approve it. But very possibly it would eventually go through.

He left the bank in a happy frame of mind.

That evening he arranged for a babysitter to take care of Taffy. He drove Susan out along the county road that brought them eventually to the farmhouse in which his parents lived. The bumpy drive made Susan a little carsick. When at last they parked, she said, "Could we sit for a while? Before we go in?"

He said, "I want to go in first anyhow." He had not told his parents about his marriage.

"That's fine with me," she said. She had put on white gloves and a hat; very dressed-up, with much lipstick, she had the same dramatic aura that he had been so taken with, that first night. But her cheeks had a hollowness, and lines had formed under her eyes. Beyond any doubt she did need a rest.

"There're a few things I want to discuss with them first," he said. He kissed her, got out of the car, and walked up the gravel and dirt shoulder to the gate.

Here it was again, the tall gray ancient farmhouse, with dry soil around it, the weeds and geraniums growing out of the bare brown earth. No lawn. No green to speak of, except the ivy growing over the fence and around the gate. On the front porch a row of flower pots had in them indistinct clumps of growth. And he saw a wicker chair, and a plantstand on which lay a stack of *Reader's Digests*.

Imagine having been born in a run-down building like this, he said to himself, as he opened the gate.

Off in the back a dog whooped noisily. He saw yellow light behind the window shades of the front room. And he could hear the boom of a TV set. Parked near the tumble-down garage was the same rusting, useless carcass of a 1930 Dodge; he had fooled around in it as a child.

I lived here while I attended Garret A. Hobart Grammar School.

The basement windows had cobwebs behind then; one showed a crack, which had been stuffed with a rag. So his father did not sleep down there any longer, now that both he and Frank had left. No doubt his father slept upstairs in one of their rooms.

His father had slept during the day, arising at ten o'clock at night, pushing up the trap door and appearing so that he could shave and eat and set off for his job. During the day he slept under their feet, beneath the floorboards. With the quart jars of apricots and the lumber and wiring.

In the morning, home from work, his father smacked off the white dust covering him; his job at the Snow White Bakery kept him buried elbow-deep in flour. Then, in the basement, he involved himself in another white dust: plaster dust, from his eternal puttering about with new partitions. He intended to make the basement into several rooms, to create a separate apartment with bath and bowl which he would rent out. The war had stopped his supply of materials. Outside the house, along the driveway, rolls of wire and heaps of beaverboard gathered bird excretion, rust, and rot. Sacks of cement became wet and sank into corruption that allowed tiny weeds to sprout within them. In the basement, before he retired at two in the afternoon, his father sawed away, filling his lungs with sawdust. He patiently breathed in wood dust, flour, plaster dust, and, in the summer, dust and weed-pollen from the fields.

Bruce, standing on the path, saw in the evening darkness that the apricot trees by the back door had died. Thank God, he thought. Nobody had ever used the apricots; the thousands of jars of them down in the basement would never be opened. As a kid he had lugged jars outdoors and hurled rocks at them, bursting them in showers of sticky juice and glass. That had brought the hornets. In summer, the pools of apricot juice had become a buzzing swamp, wriggling with the yellow backs of the hornets. Nobody had dared go within yards of them.

Up the steps, now, to rap on the front door. Under his feet the boards of the porch sagged; the entire porch leaned. At one time, years ago, the house and porch had been painted a battleship gray. Now the house had chipped and peeled until the boards themselves showed through, strips of yellowish brown beneath the gray.

He lifted back the metal knocker and let it bang.

The door opened and there stood Noel Stevens, his face smeared with day-old beard, in his suspenders, his shirtsleeves rolled up. He admitted Bruce without comment. His father, heavy and inert, lifted his hand and silently beckoned to Bruce's mother, who was in the kitchen. To Bruce, his father had always looked like a workman from the turn of the century, the massive honest not-too-bright Swedish hodcarrier or plumber who had arrived and gone directly to Minnesota and had never learned the language or visited any of the cities. The man's face was wide, shiny except for the cheeks and chin, with a long nose bent or broken in the center, and fleshy. The skin, below his eyes, showed many craters that were faintly brown, almost like liver spots.

"Well . . . by golly," his father said. His reddish hairless hand appeared, and Bruce took it.

From the kitchen his mother appeared. The tiny, tanned, clever, churchy face beaming at him, the bright eyes. Here, in her own house, she wore plain clean clothes that he identified with the rural people, the small-town Idaho people. She smiled up at him, and her grayish, transluscent false teeth, the color of a celluloid comb, caught the light and sparkled.

"Hi," Bruce said, his hand still clasped in his father's flat wet limp palm and fingers. "How have you been?"

"Fine," his father said, letting go of his hand at last and reseating himself in his deep armchair; the springs twanged under him.

His mother caught hold of him and fastened her mouth to his cheek; it happened so fast that she had sprung back before he could stir. "How nice to see you!" she cried. "How's Reno?"

"I'm not living in Reno any more," he said. He seated himself, and she did so, too. They both watched him expectantly, his father's face dull, his mother's merry and kindly, catching every move he made, every word he said. "I'm living up in Boise. I got married."

"Oh!" his mother gasped, wincing, shocked. His father remained unstirred.

"Just the other day," he said.

His father still did not respond.

"I don't believe it," his mother wailed.

To her, his father said, "He wouldn't tell you if it wasn't true."

"No," she said, "I don't believe it. Who is she?" she demanded, to first one of them and then the other.

"I don't know," his father said, tapping her on the knee. "Just settle down." To Bruce he said, "Is that her out in the car?"

"Is she out there?" his mother cried, springing up and running to the window. "How did you know she was out there?" she asked his father.

His father answered in his slow way, "I heard the car stop so I looked out to see who it was stopping."

"Bring her in," his mother said, starting toward the door. "What's her name?"

"Don't you go and get her," his father ordered.

"Yes," his mother said. Opening the door she started out onto the porch.

"Come and sit down!" his father said loudly.

She returned, flustered and red-faced. "Why did you leave her out in the car?" she asked Bruce.

"He'll tell you," his father said.

"She's feeling carsick," Bruce said.

"Tell her to come inside and lie down," his mother said.

"I want to talk to you first," Bruce said. "I'm not bringing her in her until you swear on the Bible not to say anything mean to her."

"Nobody is going to say anything mean," his father said.

"I'm not bringing her in here until you both make up your minds to do what you ought to do and not what you feel like doing," he said. "If you say anything mean to her, I'll leave and you won't see either of us again. I've thought it over and I'm sorry but I don't feel like having you give her a hard time."

His father said, "He's right."

"Yes," his mother agreed. "Well, do we get to see her?"

Bruce said, "She's older than I am."

"How much older?" his mother said.

"That doesn't matter," his father said. "If Bruce married her that's what you better concern yourself with. It's not up to you to decide."

"Ten years," Bruce said. "She's thirty-four."

His mother began to cry.

"Ten years is a lot," his father said, with gravity.

"Now I've told you," Bruce said.

They both sat unhappily, collecting their emotions.

"What did you want to discuss with us first?" his father asked.

Bruce said, "I want to see what financial shape you're in these days. Look," he said. "You sent Frank to college but I had to go to work right after high school; in fact I worked while I was in high school. What about a wedding present?"

"We'll give you a wedding present," his father said.

"I don't mean a ten-dollar bill," Bruce said. "We need thousands of dollars, six or seven thousand."

His father nodded, as if that seemed perfectly natural to him.

"I wanted to ask you first before I brought her in," Bruce said. "It's for me, so it has nothing to do with her. It's so I can get started in business." He told them a little about the store. They both listened, but he doubted that they understood. They were too numbed. Too taken by surprise. "I can't fool around about it," he said. "I can't take time to be polite; we have to have it right away. I want to get it now, before I bring her in." His voice had risen until he was shouting at them; they sat driven back against their chairs, not interrupting him. He had successfully intimidated them, which was the only way he could hope to get it. He talked on and on and they listened; he explained the whole thing to them and then he pounced on them demanding, "You sent Frank to college; it's time you did something for me, and this is the time I really need it." He ignored the fact that Frank had won one scholarship after another. "What do you say?" he said.

His father said, "We always intended to help you when you made up your mind what line you wanted to go into." He spoke with dignity.

"Good," Bruce said, delighted; he had beaten them. By the sheer weight of his voice he had made them accept what he said; he had gotten past their natural frugality and common sense. "Now, what can you do for me?" he said. "Look, I want to bring her inside; she's getting cold out there and I told her I'd be back in a couple of seconds." He leaped up and paced about urgently, forcing his impatience onto them.

His parents dithered in their desire to fix things up. His father sat down in the dining room and began searching ponderously for his check book; his mother ran upstairs for a fountain pen. A moment later he had his father's check for one thousand dollars, and his parents were telling him that they wished they could give them more. His mother, weeping again, wanted only to see Susan; she had no interest in the money. His father muttered apologetically that maybe later on, when he had a chance to take a look at the bonds he had downtown in his bank deposit box, he might be able to add something to it.

"I'll go get her," Bruce said, as if he had now been released. He strode out onto the porch; his parents accompanied him as far as the steps and stood fearfully as he opened the car door.

Susan said, "I feel better. Are those your parents?" She could see them on the porch. "I wish I didn't have to go in, but I guess I have to." Carefully holding her skirt down, she slid across the car seat; he held the door open and she stood up beside him, holding her purse and gloves, preparing herself.

"We won't stay long," he said to her as together they climbed the steps to the porch.

"It leans," she said.

"It always did. It won't collapse." He took her arm. The porchlight had been turned on, and in the uneven glare Susan's face took on a mottled cast. His parents, on the porch above them, peered down in a state of near hysteria; he had never seen anyone so deeply affected by the sight of anyone else. As soon as Susan reached the porch — she moved as slowly and regularly as possible — his mother seized her and propelled her inside. That was the last he saw of them for some time, but their voices, from different parts of the house, remained audible.

His father, accompanying him indoors, said, "Nobody would have any idea that she's older than you."

That was not true, but he felt it to be well-meant. "Her name's Susan," he said. And then, for the first time, it struck him that possibly one or both of his parents might have met her back when she had been his teacher; there had been PTA meetings — I wish I had thought of it before, he thought, because now it was too late. "We can't stay long," he said.

"How did you happen to meet her?" his father asked.

He gave him a meager account.

"Then she's from Boise," his father said, pleased. "Not Reno."

If they find out that she was my fifth grade teacher, he thought, they'll probably want the thousand dollars back. At that, he laughed.

In the kitchen his mother was showing Susan a set of hideous ornate dishes that a friend had sent her from Europe, and Susan was exclaiming at their beauty. He began to feel a little more relaxed.

ON THE DRIVE BACK HOME he stopped in downtown Boise at a drugstore, telling Susan that he wanted to pick up cigarettes. What he actually bought was a box of envelopes and some three-cent stamps. He put the check into an envelope and addressed it to himself and Susan, stuck a stamp on it, and gave it to the clerk to mail for him.

"What was your parents' reaction to me?" Susan asked several times on the trip.

"We'll see," he said. He had not told her about the check.

"How do you mean, 'We'll see'?"

"If they liked you," he said, "they'll express it concretely. With people like that, old-fashioned rural people, there's nothing to interpret. They'll give you their reaction; you'll know."

"I wondered," she said. "Because I couldn't tell a thing. Your mother was sweet and upset and he was polite, but I couldn't tell how much they meant it."

The next day the envelope with his father's check arrived at the store. He opened it and showed it to Susan.

"See?" he said. "They approve."

Transfixed, she said, "Bruce, it saves our lives. Look what you can get at dealer's cost with that." It brought about a genuine change in her morale; for the rest of the day she planned and schemed and considered an infinite number of future solutions. "What grand people they are," she said to him. "We should write to them or even go back out there and thank them personally. I feel so odd — but I guess it's all right to accept it."

"Sure it is," he said.

"Why don't I call them on the phone and thank them?"

He said, "Let me do it."

WITH THE THOUSAND DOLLARS CASH he was able to assure the loan from the bank. It came through at the end of the month; now he had twenty-five hundred dollars with which to buy goods to sell. But he still did not know what to buy. He put the money into an account that would draw four percent interest, and the interest on the total was not much less than the interest due on the fifteen-hundred dollar bank loan.

But I have to find a warehouse full of something soon, he realized. Or borrowing and begging this money will have been a mistake. As of now we're making nothing; we'll have to start dipping into the account to pay our monthly bills.

Maybe I'll wind up using the money to meet the monthly payments due on the loan. That would be a novel way of doing business.

By now he had scouted the Boise area and found nothing. To Susan he said, "I think I'll have to get out on the road."

"To where?" she said. "You mean a long trip?"

"Maybe to L.A. Or to Salt Lake City. Or Portland. Some place where I can find something warehoused. I can't let that money sit."

He began to make calls long-distance, trying to scout something in advance.

TWO DAYS LATER he had the Merc entirely lubed and checked over, its tires rotated, and then, with a suitcase in the trunk, he set off by himself on Highway 26, going west into Oregon and California.

9

THE FIRST STRETCH of driving brought him entirely through Oregon and into the northern-most part of California. Turning south he passed through Klamath Falls, through the border station, and then made the difficult drive past Mount Shasta and along the twisting grades near Dunsmuir in the deepest part of the lumber country, with lakes and fast-moving water always within sight.

Early in the morning he left the mountainous lumber country and came out onto furiously-hot flat valley farmland. Worn out, he pulled off the road at the first motel.

The motel amounted to nothing more than shack-like cabins facing one another in two lines, with gravel strewn about, and giant century plants at the office door. In a pair of lawn chairs a middle-aged couple slept, shaded by a beach umbrella. Several cars had pulled off the road and parked. He saw and heard a few children scratching in the dust in the shadows by a cabin porch.

However, he had already shut off his motor. After haggling with the motel owner he made his regular deal: use of the cabin for a period of eight hours for a dollar and a half. His tenancy did not entitle him to bathe, or to get into the bed, but he could wash his face, use the hand towel but not the bath towel, lie on the bed without throwing back the covers or touching the sheets, and naturally he could make use of the potty. At eight in the morning he locked up his car, entered the badly-ventilated cabin, and lay down for his nap.

At four in the afternoon the owner woke him. A number of cars had begun to show up, and the cabin was needed. He collected his watch, which he had taken off, and his shoes, and padded groggily outside into the still-blinding sunlight. As soon as he was out, the owner's wife hurried in with a fresh hand towel and soap.

"Any place around here I can eat?" he asked the owner, a short balding cross-looking man.

"There's a coffee shop and gas station about ten miles farther on," the man said, striding off to greet a Plymouth full of people that had come crunching over the gravel toward the motel office.

Bruce got back into his car, started up the engine, and drove back onto the road.

When he spied the coffee shop he drove up to the pumps of the gas station, told the attendant to fill the tank, and, leaving the car there, jogged across the highway to the coffee shop. While he ate a meal of meatloaf with gravy, canned peas, coffee and berry pie, he watched the attendant checking the water and tires and battery.

Lighting a cigarette he sat at his empty plate, conscious of his loneliness.

The all-night drive had not given him any pleasure. The glare of oncoming headlights had bothered him more than usual. And the straining, hour by hour, to stay awake and see each of the reflector-posts that indicated bends. He had played the car radio all night, hearing mostly static and indistinct snatches of popular tunes from stations too far off to be identified. They floated in and out. Faint voices of announcers, speaking from other states, selling products for stores that he would never see.

And of course he had run over a variety of running shapes, some of them rabbits, some possibly snakes and lizards. And just at sunup two brilliantly-colored birds had flitted directly in front of him and then vanished. Later, at a gas station, when he had raised the hood, he had found both birds dead and crushed at the bottom of the radiator. He had been unable to avoid any of the things he ran over, and that depressed him. He could not drive the highway without killing one small animal after another. And the number of already-dead animals, flattened out on the pavement ahead of him, exceeded all count.

At night, on the highway, he passed through closed-up towns in which not a single light had been left on. Those towns alarmed him. No persons, no motion. Not even cars parked at the gray-dark shops. The gas stations empty and deserted, too; a terrible sight for the driver to see. But sooner or later a lit-up gas station put in an appearance, often with one or more giant diesel trucks parked nearby with motors on, the drivers inside the cafe eating roast beef sandwiches. Spot of yellow light, with jukebox going, washroom standing door-ajar, gleaming white tiles and bowl, paper towels, mirror. Entering, he had washed his face, and looked out past the open door, at the lumber forest. At the flat blackness outside the washroom. How lonely it all was. How silent.

He thought, Once you get used to spending your nights with someone else, then you are sunk for this. Once you learn how it feels to wake up and see another face near yours. And have another person flop over against you in the early hours of dawn when the room gets cold. It's more than sex. Sex is over with in a few minutes. This is peaceful, and it goes on as long as you have her lying with you. It puts an end to an awful thing; it starts something better than anything else in life.

It changes everything, he thought. Spreads out and covers every kind of event.

That was something he had not expected or known about. Sleeping a night now and then with a girl had no relationship with it. His anticipation of what it would be like with Susan had fallen short of the actuality. It had a much greater hold on him than he would have expected. That nine or ten days could completely change him, his views and preferences, affecting even this, his sense of driving, his feel of the road . . .

After his meal he picked up his car and continued the drive on down California to the Bay Area. He arrived late at night, crossed the Bay Bridge to San Francisco, found an underpass that took him off the freeway, and at last reached Market Street. He parked and got out, feeling shaky but excited.

Something about Market Street had changed. He walked along the well-lit sidewalk, past the towering noble movie houses, and then he realized what it was. The clanking old streetcars had gone. Instead, buses shot quietly along at the curb.

Hands in his pockets he strolled in the direction of the waterfront.

When he reached First and Market he began to notice small shops that sold Army surplus pots and clothing and shoes, so he crossed to the other side and started back. At Fifth and Market he wandered off onto one side street and then another, seeing all the different small shops, some prosperous and some not. After an hour or so he found himself staring at a display of tape recorders and cameras and typewriters, among which was a small aluminum portable that he had never seen before. The brand name was *Mithrias*. Presently he noticed a cord hanging out of the back. The thing was electric. And he could make out a belt disappearing from the carriage inside to the motor, so it had an electric carriage return. Nothing on it stated that it was an import, but he recognized it as the Japanese portable Milt had told him about.

The tag could be partly read. He read it, but it gave ordinary information, in acceptable and idiomatic English. But he knew that this was the Japanesse machine. His instincts, his talent, told him.

The store, of course, was shut. But he did not have to know any more than this; the machine, to some extent, had been distributed in the Bay Area. Someone had jobbed it to this retailer. Naturally San Francisco and Los Angeles would be the most likely spots to find it, since the machines would come in by ships and these were ports. As were Seattle and San Diego. But the retail trade was higher, here.

A glance told him that this was not a regular outlet for typewriters. He saw no popular lines represented, and no display material. This was simply an enterprising small merchant who stocked a bit of this and a bit of that, from microscope sets and fancy fabrics to rocks that glowed in the dark, mother of pearl cigarette lighters and redwood wall planters. Something on the order of a gift shop, with an emphasis on metals, glass, and plastics, rather than bric-a-brac.

That raised his hopes. The Mithrias people hadn't yet worked out their franchise arrangement, or they hadn't been able to call back the machines already sold. Either way, the machines had gotten out of ordinary franchised outlets. No reason on earth why he couldn't buy on the same terms as any retailer. Of course, he would have to figure out how to transport them to Boise. But he wouldn't need very many.

Unless, he thought, I want to make it an all-or-nothing buy. Pick up as many as I can get. Make only a few dimes on each one, advertise with spotlights and free gardenias and sound trucks.

A one-cent sale. Buy an electric portable for such-and-such, get a second one for a penny.

But he still had to discover a warehouse of them, and one which the owner wanted to dump. His best bet would perhaps be — not in San Francisco or in L.A. — but in a smaller town in-between, where a local jobber had tried to do in his town what had been done elsewhere. An in-between town like Bakersfield, where perhaps an outlet of some chain drug company or department store or supermarket had been given a quota of them but hadn't made its sales.

The valley towns. Salinas, Fresno, Stockton, Livermore. He would have to comb them, one after another.

It might take weeks.

No, he could not allow it to take weeks. A week at the most. So if he seriously intended to track down a warehouse of Mithrias portables, he would have to find a direct route to them.

Goddamn, he thought. When he had worked for C.B.B. he had been on company time, free to prowl and poke at leisure. Sometimes he and his boss Ed von Scharf spent a month, off and on, digging up a buy and hazarding a variety of tenuous half-joking offers, until finally, almost out of sheer boredom, the owner let it fall their way.

Image of his boss, black mustache and all, seated among pasteboard cartons, eating a Popsicle and scratching out an inventory. A professional with two decades of buying experience, back to the days of army surplus — the genuine army surplus — and then wholesale groceries, and after that home freezers and half-cows on the installment plan, and then whole sale direct to you at no mark-up, and, at last, in with the Pareti brothers and their discount house that operated out in the open.

Returning to his Merc he consulted a map. He could take US 40 or 50 direct from the East Bay and be in Reno in four hours. The length of a long baseball game.

The time at this moment — he checked — was one-thirty. He could be in Reno before sunup. Better yet, sleep a couple of hours in the car and then start, so that he would have daylight when he reached the Sierras. Then when he got to Reno, go to a friend's house to bathe and shave and change his shirt, perhaps bum breakfast, and then drop by C.B.B. and talk to Ed von Scharf.

Starting up the Merc he drove off in the direction of the Oakland Bay Bridge.

THE HIGHWAY through the Sacramento Valley was as wide and flat as anyone could want. He made good time, rushing along between the fields and at last over a narrow bridge built not over water but over miles of reeds. The metal railing of the bridge thumped noisily, and the sound and the nearness of it made him tense. He had done this part in darkness, but now, as he entered Sacramento, the sky to the East started to turn white. If he meant to get across before the big trailers and trucks and interstate rigs blocked everyone's way, he would have to hurry.

But in downtown Sacramento he became lost, even though the streets were empty. Signs reading "truck route" pointed off in various directions. Finally he found himself driving up and down bumpy tree-shaded streets of shacks and corrugated iron machine shops and sheds. Could this be the highway out of Sacramento? He blundered across a wide intersection of train tracks and rutted dirt and a number of alley-like roads, onto a two-lane highway with closed-up diners and fruit stands and gas stations on each side of it. Making a left turn he followed the highway. It wound around a hill, rising, and on the shoulder he saw four trucks with their lights on, their diesel engines rattling away as they warmed up. The trucks were about to get back on the road. The drivers had been asleep all night but now they were awake and on the job. He put on more speed, flying around the curves.

The road rose continually. It remained narrow, but well-kept. The fruit stands fell away and he saw wooded countryside. Meanwhile, the sky became brighter. It shone a brisk white, and once, as he reached the top of a rise, he saw what seemed to be mountains.

Later on he entered a town built on a hillside, on stilts, made entirely out of lumber; he saw no stone or metal, just the reddish wood dark in the early-morning gloom. Nothing stirred. But just past the town he came across more trucks shuddering away and wanting to get back on the road. Only a question of time before he encountered a band of them already in motion. And after that he would make no time at all; he would follow them up the grades and across the top and down the other side, the entire distance to Reno.

Now the road climbed wildly. The woods became forests of pine, lumber country. It was hard to believe that this narrow road was the main highway, US 40; what had happened to the broad four-lane flat pavement between Vallejo and Sacramento? This was like some alternate route, a county or state route used by skiers and fishermen, not by the interstate carriers. Few signs marked it. The ground on each side had been piled up so that the road seemed to cut constantly through masses of reddish dirt, throwing the dirt up car-high. Every now and then he saw construction equipment pulled off and covered by canvas.

Ahead of him the back end of a truck appeared around a curve; he slowed and then shifted down and gunned past it. The first one of them, he thought to himself. And he had not reached the summit.

The Sierras around him — he had to take the word of the Standard Stations roadmap that these were the Sierras — looked like a local recreation area, marred by trail-like side roads, stacks of logs, the twin ruts left by tractors and bulldozers. Every now and then a heap of rubbish, mostly picnic plates and beer cans, reminded him of the swarm of tourist cabins just out of sight beyond the pines. Every tiny dirt road led to them. And, as he reached the summit, he realized that he would be seeing one or more lakes.

The center of the Sierras, he thought. How demoralizing it was. Ahead of him the road rose only slightly; in fact, for the first time he could not tell if he were still climbing. Possibly it was a long, nearly level grade. A sloping field tumbled away to the right side, and he saw that a couple of cars had pulled off. The summit, he decided. Suddenly he discovered that he was stiff and cold and that he needed to go to the bathroom. So he coasted the car from the road, onto the wide dirt shoulder, shut off the motor, and parked.

The mountains were quiet. No wind. No voices. And, for him, the sense of expanse. Opening the car door he stepped unsteadily out. What time was it? Seven-thirty a.m. Here he was, up here by himself. And what a desolate place. A car shot by him along the road, its tires making a furious racket. Cramped throughout his muscles, he lurched about, his hands in his pockets, feeling lousy.

This is no place for me, he decided. A sort of everyone's vacant lot with trees. He did not feel especially high up. But the air was cold, thin, and bad-smelling. It did not smell of pine needles or earth; it smelled bitter and it made his nose ache. Under his shoes the lumps of dried ground made him stumble. He stepped down the side of a pile of dirt, to a confined spot among shrubs, wee-weed, and then trudged jerkily back up to his car.

I suppose the motor won't start, he thought to himself as he slammed the door. Up this high the automatic choke always misfunctions. Imagine having to stay here a whole week . . . but the motor started.

Waiting until a car had hurtled by, he regained the road and in a moment or so had passed on by the top of the next hill. All at once the sun, which had been hidden by the hills and trees, appeared and stabbed him in the eyes; the shattering pale light startled him and confused him and he involuntarily braked his car. From behind him a small pick-up truck shot by and around.

I forgot. Hitting the top at dawn means I have to drive into it the rest of the trip. He had never seen the early-morning sun so spread-out, so large.

Presently he did get a look at the lake; at a couple of them, in fact. They were set off to one side of the road a distance below him, flat, cheerily blue, embedded on what appeared to be a plateau. The trees grew thicker near the lake. He continually glanced out of the window at the lakes, but then a sheer drop in the road, like the side of a ball, made him turn around to keep his mind on his driving. Now that he had passed the peak he found himself descending much more suddenly than he had gone up; the grade dropped him so frighteningly that for a time he did not notice that he had crossed the state line and entered Nevada.

The hills became lesser, unimportant. Once he passed between masses of rock, a dry, barren area. This really is Nevada, he thought. No more vegetation. The water has stopped. Soon he would be out on the desert. And sure enough, he soon was.

What a disappointment. As it had been before when he had driven it. Not like mountains at all . . . more like a wooded obstacle to commerce that eventually – to everyone's satisfaction – would be leveled and carted off in trucks in the form of dirt and lumber.

THAT AFTERNOON, in Reno, he and Ed von Scharf sat upstairs together in the familiar office overlooking the noisy, bazaar-like main floor of the Consumers' Buying Bureau. His former boss made it known that he was taking his coffee break, so no one tried to interrupt them. To start it off, Bruce told him about his marriage; he showed him a snapshot of Susan that had been taken in Reno the day of their marriage.

"Is she older than you?" von Scharf asked.

"Yes," he said. "She's thirty."

"Are you pretty sure you know what you're doing?"

"Positive," he said. He described the R & J Mimeographing Service. He put in every detail. His former boss listened with deep attention.

"Is sidewalk traffic fairly heavy?"

"Yes," he said. "We get a lot of people who work in office buildings, between eleven and one."

His former boss said, "I don't think you're using your head. What do you actually have? A good location and a small amount to invest, and you have some sort of an outlet with the minimal fixtures and front. Why are you thinking in terms of typewriters?"

"Because it's a typewriter place."

"No it isn't. What did you learn here? To buy whatever was to be had at a good price that we thought we could sell. You should be out searching for anything that you can get cheap that you think you can move, typewriters or vegetables; it doesn't matter what. But by insisting on a certain item you destroy your position. You enter a seller's market. The first you know, you'll start bidding against someone for these Jap machines. Look, you know nothing about typewriters. Second, you have no real reason to suppose you can get yourself a buy. I'll tell you what's hot right now. Gasoline. There's a terrible gas war out on the Coast. Retail gas, the regular, got down to 19¢ a gallon on the Coast this last month. The wholesalers are overstocked out there."

"We can't sell gas," he said. He asked him if he had ever seen the Mithrias machines.

"No," von Scharf said. "I never even heard of them. As far as I know, none of them have gotten out here."

"Then we'd have a clear field."

"How many could you buy for twenty-five hundred dollars? Suppose you have to pay one hundred dollars apiece? That's only twenty-five of the buggers. That's nonsense."

Up to now he hadn't calculated that. It made him feel cold.

"Not enough to bother with," his former boss said. "You just don't have enough capital."

"I might be able to pick up a bunch of Mithrias cheaper than one hundred apiece," he said doggedly.

"Maybe so. Well, what did you come here to find out from me?"

"I came because I thought maybe you'd know where I could pick up some of them."

"I don't," his former boss said. "I've never even seen an ad or an inventory list. I can ask around for you, if you want."

"Thanks," Bruce said.

His former boss phoned several people, including one of the Pareti brothers who had been out on the East Coast for a time. None of them knew anything about the Mithrias, but one of them believed that he had heard the name before. He thought he had read about it in a magazine article having to do with England.

"That's something else," Bruce said. "A tomb they dug up. An old tomb."

"Well, I'm sorry," von Scharf said.

"My own fault," he said. After all, he could have phoned from the Coast and saved himself the trip.

Von Scharf said, "You'd be better off putting your money into children's toy typewriters."

"Are you serious?"

"Yes. You can get a buy on them right now. Sell them at Christmas."

"What I think I'll do," Bruce said, "is try to locate the man who originally told me about them. Milt Lumky."

"Oh him," von Scharf said, smiling. "Yes, he represents some paper manufacturer up in the Northwest. Little guy with a deep voice."

"I didn't know you knew him."

"We got some paper through him, once. A hard man to deal with, but scrupulous. He told you about these Jap machines? Well, he's smart. Maybe he owns a warehouse of them and wants to get rid of them."

Bruce explained that Lumky was somewhere on his rounds, between Seattle and Montpelier.

"You can get hold of him," von Scharf said. "You could call his company and ask what his schedule is. Or you could call them and tell them to have him get in touch with you the next time he calls in. Or you could get in touch with some big paper-buyer along his route and ask them to have him call you."

He pondered. "I guess his company would know."

He called the Whalen Paper Company on C.B.B.'s phone and told them that he wanted to get hold of Milton Lumky, their sales representative for the Pacific Northwest. After some delay they informed him that Mr. Lumky was on the road between Pocatello and Boise, but that on the 9th of the month he would definitely be in Pocatello. He had an appointment to meet with the owner of a dairy who wanted to order pasteboard milk cartons of a new style. The Whalen people gave him the address of the dairy and the exact time of the appointment. He thanked them and hung up.

"This is the 7th," his former boss said, showing him a calendar.

"I think I'll drive up to Pocatello," he decided.

His former boss said, "If you want to stay here in Reno tonight you can have dinner with my wife and myself and as far as I'm concerned you can sleep on the couch in the living room."

"Thanks," he said, "but I want to get started."

"Would you resent it if I gave you some advice?"

"Go ahead," he said.

"Be sure you don't put everything you have on the block. Try to make sure that if everything falls apart you'll still come out with something. Don't wind up empty-handed."

He said, "She's putting up much more than I am."

His former boss excused himself and went downstairs to the main floor. He returned presently carrying a wrapped package, sealed with the firm's special clip that always got fixed on during a purchase. "So you won't leave here feeling bad," he said.

"I don't feel bad," he answered. But he opened the package. It turned out to be a quart of imported discount Scotch that his former boss had gone down and bought for him at the liquor department. "Thanks," he said.

"You always talk about liking Scotch." His former boss shook hands with him, clapped him on the back, and sent him out of the building and onto the sidewalk.

As he got into his car he thought, Now I have a six hundred mile drive to make. But this was one road that he knew perfectly. He stopped at a grocery store and bought some food to carry along with him, and then he set off along highway 40, going East toward the junction with 95. Off to try to find Milton Lumky, he thought. Who is somewhere in Idaho selling paper wholesale in one town or another, driving his Mercedes-Benz and wearing his lemon-colored short-sleeve sports shirt and gray slacks, listening to his car radio and smoking a White Owl cigar.

10

THE ROAD brought him closer and closer to Boise, and he began to
want to stop there. He yearned to stay overnight with Susan and Taffy
in the house. But near Winnemucca he had had a flat tire, and that
had held him up for several hours. He could not afford to cut it too
close; he needed to get into Pocatello with plenty of time to spare.

Anyhow his delay altered his schedule and brought him into Boise
at three o'clock in the morning. Of course he had a key to the house,
but if he stopped at all he would want to stay most of the next day.
There would be problems that had come up that Susan needed help
with; once that got started he might never leave.

I might simply stay, he thought.

So he drove on through dark, closed-up Boise and out the far side,
on Highway 30, the long straight stretch before the obnoxious twists
and descents began. Little traffic moved with him. He had the road
to himself.

At dawn he pulled off onto the shoulder, went wretchedly around
and crawled into the back of the car, and slept. Just before noon the
hot sun woke him up. He returned to the front and drove along the
road until he saw a roadside diner. There he ate and rested. The owner

permitted him to use the diner's washroom; he shaved, washed the upper part of his body, changed his clothes, squirted on new deodorant, and returned to the car feeling improved.

As he drove, it occurred to him that now he had entered Milton Lumky territory. At any moment he might spy the gray Mercedes. Suppose it was going in the opposite direction? Should he make a U-turn and go after it? Probably it would be going toward Pocatello, so he had only to catch up with it and go on by; his Merc had a higher top speed and that would not be hard to do. But, he thought, suppose it is not Milton Lumky and his Mercedes; suppose it is an entirely different Mercedes with someone else, a total stranger, inside. Suppose I chase it for miles, farther and farther away from Pocatello . . . but how many gray Mercedes would there be driving around this part of Idaho at this particular time? Still, it would only take one. One in addition to Milt's.

Or, he thought, I might run into him at a roadside cafe or at a gas station. At a motel. At a drugstore in some small town, both of us buying suntan oil or cigarettes or beer. I might stop at a red light and see him walking along the street of some small town. I might see him off on the shoulder napping in the rear of the Mercedes. In Pocatello, when I get there, I might see him crossing in a crosswalk, or roaming along with his satchel. Anywhere, at any moment. Now that I am in Milton Lumky territory.

He reached Pocatello that evening, just at sunset. The appointment that Milt had with the dairy did not take place until the following morning, at ten-thirty. So he had arrived with time to spare. He turned off at a motel called the Grand View Motel, rented a room, parked his car, and carried his suitcase indoors and set it down on the bed.

It's even possible, he thought, that the next car that drives in here to the Grand View Motel will be his gray Mercedes.

The evening air was warm. He left the screen door open as he took a shower in the cubicle-like bathroom.

It occurred to him that he might benefit by knowing the exact location of the dairy. So, when he had finished his shower and had put on his dressy single-breasted suit, he set out in the car to search for it. The motel owner gave him complete instructions, and he found the dairy within a few minutes. Naturally everyone had gone home. A row of trucks were parked in the rear, by a metal loading dock. The empty trucks depressed him, and he drove back into town. What a hell of a thing to drive a thousand miles for, he thought to himself. But in the daytime it would be more pleasant.

Having nothing else to do he cruised up and down the highway on both sides of Pocatello, keeping his eye out for the Mercedes. At each motel he slowed down for a good long inspection of the cars parked between the cabins or in the space before the numbered doors. He saw every make of car and every variety of motel, but no sign of the Mercedes. For hours he kept it up, driving back and forth, slowing at each motel or wherever he saw cars parked. Later in the evening the traffic began to thin, and by two o'clock he had street after street of the town to himself. But he continued to drive; he did not feel much like it, but on the other hand he did not care to shut himself up in his motel room and go to sleep. At three o'clock he became too halting in his reactions to continue. Without having had any success he drove back to his own motel, parked, went inside, and prepared for bed.

The next morning he drove over to the dairy.

In the sunlight the place struck him as much more cheerful, although he saw almost as little sign of life. Evidently the milk had been brought in at dawn, bottled and taken off to be delivered; the trucks that he had seen lined up were nowhere in sight. The office of the dairy was a small building at one end of the bottling and pasteurizing plant, and he opened the door and entered.

Behind a varnished oak desk sat a kindly-looking woman of a country sort, wearing a flowered dress. She asked him what she could do for him, and he explained to her that he wanted to see Mr. Lumky when he came in.

"He should be in any time now," the woman said. She showed him a chair in which he could sit, and some *Saturday Evening Posts* to read. But he preferred to stand by a window overlooking the company's parking lot; he watched for the Mercedes, as he had been doing now since entering Milton Lumky territory. It had become an obsession, an end in itself — not Lumky but the Mercedes was the sight he held out for.

Some time later the receptionist approached him and said, "Excuse me, but Mr. Lumky called and said he isn't going to be able to keep his appointment with Mr. Ennis."

He regarded her stupidly.

"He said he's ill," she said.

"When will he be in, then?" he said.

"He told Mr. Ennis that he'd get in touch with him very shortly."

"Is he here in town?"

"Oh yes," she said. "He's staying somewhere here."

"Did you find out where?"

"No," she said. "He said he would get in touch with us."

He left his name and the phone number at his motel, and walked out of the building.

Now he had no idea what to do. He did what he had been doing; he drove around Pocatello, up one street and along the next, searching for the Mercedes. There was nothing to think about. He had driven this far; he certainly couldn't leave. So he drove around and around, and at sunset he had still seen no sign of the Mercedes, either in motion or parked.

At six-thirty he ate dinner in a restaurant. Then he stopped off at his motel to see if Lumky had called. Lumky had not called. So again he resumed his driving.

If Lumky was sick, what was the nature of his sickness? How sick was he? Had he had an accident on the road? Or was it nothing more than an excuse to get out of his appointment at the dairy? Suppose, he thought, that Lumky had not gotten to Pocatello at all; suppose he had stopped off in some other town and phoned from there. He might not get to Pocatello at all this time. It might not be until his next round that he showed up at the dairy, in a matter of weeks.

But he kept on driving.

The traffic around him remained heavy until nine or ten o'clock and then, as it had done the night before, it began to thin. By one in the morning he saw only an occasional car.

At two o'clock in the morning he saw the Mercedes.

AHEAD OF HIM, at a stoplight, the Mercedes coasted through on the yellow. He had to stop and watch it as it continued on. When the light changed he followed after it, memorizing the pattern of its tail lights. The license plate could not be read; he could not get close enough to it. Maybe it's another Mercedes, he thought to himself. At night all cars, except bright pastel ones or very dark ones, look gray. He stuck with it, getting closer and closer, and at last he came up beside it. On the door of the car he saw the painted inscription:

WHALEN PAPER PRODUCTS
SERVE THE PACIFIC NORTHWEST

So it was Lumky. He began tapping his horn. The street being dark he could not see Lumky; he had no way of knowing if Lumky recognized him. The Mercedes kept on. He kept on with it, sometimes in front, sometimes beside it. Toward the end of town it began to pick up speed. So he did so, too.

At a stop sign he managed to stop in front of it. Setting the parking brake he jumped out and ran back to the Mercedes. It had started to back away, wanting to pull around his Merc.

"Hey," he said, banging on the door. The Mercedes continued to back, and then the driver shifted gear and moved forward, swinging out toward him so that he had to leap from its path. He managed to catch hold of the door handle and get it open.

Inside the car, behind the wheel, was a girl, wide-eyed and frightened. She wore a billowy skirt, and her hair was arranged in long curls, very blond hair, so that she reminded him of a carefully brushed and groomed grammar school child scrubbed until she shone. At a guess she was no more than sixteen or seventeen.

"I'm looking for Milt," he said, hanging onto the door handle as the car drifted forward.

"What?" she said, in a faint squeak.

"Stop your damn car," he said. "I know this is Milt's car. Why is he sick?"

The girl put her foot on the brake; she had on laceless slippers. "Milt Lumky?" she said, in her clear, high-pitched soprano.

"I drove all the way up from Reno to talk to him," he said, panting and nearly incoherent.

Staring at him, she said, "Let me get my breath."

"Pull over off the road," he said. Other cars had begun honking at them. He ran back to the Merc, hopped in, and drove to the curb. The Mercedes wobbled over behind him and also stopped. This time he came around on the passenger's side; he rattled the door handle and she unlocked the door for him. Now she did not seem as scared, but her pale, fragile features were certainly those of a child; he could not believe she was supposed to be driving the car, or any car. Her feet scarcely reached the pedals. In fact, she was propped up on a pillow. He saw, now, that she had a ribbon tied in the midst of her blond curls. The front of her dress was cut low, but she had no figure at all. It was a child's dress and a child's body.

"Are you a friend of Milt's?" she asked, in her little voice.

"Yes," he said. "I tried to get hold of him at the dairy."

"He couldn't keep his appointment," she said. "I was driving around trying to find a grocery store still open, or some place I could buy a can of frozen orange juice for him."

"Where is he?" he said.

The girl said, "He's staying at my apartment. We've been living together."

That explained why he had not seen the Mercedes parked at any of the Motels. "I noticed a grocery store still open," he said. He had gone down so many streets that he had seen every part of Pocatello. "I'll show you where it is, if you want to follow."

Shortly, they had parked in front of a dinky, family-owned grocery store that still had its lights and sign on.

"What's your name?" the girl said, as they entered the store. When he had told her she said, "He never mentioned you."

"He didn't know I was coming," he said.

While the owner of the store rang up the purchase he got the girl to give him the address. Now, even if they became separated, he could still find Milt. He became elated. What did he have to worry about? One chance in a million . . . after two days of driving around town. Because Milt wanted frozen orange juice.

Ordinarily he would not have expected such a long shot to work out, but here in Milt Lumky territory it seemed perfectly natural. Now that it had happened it failed to astonish him.

Standing beside him in the grocery store, the girl asked him what he wanted to see Milt about. In her slippers, without heels, she came up to the second button of his coat. He guessed that she was not over five foot one. Now, in better light, he saw that her skin was dry and rougher than a child's, and her hands, when she reached out for the bag of groceries, had nothing in common with a child's hands. Her fingers were knobby and the knuckles were rubbed red. Her nails, painted once but now chipped and irregular, had apparently been gnawed short. The palms of her hands had deep grooves in them. Her arms were unusually muscular; she wore a sleeveless blouse, and he saw, on her arm, a white vaccination scar that undoubtedly was years old. On one finger she had a gold band, what appeared to be a wedding ring.

He answered that he had business he wanted to discuss with Milt.

The girl nodded, evidently accepting that as natural. He asked what her name was, and she told him that she was Cathy Hermes and that she was married. Her husband, Jack, lived somewhere in Pocatello but not with her; they had separated a year or so ago. She had met Milt at the place she worked, an office in the Pocatello City Hall; she was a clerk-typist, and Milt had dropped by selling paper supplies to the city. For months now they had been living together, exactly as if they were married.

"How long has Milt been in Pocatello?" he asked her, as they walked back to their cars.

She answered that Milt had been in town almost a week; he had not gotten past Pocatello, but had come down sick on his way east to Montpelier and gone no farther.

"What's the matter with him?" he asked. He held the door of the Mercedes open for her.

She replied that neither of them knew; or, if he knew, he didn't let on. It was a chronic condition that got inflamed now and then. In a few minutes he could see for himself; her apartment was not far off.

Getting into his Merc he followed the tail lights of the Mercedes until at last she turned off into a driveway on a residential street and parked in a wooden doorless garage. He parked behind her, in the driveway itself. Cathy approached him carrying the bag of groceries.

"It's upstairs," she said. "We can go up the back way." She led him up an outside flight of wooden steps, past washing hanging on lines and piles of newspapers and bottles and flower pots, past several doors and at last to the top floor. Balancing the grocery bag she brought out a key and unlocked the door; he and she passed on inside a hallway that smelled of soap.

When she turned on a light he discovered that he was in an old, old building that still had brass plumbing fixtures and artificial candles set in the walls and the ornate egg-shaped doorknobs that he remembered from his childhood. The walls were painted yellow. The hall was quite narrow, but after that he found himself in a large front room with a high ceiling; here, the chandelier had been taken down and electric wiring ran from the ceiling to the floor, where someone had fixed up a socket for the lamp and radio.

"Milt," the girl said, disappearing into another room. Returning, she said to Bruce, "Just a minute." She carried the grocery bag back into the kitchen while he waited. The room seemed cold, and he saw her strike a kitchen match and light the oven of the black ancient stove.

"Milt," she repeated, going past him once more, into the other room. "There's a man here who drove up from Reno to talk to you." The door swung shut after her and he could neither hear nor see. He waited.

Through the closed door he heard stirrings and a man's mutterings. Then the girl's voice. They seemed to be arguing. At last the sound quieted down and he heard nothing.

The door opened and she came out and shut it after her. "Do you mind not seeing him for a while?" she asked.

"Okay," he said, struggling with his impatience.

The girl entered the kitchen and began fixing the orange juice.

"What are his symptoms?" he asked her.

"He has a constant fever," she said. "And no strength, and he's swollen up around the eyes. And he has trouble urinating."

"It sounds like a kidney infection," he said.

"Yes," she said, mixing the orange juice in a quart mayonnaise jar. "He has some pills he takes. It come and goes. It's not as bad as it was yesterday."

"Did you tell him my name?" he asked.

The girl said, "He's too dopey right now."

"You mean he didn't know who it was?"

"He feels so out of sorts that he doesn't like to see anybody until he feels better." She would not say whether Lumky had remembered him. "I know he'll want to talk to you later on when he feels improved."

He told her that he could only stay in Pocatello so long.

"Maybe tomorrow," she said. "He'll probably feel more like himself when he wakes up in the morning. Right now he hardly knows what he's saying. If you want to talk to him about business you better wait."

A disturbance from the other room caused her to put down the jar of orange juice and go out of the kitchen. He heard her and Milt talking, and then her moving about from one room to another. Water ran in a bowl; something was filled, carried; then more talking.

When the girl returned he said. "I'll drop by tomorrow morning, then."

"Yes," she agreed. "Here, I'll let you out the front door. Now that he's awake." She led him through the apartment and into the room in which Milt lay on the couch wrapped up in blankets, his head on a white pillow. Passing by him, he saw that it was Milt Lumky beyond any doubt. The man's eyes were shut and he breathed noisily. His arms had a dark unhealthy color and so did his face. The room smelled of illness. On the floor around the couch were glasses and pans and medicines.

Holding the front door open for him, the girl let him out onto a hallway. "Good night," she said, and shut the door almost at once behind him.

Anyhow he had seen him; he knew for certain that it was Milt. He returned to his motel.

11

WHEN HE RETURNED to her apartment the following morning he found the door locked and a note tacked to it.

> Dear Sir:
>
> Mr. Lumky felt better today and he went to the dairy
> to see them. I am at work. Will be home at five-thirty.
>
> Cordially yours,
> Mrs. Cathy Hermes

He tried the knob. What did this remind him of? It reminded him of the night he had gone back to Peg Googer's for his coat, found the house locked up and deserted, and had gone in through a window and discovered Susan lying in the bedroom smoking a cigarette. But how different this was . . . he wandered around to the back of the dilapidated three-story building and climbed the stairs; the back door was locked, too, and so was the single window overlooking the porch. Mrs. Hermes was too careful.

The Mercedes, of course, had gone; the garage was empty. One of them had driven off in it, most likely Milt. He wondered if Milt would come back here, or having finished his business with the dairy, would speed on to the next town to make up for lost time.

Unable to think of anything else he could do he parked his car directly before the building and, sitting behind the wheel, waited.

An hour or so later a jolt that made the whole car jump forward startled him into panicky wakefulness. The Mercedes had glided up behind him and banged bumpers; hopping out he found himself facing Milt Lumky, who grinned at him from behind the wheel of the Mercedes.

"Hello, McFoop," Milt said, leaning out the window. He shut off the car's motor and stepped out carrying his leather satchel and several packets of samples. "Think sharp, be sharp," he said. He looked the same as always; there was no sign of illness. In his jaunty bow tie, pink shirt, and sporty suit he passed by Bruce and up the steps of the building. "Come on," he said over his shoulder.

"I'm sure glad to see you," Bruce said. "I was afraid maybe you'd gone on to the next town."

Upstairs, on the top floor, Milt read the note tacked to the door and then tore it down and stuffed it into his coat pocket. As he unlocked the door he said, "What do you think of Cathy?"

"Very solicitous," he said.

"I have to pack," Milt said, holding the door aside for him. "I'm two days late on my route."

While Bruce stood by, he carried shirts from a dresser to his suitcase. In the bathroom he gathered up his shaving objects.

"I'm sorry I couldn't talk to you last night," Milt said, as he stuffed pairs of shoes into the sidepockets of the suitcase.

"That's okay," he said. "Can you talk about it now?"

"What about?" Milt said.

He said, "I'm interested in the Jap typewriters. The Mithrias. I saw one in San Francisco."

"That's right," Milt said. "You can pick them up out there on the Coast. How's Susan?"

"Fine," he said.

"Did you kick out Zoe?"

"Yes," he said. "Now we've got some working capital." For some reason he felt reluctant to tell Milt about his marriage with Susan. "What can you tell me about getting a buy on some Mithrias?" he said. "You talked about it when I saw you before."

"How much do you have to work with?"

He said, "Enough, if the price is any good."

"It's out of my hands," Milt said.

"Does that mean you used to have an interest?"

"No," he said. "But I used to know more about it. I was thinking about buying in."

"And not any more?"

"If I got them there's nothing I could do with them. I'd have to hold them and try to turn them over as a job lot to some retailer."

Bruce said, "What I want to do is sell them. Advertise. But it all depends on the price."

"Is it your money?"

"Mine and Susan's," he said.

"All I can tell you is that there's one warehouse I know of for sure. But it's not out here. It's in Seattle."

"That's okay," he said. He had expected it to be on the Coast; if any existed here, then something had gone wrong.

"That's right," Milt said, closing up his suitcase. "You're a great one for driving around. Cathy says you came up from Reno." He stuck several objects in his pockets and glanced around for more. "When did you want to get them? The trouble is I'm not going to be back in Seattle for a couple of weeks."

"I want to get them as soon as possible. If I get them at all."

"Have you tried one out?"

"No," he said.

"Don't you think you better?"

"I will," he said. "Before I put any money in."

"You know, you're a real buyer. You're not a damn bit interested in the machine; you're just looking at it as an investment. You're detached. Aloof, like a scientist." He slapped Bruce on the arm. "Come on. We're finished."

They walked downstairs. "I want to settle this," Bruce said, "and I don't see how I can if you hop in your Mercedes and drive off."

"Can't you come along?" Then he noticed the Merc. "Oh," he said. "I just figured I'd give you a lift to Montpelier and we could chew the fat as we went. I was looking forward to company. Why don't you leave this tank here? I'll be in Montpelier a day or so and then I'll be heading back here. You can pick it up again then."

"And then what?" Bruce said.

"It depends on what we hatch up." Suddenly Milt became serious; in a low, humble voice he said, "You know, I almost go nuts driving alone on the road. I can really stand company; I mean it. And I'm positive we can figure out something on the Jap machines."

It occurred to Bruce, then, to wonder how ill the man was. If he required constant care. He quailed from the notion of being Milt Lumky's nurse, as Cathy Hermes was. And as perhaps other persons throughout Milton Lumky territory were. But he had to settle the business about the typewriters. And if he said no to the idea of going to Montpelier, then Milt would simply wave good-bye and ride off; he had already started the motor and was behind the wheel. Obviously he was in a genuine hurry. It was a wonder he had come back to the apartment at all.

"You can't stick around here long enough to discuss it?" he said.

"It isn't a question of that, it's a question of gettng some action started on the thing. Throw your stuff into the back and we'll be in Montpelier in a couple of hours. Your car'll be safe here; just get everything out of it and lock it up."

Reluctantly, he did so. He added his suitcase to the heap of sample cases in the back of the Mercedes, and a moment later Lumky sped out into the mid-morning Pocatello traffic.

THE TRIP between Pocatello and Montpelier was by no means as bad as the trip between Boise and Pocatello. They made good time, seeing mostly farms and orchards; the pavement itself was in fair shape and several portions had been recently laid down. Traffic was light. Lumky did not drive fast, but he kept up a good professional pace, passing slow vehicles and getting out of the path of new Buicks and Cads that wanted as much speed as they could flog out of their three hundred horse engines. He averaged something over fifty-five, which, on that road, was not bad.

That afternoon they reached Montpelier. The local streets were in terrible disrepair, almost a form of degeneracy. In some spots the pavement had entirely broken down, leaving nothing but rubble. All the houses had an archaic, woebegone appearance; they did not need paint or obvious work, but each was a somber neutral color, as nondescript as possible. The houses looked like farmhouses brought together, with weedy lawns and flower beds in between. Many of the cars they saw parked had winter tires, suggesting that during rains the mud made the roads into pigwallows. The first motel they saw had only a dirt pasture in which to park; the cabins were clapboard shacks and the sign was hand-painted on the wood, not neon. They next passed a tumble-down garage and then two or three gas stations, an ice cream stand, and after that the main street of town with its bars, workman's clothing stores, tiny theater, and abandoned warehouses that had once served the train during the decades of heavy freight. The air was filled with dust. All the cars they saw were gray with dust. The men on the sidewalks wore wide-brimmed western hats. The sight discouraged both him and Lumky.

"What a place," Lumky said. "I stay here as little as possible. And right across the border from Utah . . ." He pointed. "As soon as you go down there you find yourself in a forest, and then you come out in Logan. That's where I'd like to be. It's clean. All Utah is clean."

"I know," he said. And he thought, This is the extreme edge of Milton Lumky territory. Its frontier.

"In Utah they'd never let this dust blow around," Lumky said, searching for a parking slot. Mud-spattered pick-up trucks had most of them already, the work vehicles of a farm area. "They have water running down the gutters. Everything's fertile. They make it that way; it's due to L.S.D."

"L.D.S.," Bruce said.

"That's right. I'm thinking of 'LSMFT.' Of course that's the joker. If you live in Utah you have to join the Church. It's a hell of a thing — they won't let you alone. You can't buy cigarettes or booze; they look at you funny if you drink coffee. You can't rent a room or go to the toilet." He found a parking slot and parked the Mercedes. "These people up here don't give a damn about anything. The whole town's collapsing in ruins." He got out of the car and stepped up on the sidewalk, fastening his belt; while driving he had undone it.

On the drive both of them had felt under the weather. Bruce was not used to being a passenger while someone else took the wheel and he had quickly become a thorn in Lumky's side. But now that they were out of the car they both began to feel better.

"How about something to eat?" Lumky said.

"When do you have to see these people?"

"As soon as possible. But I'm hungry. If I go without eating my gut will growl." He started off. "And that kills sales."

They found themselves in a long dark tunnel-like cafe, filled with the screech of electric guitar music from the jukebox in the back, gray with the smoke of burning grease. At the counter a row of men sat, all with hats on, eating from platters. The walls of the place had been painted black. Three tired middle-aged women washed dishes ceaselessly.

"This is limbo," Milt said. " But the food's good. Have some fried ham." He located two vacant stools and climbed over one. Bruce took the one beside it.

The food, when it arrived, was not bad.

"There're worse places than Montpelier," Milt said, as they ate. "Don't let it get you down."

He said, "The worst I've ever seen is around Cheyenne, on the road up from Denver through Greeley."

"Cathy's husband owns some of those auto wrecking yards in Colorado," Milt said. "A littering moron. It never occurred to me that anybody deliberately put that junk along side the highway. But she says he dumps it there very carefully. He probably thinks it's pretty."

They ate their meal, drank their coffee. "I wonder what I can get the Jap typewriters at," Bruce said. "Per each."

"The things have been in warehouses for a couple of years, now," Milt said. "This whole Jap import business is a mess. They shouldn't run you too much."

"Less than a hundred dollars?"

"Much less."

That raised his spirits radically. "Give me a general idea."

"Seems to me it was around forty dollars a machine. In original cartons. There were about two hundred of them in this particular warehouse, when I saw them. That would make it —" He calculated. "About eight thousand dollars for the lot. Do you have that much on hand?"

"No," he said. "More like twenty-five hundred."

"It sounds as if you sold your car." Milt chuckled. "That's about one used Mercury. In fact it's exactly what I paid for this Mercedes, and it was used when I got it. Of course, you don't need two hundred. You could pick up sixty; that would be about right, for a shop the size of yours. But the problem is, will they sell sixty of them at that price?"

"Sixty would be a big help," he said. A lot bigger help than twenty-five. So maybe is had been worth it after all, the long drive, all the difficulty tracking down Milt Lumky.

"I understand they've been retailed at around a hundred and eighty dollars," Milt said. "To compete with the Smith-Corona. You'd have to figure on some kind of guarantee, I suppose. That's something I know nothing about. You better investigate that pretty thoroughly." He fooled with a crumb of food and then he said, "Maybe I could loan you some more money. Enough to take the warehouse as is. If they won't break it up for any decent price." He eyed Bruce. "I mean Susan. For Susan. Not for you as an individual."

"It could be a wedding present," Bruce said jokingly, and then he realized what he had said.

At once the man's face tilted back and expressed, for him to see, his different reactions. "You and Susan?"

"Yes," he said.

Milt said, "When?"

"Just a few days ago."

They sat in silence.

"No kidding," Milt said, in a subdued voice. "I can't get over it. Well, congratulations," he said, sticking out his hand. They shook on it. His hand was damp and trembling. "You know, I had a hunch about it that night when I dropped by and you were there. But I dismissed it. Were — you married then?"

"Not yet," he said.

"It's amazing. I didn't think she'd get married again so soon. Well, you live and learn. That's certainly no lie. I'll pay for your meal." He picked up the two checks and slid back from his stool. Without another word he walked to the front of the cafe and got out his wallet to pay the cashier.

Bruce, joining him on the sidewalk, said, "I don't know why I didn't tell you right off the bat."

"You told me right off," Milt said brusquely. "It seems right off," he said, as he got into his car. His face had a gray, pushed-in quality. "Maybe I'll phone her up and congratulate her," he murmured, sitting at the wheel without starting the motor. "No, I have to see these people." He examined the dashboard clock. "It's about paper cups or something. Can you imagine driving thousands of miles to sell some guy in a small town on buying paper cups? Selling's a hell of a strange business."

"That's true," Bruce said, feeling uncomfortable.

"Reach around back in the back," Milt said. "There's a long thin carton. Full of cups."

After Bruce had found it, Milt opened it and made sure that the cups were intact.

"You stay here," he said, climbing out with the cups. "I'll go drop them off and then come back. It's that hotel down a couple of doors. I'll tell them to call us if they want the cups. They ought to be able to decide." He went on, leaving Bruce and the car and his satchel.

Time passed and at last he returned, without the cups.

"That's that," he said, sliding in. He started up the motor and began backing out into traffic. "Let's head for home. The hell with Montpelier, Idaho."

A Greyhound bus honked at him. With a savage swipe at the horn ring he honked back.

AS THEY DROVE BACK, through farmland they had seen only an hour or so earlier in the day, Milt sat hunched over, his chin out, his eyes fixed on the road. The car radio, which he had turned on, blared out and destroyed the possibility of conversation. Milt gave every indication of having gone into a glowering lethargy; his control of the car became dim and he did not respond quickly to changes in the traffic. But finally he roused himself, shut off the radio, and took hold of the wheel with both hands.

"I'll drive back to the Coast with you," he declared.

"To Seattle?"

"Yes," Milt said. "We'll get you your typewriters."

"Terrific," he said.

"How long do you think it'll take?"

He said, "It depends on whether we take both cars. It'd be faster if we took one and alternated the driving."

"I have to get back out here again," Milt said.

"I'll drive back out here with you."

They discussed the choice of cars. The Merc, being larger, might be more comfortable. And in it they could make better time. On the other hand, the Mercedes would use less gas.

"How do you feel about somebody else driving your car?" he asked Milt. "I don't care who drives the Merc."

Milt said, "Parts would be easier to get for your car. Tires and fuses and shit like that." He gave no direct answer to the question.

In the end they decided on the Merc; he who was not at the wheel could stretch out and sleep more easily in the larger car.

An hour or so later they re-entered Pocatello. A funeral in progress blocked their movement; car after car with headlights on passed haughtily in front of them, protected by special police wearing brilliantly shiny uniforms and helmets. Milt, at the wheel, stared at it silently at first, and then he began to curse out the cars. "Look at them," he said, interrupting himself. "It must be the mayor." The cars, most of them new and expensive, passed into what seemed to be a public park but which was probably the town's finest mortuary. "The goddamn dead bad-smelling dirty nasty-minded mayor of Pocatello." His voice rose. "Look at the lacquered helmets on those cops. It's like living in Nazi Germany." With the window down he said loudly out into the street, "Bunch of goddamn Nazi S.S. men strutting around."

The police paid no attention to him. Eventually the last car of the funeral procession passed before them; the police blew their whistles, and traffic once more began to move.

"Fuck," Milt said, starting the car up and gunning the motor in low.

"Actually we didn't lose much time," he said, but Milt did not respond.

When they reached the house they parked the Mercedes in the doorless garage and started transferring their luggage from the back seat and trunk to the Merc.

While they were doing that a car drove up to the curb. Its door opened and Cathy Hermes hopped out, slammed the door, and waved good-bye. The car, a 1949 Chrysler, started off and made a left-turn at the corner.

"Her husband," Milt said, lifting an armload of samples from the back of the Mercedes. "He drives her home from work and leaves her off. This is home."

Her brown cloth coat flapping behind her, Cathy hurried toward them. "Are you back so soon?" she called, clutching her purse and beginning to run. "What are you doing? Are you going to go some-where in his car?"

Milt said, "We're taking off again."

"Where?" She reached him and placed herself in front of him, keeping him from carrying any more to the Merc.

"Seattle," he said.

"Now? Right away?" She breathed rapidly, frowning at him in the late-afternoon glare. "What's the rush? I thought you weren't starting back for three more days. You were going to rest around here until Tuesday at least."

"I'll be back," he said.

At that, she fluffed up and said in her tiny insistent voice, "You're not supposed to take such a long trip at one time. You know it's too hard on you. Why do you have to go with him anyhow? Are you leaving the Mercedes here?"

"You can use it," Milt said, setting her to one side so that he could load the samples into the Merc. "Here's the key."

"I have a key," she said. "Will you explain to me what this is all about? I think I have some right to know, since it'll be me who'll have to take care of you."

Milt said, "He and a friend of mine got married and I want to get this business settled for them as a wedding present."

Both of them retired off to one side to argue. Bruce did not want to mix into their argument, so he continued loading up his car with whatever he could find in the Mercedes.

Beckoning him over, Milt said, "I have to get some junk that's upstairs. I'll be back down in a couple of minutes." He entered the building, dragging his feet, sullen and taciturn.

In the driveway Cathy remained behind, holding her purse, shut off by his going into the house.

"I guess it's my fault," Bruce said, as he loaded.

"He knows he shouldn't go," Cathy said.

"I'll do most of the driving."

Her cheeks flushed, she said, "He isn't supposed to sit for so long, and when he's on the road between towns he doesn't stop to go to the bathroom often enough. That and the bouncing around. Couldn't he just call on the telephone about his business for you?"

"He would know that," he said uncomfortably. "Not me."

When Milt returned, Cathy said to him, "Why don't you just phone?"

"No," Milt said. He put the things he had brought down into the

Merc. "I'll be okay," he told her. "I'll lie down and stretch out in back and let Bruce drive."

"This woman must be an awfully good friend of yours," Cathy said. "Maybe she can take care of you. If you get sick because of this, I'm not going to take care of you." She started into the house.

"Suit yourself," Milt said, getting into the Merc. "Let's go," he said to Bruce.

Standing on the porch Cathy called down, "Don't come back here."

"Okay," Milt said.

She threw down the key to the Mercedes; it landed in the dirt of the driveway. "Let your Boise friends take care of you," she said. She opened the front door of the house, entered, and slammed it after her.

"Let's go," Milt repeated.

Behind the wheel, Bruce started up the Merc. They drove away, both of them silent.

"We'll see what she says when I get back," Milt said, sometime later. By now he had taken the wheel himself.

"She really takes an interest in your welfare," he said, with a deep sense of having been responsible, but at the same time knowing that if they wanted to get the typewriters this was probably the only way.

Milt said merely. "Susan probably feels the same about you. She probably thinks I'm a bad influence on you."

"She doesn't know where I am," he said.

"If she knew she'd warn you away from me. Women always feel like that about their husbands' friends. It's instinctive. Fear that their husband is really a queer."

"I don't think that's why she's sore," Bruce said. "Do you?"

"No," Milt admitted.

"I don't see that there's any inference in this that either or both of us is queer." That did not set well with him, even the idea of it.

Milt, smiling a trifle, said, "It's just a manner of speech."

After a time Bruce said, "How does it feel to drive an American car, after your Mercedes?"

"Like driving a tub of blubber."

"Why do you say that?" he said with resentment.

"It slides around like a loose goose," Milt said, waggling the power-assisted wheel so that the car steered from side to side, across the white line and then onto the shoulder. "Are you sure this wheel is attached to anything down underneath? It has no road-sense. Like driving a bag of chicken feathers. Lots of nice window, though." He poked Bruce in the ribs. "Like that vista-dome train."

"You try opening it up," he said. "Then you'll see the difference. This car'll cruise at ninety all day long."

THEY CONTINUED UP HIGHWAY 30, into northern Oregon, not stopping in Boise. Sometime early in the morning, before dawn, Milt suggested that they pull off and eat. They found a roadside cafe, ate, and once again returned to the road. But now Milt seemed sluggish and uncomfortable. He let Bruce take the wheel; settling against the door on his side he wrapped his arms around his body but did not sleep. At the wheel, Bruce listened to the man's breathing.

"You okay?" he inquired.

"Sure," Milt said. "Taking a nap."

"Your kidneys bothering you?"

"I don't have any kidneys," Milt said.

"Maybe we ought to find a place to stay," he said, but his own urge was to keep driving. They might possibly reach Seattle without stopping, make the entire trip in a single dash. The excitement of the drive itself began to take precedence, in his mind, over their purpose in going to Seattle in the first place. Most of his long trips on the road had been lonely ordeals, with no one to share the job or talk to. He could understand why Milt had wanted company. It made a difference. Here they were together, the way he and his former boss Ed von Scharf had been originally, before he had learned enough to go out and buy on his own. How much this reminded him of those days . . . except that in a sense the situation had been turned around. Now he did most of the driving and made the choices as they showed up. Beside him, his companion became more and more inert. Eventually it would all be up to him.

But in a certain respect he enjoyed this, having the wheel to himself with Milt taking it easy in the seat next to him. It made him aware that without him they could not possibly get to Seattle; at least, not in this fashion, driving on and on without stopping. Partly it had to do with age. And with general all-around physical health. But also, this was his dish. Growing up in Montario he had been born to the road; in his high school days he had made the drive down to Reno, seventeen years old and already yearning to —

Milt interrupted him. "What's wrong with you?" He glared at him, and, drawing himself upright, croaked, "How do you get the way you are? Is it some kind of pose?"

Taken by surprise, he said, "Explain what you mean."

Thrashing about, Milt indicated the road and the land beyond it. "You *thrive* on this. I've been watching you — you eat it up. The more the better. How does a person get like that? I've been asking myself that over and over again. Don't you need anything outside yourself? Human beings mean nothing at all to you."

The tirade, coming without warning, and being in such a jumbled fashion, made him wonder what could have gotten into Milt. "What's this all about?" he asked.

Subsiding somewhat, Milt said, "You're so damn self-sufficient. No, it's worse than that. You don't care anything about anybody else; maybe you don't even care about yourself. What are you alive for?" Accusingly, he said. "You're like one of these millionaire tycoons that rides rough-shod over mankind." He spoke with such fervor and righteous sincerity that Bruce had to laugh. At that, Milt became even more incoherent. "Yes, it really is funny," he managed to say. "Do you even care about your wife? Or did you just marry her to inherit the business? Hell, you're a madman." He stared at him.

"I'm not a madman," Bruce said, and he had to fight down fits of laughter; there, beside him, dumpy, cross Milton Lumky had turned red-faced and his eyes prepared to pop from his head. And what about? Impossible to tell. "Listen," he said, "if I made you sore by —"

"You didn't make me sore," Milt interrupted. "I pity you."

"Why?" he said.

"Because you don't love anybody in the world."

"You have no way to know that."

"You have no bonds of affection with anybody. I've got you figured out. You have no heart." Abruptly, with passion, he smacked himself on the chest and shouted, "You have no fucking heart, do you? Admit it."

Incredible, Bruce thought, that anybody could really talk like that. Believe in such empty phrases. Trash he had read emerging from him, using his mouth and voice. But beyond any doubt, to Milt it was a critical matter. That sobered him and he said, "I have a good deal of feeling toward Susan."

"What about me?" Milt said.

"What do you mean, 'what about me'?"

Milt said, "Forget it."

In his life he had never heard anybody talk like that before. "I know what's bothering you," he said. "This scenery depresses you and it doesn't depress me. That makes you mad and it worries you."

"Do you ever feel depressed? About anything?"

"Not about scenery," he said. But then he remembered how he had felt going through the Sierras. The littered, abandoned quality of the mountains. The sparse vegetation. The silence. "Sure," he said. "Sometimes it gets me down. I don't like it so much out between towns. I think anybody who's on the road feels like that, especailly out here where we have to get on the Great Western Desert."

"I can't drive that desert," Milt said. "Down into Nevada." Now he had grown ill-looking and weak once more; he settled against the door. The flush had faded from his face, allowing it to collapse. For a long time neither of them said anything. At last Milt stirred about and said, "Let's pull off and get some sleep." He shut his eyes.

"Okay," Bruce said, with reluctance.

At dawn they reached a small motel set back from the road, with its vacancy sign still lit and blinking. The owner, a middle-aged woman in a bathrobe, led them to a cabin, and soon they had locked up the car, carried their suitcases indoors, and were crawling into the two single beds.

As he fell asleep he thought triumphantly, Only about two hundred more miles left to go. We're almost there.

No, he thought. More like three hundred. But it made no real difference. We can make it with no trouble at all.

AT ELEVEN the next morning he awoke. Getting out of bed he padded into the bathroom, struggled out of his wrinkled, unpleasant-feeling clothes, and enjoyed a shower. Then he shaved, combed his hair, and put on clean clothes, a fresh starched white cotton shirt in particular. That made him feel better than ever. And yet something dangled in the back of his mind that depressed his spirits. Something dragged him down. What was it? An only partly-remembered unpleasantness. In the bathroom he stood at the mirror fussing with his talc, trying to detect the nature of the weight on him. Outside the motel, the warm sun sparkled off cars moving along the highway, and he became ready to leave; he at once wanted to get started. With impatience, he left the bathroom and returned to the front room.

In his bed Milt Lumky lay on his side, his legs drawn up, his face obscured by the covers. He did not stir but he was awake. Bruce could see his eyes. Without blinking, Lumky stared off into the corner.

"How are you feeling?" Bruce asked.

"Okay," Lumky said. He continued to stare and then he said, "I hate to have to tell you this, but I'm sick."

Picking up his suitcase, Bruce began the job of returning his things to it. "How sick?" he said.

"Darn sick," Milt said.

Hearing that he felt fright. His legs shook under him. This was the awful thing in the back of his mind, and now it had come forward. He went on packing, however. In the bed Milt watched him. "That's too bad," Bruce said. "I'm sorry to hear that. Of course it isn't exactly a surprise to either of us. We sort of expected it from yesterday."

Milt said, "I'll have to stay in bed for a while." He spoke slowly, but without any sign of doubt. As if he knew his own situation so well that there could not be any argument.

"Then maybe she was right," Bruce said. "Is that so?"

"She was right," Milt said.

"God damn it," he said. "This is a hell of a thing." He ceased packing and stood aimlessly.

"This is a hell of a thing to wish onto you," Milt said, "but there's nothing we can do about it now." Evidently he felt no need of apology; his voice was gruff.

"You want your medicine?" he said.

"Maybe later," Milt said. "I'll just take it easy for now." He made no move to get up. He seemed calm about it, not in any pain or even alarmed. Only resigned, and somewhat subdued. Not trying to make any jokes about it.

Did he know this was going to happen? Bruce wondered. I'll bet he did. Maybe this is his getting back at us. Getting even because we got married. Jealous of me, he thought. Thoughts of that sort entered his mind as he gazed down at Milt Lumky in the bed. After all Milt said himself that he was interested in her.

"I guess we don't get into Seattle," he said.

"Later on," Milt said.

"I mean, maybe we don't get in at all."

Milt said nothing. Then he grimaced, either feeling pain or thinking of something. He stirred about in the bed; his short, stubby fingers appeared and he grabbed at the pillow to tug it under his head. The covers fell across his face. His back was to Bruce.

After some time had passed, Bruce opened the cabin door and walked outside, onto the parking area by the car. They had rolled up the car windows and he could see that the interior of the car was dank and oppresive. So he opened the car door and rolled down the windows. The upholstery burned his hand as he leaned against it. The car smelled of fabric and dust, as it always did in the mornings. He sat behind the wheel and lit a cigarette and smoked.

I can't leave him, he realized. I can't drive off leaving him here by himself. Undoubtedly he actually is sick. And anyhow, I can't arrange for the typewriters without him.

Without Lumky he could do nothing; his hands were tied. All he could do was stand around and wait and hope that Lumky would recover.

Lumky had him stuck here. He couldn't go back to Susan at Boise, or up to Seattle for the typewriters, or back to Reno or anywhere. Stuck in a second-rate motel off the highway, somewhere in Northern Oregon or possibly in Washington; he did not even know if they had crossed into Washington or not. He did not even know the name of the motel.

12

HE WALKED DOWN THE PATH to the motel office. Inside, the middle-aged bright-eyed woman who owned the motel was busy scrubbing the white enamel Seven-Up machine; she smiled at him as he entered.

"Morning," she called, resuming her scrubbing.

In one corner of the office a child sat reading a comic book. Next to the door was a revolving rack of picture postcards of Washington and Oregon scenery. To the left he saw the counter and to the right was the pay phone. The office was clean, pleasant with sunlight.

"Do you know a doctor around here?" he asked. "Who you'd recommend?"

"Is your companion sick?" She stopped scrubbing and straightened up. "I noticed you didn't stir around much this morning. Last night when you came in I thought to myself that he looked extra tired." She put away her rag and the can of Dutch Cleanser. "Are you related?" she asked, facing him across the counter.

"No," he said, irked.

"I thought possibly he was a relative, possibly your older brother." Laughing nervously she reached under the counter and produced a notebook. "There's several good doctors around here . . . just a minute." She turned pages.

From the rear door her husband, a thin, dour-looking, Oklahoma type of man, appeared. "What's it for?" he asked Bruce. "What variety of illness?"

"I don't know what's the matter with him," he said. "Some chronic thing." Since the two of them were regarding him intently he said, "I don't know him too well; he's a business acquaintance."

"You better find out what it is," the man said. His wife nodded.

"I guess so," Bruce said.

"Go ask him what it is," the woman said. They exchanged glances and she said, "Find out from him if it's contagious, will you?" She and her husband followed him to the door of the office.

"I know it's not contagious," he said. "It's a kidney ailment."

"There's contagious kidney ailments," the man called after him, from the doorway of the office.

As Bruce walked back up to the cabin he could hear the two of them behind him in the office, talking in low tones.

They'll probably tell us it's against the law to have him stay here, he thought to himself. They'll probably make us leave.

Of course, there were other motels. If Milt was well enough to be moved.

He did not feel like going back inside the cabin, so he stood outside on the porch. Along the highway one vehicle after another passed. From where he stood he could not see their wheels; they appeared to be sliding. Like metal toys pulled along on a string, over the pavement, faster and faster. The sight filled him with uneasiness and he opened the cabin door.

"Hi," Milt murmured from the bed.

"Do you know how I can get hold of Cathy?" he asked.

"Why?"

"I want to get her advice."

"There's nothing she can tell you. Don't you think I know what's wrong with me?"

After arguing with him he managed to get the name of Cathy's office at the Pocatello City Hall, the city tax assessment office.

"I don't want you to call her," Milt said, sitting up in bed. His face showed that he had begun suffering a great deal of pain; the flesh below his eyes had sagged downward and become twisted and creased. "I'll be okay after I get some rest. I just have to be off my feet and lying down. Probably by tonight I'll be back in shape."

"Tell me exactly what's wrong with you."

Milt said, "Nephritis. I got it because of an attack of scarlet fever when I was a kid. Bright's disease, they usually call it."

"How bad do you have it?"

"It comes and goes. It's the son of a bitch pains in my back that get me. There's nothing you can do. So don't call Cathy. Don't worry about it. We'll be in Seattle by tomorrow night." He lay back in the bed, his arms at his sides.

"You're positive I can't get you anything?"

"Go on out and get yourself some breakfast."

He left the cabin and roamed around, across a field, past a fenced-in pasture in which a pair of horses cropped grass. The air smelled of dung and hay. Under his shoes the ground crumbled away as he stepped onto a rodent burrow. Bending down, he watched big red ants at work. Far off, on the highway, the cars moved along.

One day, in July, he had broken down outside of Wendover, Nevada. Pulled over on the shoulder of the highway he had fussed with a broken oil line from ten in the morning until one-thirty in the afternoon, knowing even as he fussed that he had no chance of repairing it. What he had been trying to do was show the cars going by that he was okay, that he would be back on the road soon. During that whole time he had kept his back to the road and his head down under the hood where the motor was, ashamed and filled with rage, but hoping that none of the cars would stop. Finally a tow truck had appeared from Wendover; a motorist who had noticed him had gotten hold of it. Why had he felt so guilty to be stuck on the shoulder? I don't know, he thought now. He had not known then. But here once more he was stuck, and for a much longer time. The thing he most dreaded.

Do I think they're laughing at me? he wondered.

He thought, Like Old Man Hagopian when I was buying the box of Trojans. Everybody getting a kick out of it.

Remembering that, he found himself blushing.

Christ, he thought. What was so funny about that? Anyhow everybody has to buy them sooner or later. Until they get married, and then the woman buys something instead that comes in a tube. More like a medicine.

One day he had seen a little colored boy who had found a discarded rubber, probably in the gutter. The colored boy, as he strolled along, was blowing the rubber up like a balloon.

God, and it undoubtedly had been used. He hadn't known whether to laugh or be disgusted. Or knock it out of the kid's hands. Anyhow he had gone on straight-faced, pretending not to notice.

It really was funny.

Wouldn't anybody laugh at a thing like that?

I really have to get out of here, he thought. Even if Milt was a blood relative, like the lady thought, I'd still have to leave.

But it sure would be dirty to leave him here. Somebody had to be with him.

He recrossed the field, back to the motel, to the office. The lady and her Oklahoma husband were not in sight. At the pay phone he laid out the slip of paper with Cathy's number and put a dime into the phone. The operator told him how much to deposit and he dropped in the proper amount. The connection was made. A woman, not Cathy, answered the phone. He asked for Mrs. Hermes, and after an interval he found himself talking to her.

"This is Bruce Stevens," he said.

"How is he?" Cathy asked, without a pause, aware at once why he had called.

"He's in bed," he said. "He's worn out."

"How far did you get?"

"Pretty far," he said. He knew now that this was Washington, just outside a town called Pasco. "But we're off the road now at this motel. We stayed here overnight. I didn't realize until this morning how bad he was. I recall that you warned me, but anyhow here we are. What are your feelings?" he asked her.

"I can't do anything," she said.

"You have his car. You could drive out after work." He began to tell her where the motel was, but she broke in.

"I don't have the key. I threw it to him."

"It's in the driveway," he said.

"No it isn't," she said. "I looked this morning and I didn't see it. As a matter of fact I was late to work because I spent so much time looking all around for it."

"I know it's there," he said. "He didn't pick it up."

Cathy said, "I know it's not there."

"Could you come out on the bus, then?" he said.

"No," she said.

"I have to drive on to Seattle," he said. "I have to settle this business."

"Are you telling me the truth? Would you actually drive off and leave him when he's flat on his back sick in bed in a motel?"

"I have to," he said. When she said nothing he said, "Anyhow it's my car."

She said, "I do have the key to the Mercedes."

That did not surprise him. "Then drive out here," he said. He gave her a long complicated set of directions.

"It'll take me a long time," she said, in a balking, frantic way. "I can't drive that far in one hop. I'll have to stop along the way; I don't think I can get there until the day after tomorrow. I'll have to arrange for time off from work. I don't even know if I can do that. Does that mean he'll be alone until then, or will you stay with him until I get there?"

"I should leave now," he said.

Near tears, she said, "Then there's no point in my coming. Suppose you leave him, and then while I'm trying to get there he leaves?"

"He can't leave because he won't have any car to leave in."

"That's so," she said. "No," she decided. "I won't do it. You have to stay with him. It's your fault anyhow." The phone clicked. She had hung up.

Now what should I do? he asked himself.

He hung up the receiver. Should I call her back? But there's nothing I can do over the phone; I can't make her drive out here, or come out on the bus. If she won't come then that's it. And when she says it's my fault she's right.

But I don't see how she can't come, he thought to himself. I would have thought she'd jump right in the car and drive on out. Didn't she drive all over Pocatello that night searching for orange juice for him? And it's an easy car to drive. And she's familiar with it.

Leaving the motel office he looked around outside, among the cabins, for the owner. He found her in an empty cabin, fixing fresh towels. "Can I get some change from you?" he asked her. "For the phone."

"Did you find out from your friend what he has wrong with him?" she asked, as they returned to the office.

"It's nephritis," he said. "It's not contagious."

Back in the office she changed a five-dollar bill for him. "Has he got a family?" she said "A wife?"

"I think so," he said. Putting money into the phone he called Susan in Boise. The motel woman hung around for a moment, and then she left the office. "I have some bad news," he said into the phone. "I'm up here in Washington with Milt Lumky, and he's sick." He explained to her along the lines that he had explained to the motel woman, but she interrupted him.

"I know about Milt's kidney trouble," she said.

"He's apparently had it most of his life," he said.

"You better stay with him," Susan said. "Do you have enough money with you? I can wire you some." They had arranged it so that when the time came for him to buy she would wire him the money.

"I'll be okay," he said.

"When he has an attack he's usually laid up flat on his back for a couple of days," she said. "And it's very painful."

"I had plenty of warning," he said. "The girl he's been living with in Pocatello told me, and when I got there he was already sick. So I have nobody to blame; I certainly can't blame him."

"You can to this extent," Susan said, in a careful, rational tone. "He's the one who's in the position to judge, and if he went along with you, then it's not your fault. You have to assume he knows what he's doing; he's a grown man. You can't be expected to make judgments about somebody else's illness, especially somebody you barely know. Why doesn't she come out and take care of him, this girl?"

"I talked to her on the phone," he said, "but she said she didn't feel like it."

"It's not your worry," Susan said. "Unless you want to make it your worry. Unless you feel responsible. There's the intangible aspect to it."

He said, "I feel it's my fault, because if I hadn't started talking to him about the typewriters he wouldn't have come along; after all, this trip is so I can get the typewriters. He gets nothing out of it. It's a favor he's doing for me."

"You can't afford to be bogged down very long," she pointed out.

"True," he said. "But I feel I have to."

"Okay," she said. "Keep in touch with me."

"I'll call you again," he said. He told her not to worry and then he hung up. After a moment or so he left the motel office and trudged back in the direction of the cabin.

It's just one of those things, he thought. When a person is ill it takes precedence over everything else, especially questions of what's practical. You can't always do simply what you consider to be in your own best interest. Nobody can live like that. Economic gain isn't everything, he thought. Or even the most important thing. I know if it was me who was sick Milt would stay.

That's why he's here in the first place, he thought. Because he put his friendship with me over practical considerations. So that's the hell of it, he thought. And there's just nothing that can be done.

When he opened the cabin door Milt, in the bed, murmured, "I feel better. This god damn business comes and goes." He had propped himself up to a sitting position, the pillow behind him. "Close the door," he said. "The light's blinding."

Closing the door, Bruce said, "The motel people are afraid it's the bubonic plague."

"Then tell them to start fleeing," Milt said. "Listen," he said. "I've been thinking about this. Maybe you should drive on. Look in my coat pocket in my wallet. I've got the name of the man written down on the back of a card. The guy who owns the machines."

"That's okay," Bruce said. "I'll stick around."

"Bring it," Milt said.

Carrying the wallet over to the bed he handed it to Milt. Grunting with effort, Milt sorted through the cards and folded slips of paper; as he examined each he took an interest in it, halting to ponder and recall what it meant and why he had kept it. Some of the cards had stuck together, and he put his eyes close to them as he cautiously pulled them apart. One of the cards sent him off into reverie, and for a considerable time he neither spoke nor moved.

Finally he resumed and found the one he wanted. "Phil Baranowski," he said, reading the back of the card. "Here's his address and phone number. Phil is a funny guy. I met him at a wholesalers' party. Then later on he showed me the machines, among the rest of the junk he had hold of that he wanted to peddle. That was six or seven months ago. He's probably still got all of it plus a ton more."

"I'm not going," Bruce said. "Partly because it's obvious that if you're not along he won't sell me the machines, and partly because I don't think you should be left alone. I don't think you're well enough."

"He'll sell them if you use your intelligence. Make it clear that you know me."

In the end he wound up accepting the card. But the worry continued to nag him. He might make the trip by himself, arrive at Seattle, and have Baranowski refuse to do business with him. Even though he did not intend to go, even though he meant to remain in the motel with him, he said, "Could you write some sort of note to him? Or phone him?"

Milt shrugged. "Not necessary," he said, scowling.

"If we get to discussing it, can I have him phone you?" He felt guilty, but he could not afford to take chances with the matter.

Rousing himself, Milt said, "If you want. If you can get hold of me. There's no phone here."

"There's one in the motel office."

Milt nodded.

Seating himself in the chair in the corner, facing Milt in the bed, he tried to relax. But his restlessness grew. "Listen," he said, standing up. "I think I'll go roam around and maybe buy something to read. Do you want anything? A magazine or a book?"

Gradually Milt had sunk down in the bed. He opened his eyes and regarded him and then he said, "Bruce, there's something I've been going to say to you. I've been thinking about it, trying to figure out what it is that's wrong with you, why you're the way you are. I think I've finally got you figured out. You don't believe in God, do you?"

This time he did laugh. This time the question was too inane and too seriously asked; he began to giggle and once he had started he could not stop. He found himself lying back in his chair, his hand over his eyes, wheezing and weeping, gasping, while across from him Milt continued to watch him somberly. And still he could not stop. The more he tried to stop, the harder it became to stop. At last he lost the ability to make any sound at all. Even his laughing was soundless. Not since his grammar school days, not since Saturday afternoon at the Kiddies' Matinee at the Luxor, watching a Three Stooges comedy: he had not laughed so much since then. He knew that Milt was kidding. Now he realized that Milt had been kidding before, in the car. The whole time he had been kidding straight-faced. Looking back, realizing that Milt had been pulling his leg, he laughed harder and harder, until his ribs ached and he had exhausted himself and become dizzy.

When he was able he got to his feet. "Excuse me," he managed, and walked step by step into the bathroom. There he shut the door and rinsed his face with cold water. He rubbed his face with the towel, combed his hair, glanced at himself in the mirror, and then he returned to the room.

In the bed, Milt lay as before.

"I'm sorry," Bruce said shakily, sitting down again in the chair.

Milt said, "I must be dreaming or something. I ask you a perfectly simple question and you laugh your head off."

"Not again," he said weakly, lifting his hand.

"Not again what?"

"I can't stand it."

Milt stared at him and then he said with ferocity, "Are you out of your mind? Stand back and take a good look at yourself. What kind of a person are you to laugh at a question like that?" He sat up in bed and smashed the pillow into place behind him. His face had flushed and become wrinkled, as if the bones and teeth had been removed, had slipped back down inside and been dissolved.

"I told you I'm sorry," Bruce said. "What else can I say?" He got up and came over, holding his hand out.

Milt shook hands with him, and at the same time said, "I'm deeply worried about you. I wouldn't try to talk to you seriously if I wasn't worried about you." He let go of his hand. "You're smart and personable; there's no reason why you won't go far. I can't stand seeing you settle for a compromise."

"What compromise?" he said.

"Giving up what you really want. You've set your sights on a material life of getting a buy and making a profit. You were cut out for —" He searched for the word. "You ought to be after something spiritual."

Bruce said, with difficulty, "I'm sorry, but I'm going to start laughing again." His jaw began to tremble of its own accord; he had to sit with his chin in his hands to keep it still.

"Why does that strike you as funny?"

"I don't know," he said.

"There's only one reason why a person goes into business," Milt said. "To make money."

"No," he said.

"What else, then?"

"There's a satisfaction in it," he said.

"Balls," Milt said.

He said, "You mean I should be a fireman or a cowboy?"

"You should have some values in your life, something permanent."

"Like you have?" he said, laughing, unable to stop laughing.

"I don't want you to be like me," Milt said.

"You shouldn't have become a salesman, if you feel like that," he said. "Personally, I don't see anything wrong with it."

"That's what I mean."

Bruce said, "Wanting to make a store run is a permanent value, for me. I've always wanted to do it. Since I was a kid."

"Maybe you think that now," Milt said. "That's self-deception."

"Wouldn't I know? Better than you?"

"An outside person can tell better," Milt said. "Nobody has any insight into themselves."

"Can you tell me what I want better than I can?" he said. "You can't read my mind. You don't know what's going on in my mind."

"I can tell you what's best for you. What you ought to be doing, instead of wasting your life."

"I'm not wasting my life," he said.

"Sure you are," Milt said. "What are you, if not a punk kid trying to hustle some cheap Japanese typewriters. What's there to be proud of in that?"

"The hell with you," he said.

"Yes," Milt said. "The hell with everyone. Me, Susan, everybody else. But face the truth about yourself. I know what's the matter with you. You don't have the maturity to care about anything but teen-age values. You're selfish and immature. You're a good kid and everybody likes you, but you're just not an adult, as much as you'd like to be. You're still a long way off, and if you expect to get there you better learn what's worthwhile and spiritual in life."

"Take your own advice," he said.

"I know why you're the way you are," Milt said, nodding.

To Milt he said, "I guess I'll go roam around and get something to read." He opened the motel door; sunlight blinded both of them.

In his bed, Milt said nothing.

"See you later, then," Bruce said, still lingering. But Milt said nothing more.

Stepping outside, he shut the door after him.

AN HOUR OR SO LATER, when he re-entered the cabin with his magazine, he found Milt sitting up in bed writing a check.

"Here," Milt said, handing the check to him. "This is what I promised you. Your wedding present."

The check was made out for five hundred dollars.

"I can't take this," he said.

"You won't get the machines without it," Milt said. "Anyhow I'm not giving it to you; I'm giving it to Susan. This is my last chance to let her know how I feel." He smiled slightly. "After this it becomes a crime. Anyhow, I've got plenty of money and no one to spend it on."

Putting the check in his wallet, Bruce said, "Thanks."

Neither of them said anything about their argument.

"Did I tell you I called Cathy?" Bruce said.

"No,"Milt said.

"She found the car key. So she can drive out here. I gave her the address of the place."

Milt nodded.

"And the motel people are conscious that you're sick. They have the names of local doctors; I was asking them about it."

"Fine," Milt said. "They probably can bring me what I need." He seemed impassive.

"How would you feel, then," he said, "if I did drive on?"

Milt said, "I told you to."

"If you feel you'd be okay, I think I will."

"Are you driving back this way after you finish up in Seattle?"

"No," he said. "I thought I'd drive down the Coast and back up by US 26, through Oregon."

Milt said, "I'm sorry you called Cathy. There's no reason why she should have to drive out here. I'll be up and around in a day or so and there's no reason why I can't go back there on the Greyhound." He lay back and stared up at the ceiling. Presently he said, "I hope you swing the deal for the typewriters."

"I hate to leave," he said, "with you still sore at me."

"I'm just upset," Milt said.

"Don't worry about me," he said.

"Okay," Milt said.

"Even if I don't believe in God," he said, "I can still have a full life."

Milt said, "There's just something dead in you."

"No," he said.

"You're like these scientists making H-bombs," Milt said. "Cold as hell, rational as hell."

"But no soul," Bruce said.

Milt nodded.

"Maybe we'll all be blown up," Bruce said. "And then it won't matter."

"I'd be willing to bet that even that wouldn't faze you."

"It would," he said.

"You wouldn't even notice," Milt said.

He began gethering up his things from the bathroom, packing them into the opened suitcase.

"Maybe it would be a good thing after all," Milt said. "The bomb, I mean. Maybe it would wake people up."

"I doubt it," he said. "I doubt if it would be a good thing."

"People have to face reality sometime." He said it with bitterness and conviction.

After he had packed up his things, Bruce went down to the motel office and told the owners the situation. He gave them Cathy's phone number, and, as an afterthought, Susan's and his own in Boise. To wind it up he wrote out the name and address of Milt's company. And he made it clear to them that Milt had enough money to maintain himself; he wanted to be sure that Milt would be well-treated after he left.

"Don't worry about him," the woman said, accompanying him to his car. "We'll keep our eye on him." Cheerfully, she helped him unload Milt's things.

He carried the bundles and suitcases into the cabin. "Well, I'll see you," he said to Milt. He paused in the doorway. "Take it easy."

"Take it easy," Milt said, not looking at him. "Don't take any wooden nickels."

Presently he had driven out onto the road, leaving the motel and Milt behind.

13

He reached Seattle that evening and at once parked at a gas station and telephoned Phil Baranowski at the number Milt had given him.

"It's pretty late," Baranowski said, when he had explained what he wanted and who he was. "It's ten o'clock."

Not having realized how late in the evening it was he said, "What about early tomorrow?" Anyhow he needed sleep; he did not feel fit enough to talk business after having been all day on the road.

They agreed to meet at nine-thiry in the morning at a downtown street corner that Baranowski assured him he would have no trouble finding. Baranowski gave him no clue to his chances; he simply said that he would be willing to discuss the machines and that was that.

Hanging up, he felt disappointed. All the distance he had covered . . . here he was now, face to face with the man who actually owned a warehouse of the machines. And it was an ordinary voice on the other end of the phone, a business-like voice much the same as any other.

The next morning he parked at the corner and waited for Baranowski to show up.

At a quarter to ten a thin, dark-haired man wearing a shiny blue double-breasted pin-stripe suit came striding along the sidewalk toward the Merc. He appeared to be in his middle forties. Waving to Bruce he leaned down to the window and said, "Want to go in your car or mine? Might as well take yours." He jumped in beside Bruce, and they drove off, Baranowski giving him directions. The man had an animated, terse manner; his eyes shone and he gestured continually. He seemed honest but overworked. Bruce had the feeling that to Baranowski the stock of typewriters did not amount to much. The man had a fixed idea of their worth and he would not let them go for less. But to him the amount was small; it was one inventory from among many, and as they drove from downtown Seattle toward the warehouse, Baranowski gave him an idea of some of these other involvements. Evidently the man's main interest lay in the direction of imported optical equipment from Japan and Europe, lenses and prisms and binoculars and microscopes. He told Bruce that he had started out years ago as a lens-grinder for a Portland firm that made eyeglasses; eventually he had opened his own shop in partnership with an optometrist, and then he had gone into warwork during the 'forties, and now into this. He no doubt had direct contact with exporters in Japan who supplied him his lenses, and the typewriters had shown up as one of their sidelines.

"Milt thought I could pick them up for around fifty dollars each," Bruce said, as he parked near a large wooden warehouse across from a chemical company which had its tanks up on stilts. The pavement was irregular, broken down by trucks.

"Milt was being optimistic," Baranowski said, getting out of the car. "Did he mention that they're all in original cartons?" With a key he unlocked a side door of the warehouse and the two of them entered.

The place was dark and dry. Baranowski switched on several overhead lights. "I can give you up to four hundred of them. Absolutely identical." He reached up to the top of a pile of small square cartons and lifted one down; handing it to Bruce he showed him the stencilled code markings. "You'd be surprised how many times we run across other stuff in cartons, not what it's supposed to be. But these are what it says. We had them checked over before they left the shipper." He told Bruce, then, about a wealthy retired broker who had ordered a case of Cutty Sark Scotch, and when it had come he had opened it and found the wood crate filled with bricks. "And that was from Scotland," Baranowski finished up.

"Can I open this?" Bruce asked.

"Please do."

He opened the carton and lifted out the typewriter. Sure enough, it was what he had seen in the store window in San Francisco. "Can I plug it in and try it?" he asked. The machine seemed unexpectedly light. No heavier than a book. And smaller than he remembered. But the workmanship appeared good; he examined the various screws, and they had all been driven in properly and finished up with the heads evenly countersunk.

Baranowski patted him on the shoulder. "Take it along with you," he said. "I'm in kind of a rush. You go back to your motel or wherever you're staying and give it the works. Give it the hardest treatment you can. I've got one I've been using for six months; no trouble at all with it. They're beautifully built." He switched off the lights and led Bruce toward the door. On both sides of them, in the gloom, the cartons of Mithrias had been piled up, one on top of another, an entire cavern of them. And, beyond them, he saw larger cartons, other machines. "You make certain you're satisfied and then you give me a buzz. Okay? You know where to find me."

They drove back to the downtown business section, and Baranowski told him where he wanted to be let off. The last Bruce saw of him he was striding off into an office building, his hands thrust deep in his pockets. The Mithrias remained on the car seat beside Bruce. The man, without hesitation, had left it with him, without ever having laid eyes on him before.

IN HIS MOTEL ROOM he set the typewriter up on the bed, plugged it in, and placed a batch of typing paper and carbon paper beside it. Too bad, he thought, that I'm not a typist. He switched it on and the thing began to hum. But he did know something about machinery. Almost at once he could see that a great deal of ingenuity had gone into it. The carriage return intrigued him; it did not operate by means of a pulley, but by the use of a simple spring and lock system, like the release of a crossbow. Two strike pressures could be obtained, *light* for one carbon, *heavy* for several. The key-touch pressure could not be changed except by adjusting a screw from the back. Tabs had to be set from the back, too, and manually, as on the old pre-war machines. That did not matter, however. The main thing was the sturdiness of its construction and the general swiftness and dependability of its action. Rolling in two sheets of paper he began to type. The thing was noisy — the keys struck with a sharp clack — but such was the case with all electrics. He discovered that once a key had been pressed down, the letter would not restrike until the key had been let completely up. So there was little chance of accidental multiple strikes. With two fingers, the best he could manage, he began typing the letters *f* and *j* as rapidly as possible. He found that he could not confuse the action; it kept well ahead of him. So it represented a genuine electric, in its speed and in its light touch.

With a screwdriver he removed the bottom plate and inspected the works. The machine used an old kind of rubber roller that threw the key up and simultaneously released it. The belt from the roller to the tiny electric motor seemed to involve a good deal of friction; probably it would have to be replaced from time to time. In fact, throughout the works many friction points could be noticed. The motor would be under considerable strain. Wear would be fairly intense. He left the machine on, with its motor running, for a good part of the day. It did not get especially hot. Keys left jammed, he realized, would probably set up a process of binding that would burn out the motor in an hour or so. But that was a risk in most electrics.

The style of type, although not unusual, was effective. Copied no doubt from conventional American machines.

Making himself comfortable he began to load the machine up with work; he pressed the carriage return button again and again, for over an hour. The carriage shot back and forth, causing the machine to lurch gradually across the bed. But the mechanism never failed to operate. In the same fashion he repeatedly tried every control. It stood up perfectly, although several times, when he started to type, he jammed the keys and had to shut off the motor to unjam them.

The carbon impression appeared to be uniform enough. The keys all hit with equal force. He tested the strength of the type-bars. They seemed somewhat flimsy. Probably they would have to be realigned from time to time. The *n*, he discovered, had already gone out of alignment.

Putting in a fresh sheet of paper he laboriously typed a letter to Susan. Two-finger typing was a slow business, but at last he had what he wanted. He informed her that this was a sample of the work put out by the Mithrias, and that it was up to her to make the judgment on it; his knowledge began and ended with the mechanical aspect. After all, she had been making her living as a professional typist. As to the sales possibilities, he believed that if he could get the machines cheap enough, nothing stood in the way of their unloading them. Then he told her to phone him as soon as she had decided. He typed out the phone number of the motel, sealed up the letter plus a first and fifth carbon, carried it downstairs to the main postoffice and mailed it off to Boise special delivery air mail.

The next day he carried the machine to a typewriter repair agency that offered service on "all makes and models."

The plump, curly-headed young man behind the counter examined the machine and said, "What the hell is it? One of those Italian portables? The Olivetti?" He turned it upside down and peered up into it.

"No," Bruce said. "It's Japanese."

"What's wrong with it?"

"Nothing," he said. "I just want to find out if you can service it when it needs service."

"Wait'll I get the repairman," the curly-headed young man said. He went off behind a curtain, and when he returned he had with him a massively-built older man with dark hair and bare, hairy-black arms. The man wore a blue apron and he had ink and grease on his hands. Without a word he picked up the machine, plugged it in and turned it on, listened to it and poked at it.

"It's built in Japan," Bruce said.

The repairman scrutinized him. "I know," he said. "Where'd you get hold of it?"

"In San Francisco," he said. "In a shop there."

"What kind of guarantee did they give you?"

He said, "Why?"

"Just curious."

"None," he said.

The repairman said, "Well, I'll tell you. I wouldn't have one on a bet."

"Why?" he asked. This was why he had brought it here, to get an opinion from a trained typewriter repairman.

"You can't get parts. Where're you going to get parts? Write to

Japan? Does anybody in this country stock parts?" He turned the machine on and off, jiggling the switch.

"I guess not," he said, acting out his role.

"It's not badly put together," the repairman said, shaking the machine and operating the carriage return. "Those people are clever and they've got little fingers; they can get in and assemble where there's no space for a white man to stick his thumb. Look at this." He showed Bruce how close together the moving parts had been placed. "That's why they can build it so small. But hell, when you want service, how's anybody going to get a tool into it?" He stuck the end of a screwdriver down and showed Bruce that it could not be fitted into some of the visible screws. "You practically have to disassemble it to clean it."

"Have you had any in here for service?"

"A couple," the curly-headed younger man said.

"Better stick to American products," the repairman said. "It's like anything else; buy a brand you know."

Picking up his Mithrias, Bruce thanked him and left the repair shop.

For the heck of it he tried one more shop. A moody-looking man waited on him. Apparently he had never seen a Mithrias before; he viewed it from every angle, saying nothing, not plugging it in or asking anything about it. Finally he turned his head and said, "Is this something new they're bringing out? Some of the bolts are metric. We're going to have trouble with these."

"Can you work on it?"

"Oh sure, we can work on it. What's the matter with it?" Now he plugged it in and ran a piece of folded paper around the roller.

"Nothing right now." he said.

"Oh, you're just getting the news in advance. Is it yours?"

"Not quite," he said. "It may be. How much do you think I ought to pay for it?"

"Is it new?" The man tapped at the rubber roller. "It's been used. Look at the key-strikes in the platen."

They discussed it and decided that the Mithrias electric portable, when new, was worth about two hundred dollars. Probably he would have perpetual trouble getting service on it. But it seemed well-built and if he was lucky he would get a lot of use out of it. The repairman tapped out laboriously a few words, with one finger instead of two, jamming the keys and at last giving up.

"I'm not much of a typist," he admitted.

"Neither am I," Bruce said. He thanked the man and departed with his Mithrias under his arm.

So it could be worked on, if the repairman was willing. The problem was no greater than with foreign cameras or cars; maintenance was a calculated risk. That cheered him up. They could sell the Mithrias in good conscience.

He drove to the downtown address at which Phil Baranowski operated. The legend on the office door read WEST COAST OPTICS, and when he opened the door he found himself facing an illuminated and velvet-draped display table of optical equipment.

"Made up your mind?" Baranowski said, from somewhere out of sight. He appeared, his sleeves rolled up, carrying a pry bar. Off the office Bruce saw a small store room; Baranowski had been getting the lid from a packing crate. "Don't mind if I keep on working." He returned to the crate and picked up a cigarette that he had left lying on top of it.

Bruce said, "Depending on what you want for them, I'm definitely interested."

"They're nicely put together, aren't they? Overseas they don't have assembly lines like we have; they don't shoot them out one after another. The things are made stationary. First one man works on it and then he goes down to the the next one and the next man takes his place. They can turn out professional-quality equipment in a garage. In a basement. With a couple of belt-driven lathes. During the war they hand-ground lenses and mirrors in bombed-out cellars. They made the most intricate electronic equipment with a hundred dollars' worth of bench tools. If a Japanese shop had had what the average do-it-your-selfer has in his garage today, they would have got the A-bomb before we did."

"How much do you want for the portables?" he said.

"You want them all?"

"No," he said. "I couldn't hope to unload them all. At any price. Too much of a service problem."

"There's no service problem." Baranowski paused in his work and gestured with the pry bar. "What do you mean?"

"No parts. And metric bolts. And no space to work; everything packed in tight. You can't get at anything."

"Do you expect them to break?"

"Every machine breaks. Any electric typewriter needs constant maintenance."

"Leave that up to the customer."

"We have to put some kind of guarantee on them."

"Don't play up the imported business. You're not going to notify them that they're made in Japan, are you?"

"No," he said.

"Well, that's fifty percent of it. If they think they're made in this country it won't occur to them to worry about service."

"We're not a schlock outfit," he said. "That's not the way we do business."

"And this isn't a schlock typewriter," Baranowski said sharply. He gave up his unpacking and came back into the office, swinging his pry bar around. "It's a good sound piece of workmanship and anybody who knows anything about machinery'll recognize that."

"How much?" Bruce said, feeling that he had the man on the defensive.

"For how many? I don't want to break the warehouse down. If I keep it intact I can offer somebody an exclusive. If I sell you some and somebody else some, you'll be in competition."

"I'm not selling them in this area," he said.

"Where, then?"

"The southern part of Idaho."

"Around Boise?"

"Yes," he said.

"Anywhere else?"

"No."

"I could sell you two hundred."

"At how much?"

Baranowski sat down at his desk and began writing figures. At last he said, "Fifteen thousand."

It stunned him. He computed it and arrived at a figure of seventy-five dollars a machine. "Too much," he said, "and too many."

"How many, then? That's as low as I can cut it." Baranowski scowled.

"What about fifty of them?"

In a quiet voice Baranowski said, "Are you kidding? That's almost a retail quantity."

"Nobody walks into a retail outlet and buys fifty typewriters."

"What sort of price do you think you can get on a quantity like that? What sort of selling are you in? Evidently you have no experience in this." Baranowski started back to the store room.

"All right," he said. "Let's make it seventy-five."

"Seventy-five," Baranowski said, "at around one hundred dollars each."

"No," he said. "Seventy-five at forty dollars."

"Well, glad to have met you." Turning his back, Baranowski resumed his unpacking.

Bruce said, "I'll buy seventy-five machines at forty dollars apiece. Three thousand in cash. I have the cash. No guarantee, but they have to be identical with the machine you loaned me, and in sealed original cartons."

In the store room Baranowski said nothing.

"I'll give you a call in a day or so," Bruce said. "So long." As he started out into the hall he said, "I'll leave the machine you loaned me. It's on the table."

The door closed after him. Somewhat shaken, he walked downstairs to the ground floor and outside onto the sidewalk.

THE NEXT MORNING Susan telephoned him. "I got your letter," she said. "It looks wonderful. Go ahead and buy them. I'm really excited about it. How many do you think you can get?"

"Time will tell," he said.

The day dragged by. Late that afternoon the phone in his motel room rang. Sure enough, it was Baranowski.

"I'll make one proposal," Baranowski said. "Take it or leave it. I don't go in for haggling. Sixty machines at fifty dollars apiece. I know you've got three thousand to spend, and that's what it comes to."

"It's a deal," he said.

"All right," Baranowski said. "I'm not happy about this, but evidently you're inexperienced at this so what the hell. Only next time don't come to a jobber and try to buy a pissant quantity like that."

Shortly, Bruce had driven out to meet Baranowski at the warehouse in the industrial section. A contract was typed out on one of the machines, the money passed over in the form of a cashier's check, and then together they loaded sixty of the sealed cartons into the Merc.

Bruce examined each one to be sure that the coded markings were identical.

"I think I'll open them up," he said suddenly.

Baranowski groaned.

"Since I'll be selling them direct," he said. "And you don't care if I do." While Baranowski stood unsympathetically by he carried all sixty cartons from the car and piled them back on the loading platform. One by one, with the blade of a screwdriver, he slit open the cartons, lifted out the machines, and made certain that he was getting what he had paid for. In all sixty he found no variation at all, except that one machine showed a dented side. Baranowski, wordlessly, grabbed up another carton from the warehouse and shoved it in his hands.

"Good luck," Baranowski said, and then he disappeared inside the warehouse, for good.

Bruce drove away with his sixty portable typewriters, feeling the sluggishness of the car under the weight. Had he done right? Too late to worry about that now.

Returning to his motel he packed his suitcase, paid what he owed, and started the drive back to Boise with his typewriters.

14

THE FOLLOWING NIGHT, at one A.M., he entered Boise. Parking in front of the house he locked up the car and climbed the stairs to the front porch. Letting himself in with his key he went into the bedroom and stood at the end of the bed until Susan awoke.

"Oh!" she said, staring at him.

"I'm back," he said.

At once she slid from the bed and picked up her robe. "Let's see them," she said, buttoning her robe. "They're still in the car, aren't they?"

He said, "I'm too tired." Seated at the end of the bed he began removing his shoes. "I took it as fast as I could. I only got a few hours sleep."

Bending down, she kissed him. "I'm glad you're back."

"What a grind," he said. He finished undressing, and, without putting any pajamas on, got into the bed where she had been. The bed was warm and it smelled of her. Almost at once he was off into sleep.

"Bruce," she said, awakening him. "Can I go out and get one? I want to see what they look like."

"Okay," he murmured. And again he fell asleep.

The next he knew she had seated herself on the edge of the bed, in her robe and slippers. He had the feeling that a good deal of time had passed. "Hi," he muttered.

Susan said, "Bruce, are you awake enough to look at something?"

The tone of her voice caused him to come fully awake, worn-out as he was. He sat up and looked at the clock. An hour and a half had gone by. "What's the matter?" he said.

Arising from the bed, she walked to the door of the bedroom. "I want you to look at something."

He got up, put his trousers on, and followed her down the hall to the living room. On the table a familiar Mithrias portable had been placed between two stacks of typing paper, one white and one yellow. She had been typing.

"Here," she said. She handed him a small booklet, which he recognized as the book of instructions.

"What about it?"

"Open it," she said.

He opened it. The cover had only the word *Mithrias* on it, and the first page was a diagram of the machine with each control numbered. He examined the second page.

The instructions were in Spanish.

After a moment he said, "Then these didn't come in to Seattle by ship from Japan. Directly. They must have originally been shipped to Mexico or Latin America."

Susan said, "I'm afraid to tell you." She had a dry-eyed wild expression. "The keyboard isn't standard."

"What's that mean?"

"A touch-typist can't use them. I brought in ten of them." She pointed, and he saw that she had carried ten cartons in, opened them, and gone over the ten machines. "They're probably all the same."

"Explain it to me," he said. But he understood. "I thought keyboards were standard everywhere."

"No," she said. "It's different in different countries. This is a Spanish keyboard. See. The upside down question mark. The special *n* with the tilde over it. The acute mark." She typed the marks. He had paid no more attention to them than he had to the percent sign or the etc sign. "Some of the letters are in the same position as English keyboards, but some aren't. Even in this country there used to be several different keyboards; just in this one country alone."

Both of them were silent, for a time.

"Would any typist know that?" he said finally.

"Yes," she said. "As soon as they started to touch-type."

"Would that mean almost anybody?"

She said, "We couldn't sell them unless they had a standard keyboard. There aren't any machines sold any more without standard keyboards. There haven't been in years. It's implied. It's taken for granted. What did the man who sold them to you say? I want to see the contract."

He got out the contract and they examined it. Naturally it said nothing about the keyboard.

"Has the check had time to go through?" she said. "Anyhow it was a cashier's check, wasn't it? So that's out. We can go to Fancourt and see what he says. I thought you'd want me to wake you up and tell you."

"I guess so," he said, numbed.

"Do you have any money left?"

"No," he said.

"How were you going to advertise them, then?"

"Sell a couple," he said. "Then buy space."

"I'm going to get dressed," she said. She returned to the bedroom and presently she reappeared wearing a dress, her hair tied back. "Do you have a cigarette?" she said, searching around in the living room.

"Here," he said, handing her his pack. "I wonder if Milt knew," he said.

"Of course he didn't know," she said.

"I think he did," he said.

"Milt would never have let you buy them if he had known," she said. "I've known Milt Lumky for years."

"Don't you think it's possible that he was sore and getting back at us?"

"For what?"

"For getting married."

"Why?"

He said, "Because of his interest in you."

"I suppose," she said, "now you want to drive back up there and ask him."

"It doesn't matter," he said. In his own mind he was convinced that Milt had known. "I guess we'll have to get rid of them," he said.

"Yes," she said. "If we can."

"It's possible to sell anything," he said. "It all depends on the price. Maybe they could be worked over. Keys changed around."

"We don't have any money," she said. "If you had saved some money out, maybe we could do that."

"If I had saved any money out," he said, "I wouldn't have been able to get the typewriters."

With fury she said, "Wouldn't that have been a shame."

"I spent two days looking over the thing," he said.

"And you never noticed the keyboard."

"I don't touch-type," he said.

"But it never occurred to you."

"No," he said. "It never did. Well, these things happen."

"I'm not used to it," she said in an almost unrecognizable voice. "I never worked for a discount house that buys up things that are being dumped for one reason or another."

"The trouble is," he said, trying not to pay attention to what she was saying, "that we don't have enough working capital to write this off. That's the part that gets me. It's too bad." He did not look at her because he was unable to stand the expression on her face. The grim, hard look that he remembered back into the past, the anxiety and impatience. "Let's go to bed," he said. "We'll take a look at the rest of them tomorrow. Maybe they're not all like that."

Susan said, "This is why I wanted to get out of owning a business. Dreadful things like this, when somebody swindles you."

Shrugging, he said, "Well, there had to be some reason why they were selling so cheap. Now we found out. But we can probably do something. Don't —" He broke off. "We'll fix it up," he said.

"More deals?" she said.

"Something," he murmured.

"I feel so strange," she said in a thin, shrill voice that shook. "It's my own fault for getting mixed up in this kind of way of doing things. I'm not blaming you."

"There's no issue about blame," he said.

"True," she said, clasping her hands together. "I mean, it's my own fault. I wanted somebody who could talk this kind of language. I got what I wanted, so why dwell on it?" She began to pace about the living room, straightening things on the mantel, rearranging the magazines on the coffee table. "This is my punishment. I should simply have gotten out of it entirely. Sold my share to Zoe."

He said nothing.

"After all," she said, "I ought to know how discount houses operate."

He said, "We can get rid of them."

"How?"

"In a group," he said. "At what we paid. To somebody who can afford to work them over. If we had the captial we could probably do it ourselves."

"Of course," Susan said, "you could try to do what that man did to us. You could see if possibly someone wouldn't notice. If you didn't notice, maybe there's somebody else."

"That's right," he said. His mind began to tangle with it. "I might drive down to Reno," he said. "It's just a thought. I'll talk to my former boss. It's perfectly possible that I can interest him in them. It would make a good deal for them."

"Would you tell him?" she asked. "About the keyboard."

He said, "Well, as they say — Buyer beware."

"If you do that," she said, "don't think about coming back here."

"What?" he said.

She said, "If you drive down there I will call him on the phone; I know his name. I'll tell him about the keyboard."

"Why?" he demanded.

"I don't want to pass them along to somebody else. I've never done business that way. I'd rather take the loss."

"We can't take the loss," he said.

"You mean I can't take the loss. It's my place, not yours. I can take the loss. I'll go out of business before I'll stick somebody else with them. If anybody wants them knowing what's the matter with them that's fine. You don't understand that, do you?"

"I understand that you're sore and both of us need our sleep," he said. "Let's go to bed, for Christ's sake! I've been on the road for a week." Turning, he walked down the hall and back into the bedroom. Sitting down on the bed he unfastened his pants, stood up and stepped out of them and crawled into the bed.

Susan appeared at the door. "Listen," she said. "I've had enough. I've had all I can stand."

Getting out of bed he dressed once more, this time completely.

He put on his shirt, his tie, his shoes and socks, and then his coat. "I'll see you," he said.

"Where are you going?" she said, following him down the hall to the living room.

"Who gives a damn?" he said. He opened the front door. "I'll see you," he said, starting down the steps toward his car.

Behind him she slammed the door so loudly that the sound echoed for miles, up and down the dark deserted street. Dogs, a long distance off, began to bark.

He got into his car and started it up. A moment later he had started out from the curb and was driving away from the house.

FOR AN HOUR OR SO he drove aimlessly, and then he found himself on US 95. Presently he turned in the direction of Montario. Why not? he asked himself.

When he reached Montario he took the familiar route to Peg Googer's house. As he parked he noticed no sign of lights. Naturally, he said to himself. The time was three or four o'clock in the morning. He got out of the car and walked up the path to the porch. For some time he knocked. Nobody answered. So he walked around the side of the house and rapped on what he knew from experience to be her bedroom window.

The back door opened. Peg, wrapped up in a white robe, whispered, "My god, it's Bruce Stevens." She fluttered uneasily. "What's the matter? Forget your coat again?"

He said, "How about letting me stay the rest of tonight? I just got back from Seattle."

"Oh no," she said, blocking the door. "You have a wife now. Or did that slip your mind?"

"I'm too tired to drive to Boise," he said. He pushed past her and into the house. When she had managed to lock the door and pursue him he had already begun hanging up his coat in the bedroom closet. All he wanted was sleep; he paid no attention to her as she stood clamoring at him. As soon as he had gotten his clothes off he threw himself into the bed and pulled the covers up over him.

"And where am I supposed to go?" Peg demanded, a little hysterically.

He shut his eyes and said nothing.

"I'll sleep in the other room," she said. She gathered up her clothes, and the bottles on the vanity table, and left the room. When she returned she said, "What's all that in your car? Did you pack up all your things and move out? I'm so curious." She hung around the bed, waiting for an answer. "If you're going to sleep here you better tell me. I think it's against the law or something, isn't it? Now that you're a married man. Is Susan going to come looking for you?"

"No," he said.

"Don't go to sleep," she said merrily. "I want to talk to you." She switched on the lamp by the bed. "You really are beat. You look as if you haven't shaved for a month. Have you been on one of those lost weekends?"

He said nothing. Finally Peg shut off the light and left the room.

"Good night," she said, from the hall. "I have to get up early and go to work tomorrow, so I probably won't see you. There's eggs and pork sausage in the refrigerator. Lock up the house when you leave. You are leaving, aren't you?" She hovered about once more. "Yes," he said.

Finally she shut the door, and he at last was able to go to sleep.

AT NOON THE NEXT DAY he got out of bed, bathed, shaved, dressed, ate breakfast in Peg's kitchen, and then drove back to Boise.

He found Susan down at her R & J Mimeographing Service office, sitting behind one of the desks with a great batch of papers before her. Seeing him she at once put down her cigarette and said in a low voice, "Hi."

"Hi," he said.

"I'm sorry we had a fight," she said. She sat with her chin in her hands, rubbing her forehead and staring down hollow-eyed. "Bruce," she said, "this is the end of this place. I just hope it isn't the end of us."

"I hope so, too," he said, going over and drawing up a chair so that he could sit beside her. He put his arms around her and kissed her; her mouth was dry and only barely responsive.

She said, "If you want to try to fool somebody else into buying those machines —" Her eyes filled with tears. "It's my fault. I'm responsible."

"Why?" he said.

Under her eyes dark heavy pouches had formed, and, he saw, her throat was wrinkled with despair. "After all," she said in a wavering voice, "I was your teacher. I helped form your morals."

At that he had to smile. "Is it such a moral lapse?" he said. "What do you do when somebody hands you a counterfeit bill? Don't you pass it on to the next fellow?"

She said, "No."

"Really?" It appeared to him that she was saying it only for the record. "Everybody passes them on," he said.

"Don't you see?" she said. "That's the difference between us. You think I'm kidding."

"I don't think you're kidding," he said. "But I think that in practice —" He changed what he had intended to say. "Theory is one thing," he said. "We have to get rid of them. Isn't that right? We can't absorb the loss. A big place, like C.B.B., could absorb the loss and never know it. They take a certain percentage of losses every year; they buy into bum deals and they expect to. They make thousands of deals a year and by the law of averages, some of them have to go wrong."

She nodded, following what he was telling her.

"But," he said, "with us it's different."

"Everybody in the business world feels like you," she said. "Don't they? It's just another world from me, Bruce. It has nothing to do with right or wrong; I just know I can't do something like that. We're stuck with them, or maybe somebody else can do something with them, but you have to tell them what they're getting. I meant what I said. If you drive down to Reno I'll phone him; I remember his name. Ed van Scharf or von Scharf." She showed him a notebook. On a page she had written the name down, and the phone number of the discount house.

"Can I stay at the house tonight?" he said presently.

"Of course you can," she said, caressing his arm and shoulder and staring at him with intensity, as if, he thought, she were searching for some sign. Something to tell her what to do. "You could have last night. You didn't have to leave. Where did you go?"

"I slept in the car," he said.

"You don't ever have to do that. I didn't go back to bed; I stayed up until morning, thinking. I shouldn't have upbraided you about your having worked for a discount house. But it is true, Bruce. Your training and outlook are different from mine. I called Fancourt and he's coming by after I close, around six. I want to tell him the situation. I know there's nothing he can do, but I want to make sure."

"It's a good idea," he said, although he saw no use in it.

"And then I'm giving up this place," she said. "It's taught me a lesson. Out of the three thousand we just owe one half. We can get enough out of this to pay the loan easily and have a good deal left over. It might even be that Zoe would want to buy it. I think I'll ask around five thousand for it. I just want to get it off my hands and get out of here. And then when that's done, we'll look around and see what we want to do." She smiled at him hopefully.

"You don't want to make one try to dump the machines?"

Hesitating, she said, "I — don't think we can."

"We can," he said.

"You don't know that, Bruce."

Getting to his feet he said, "I'll go up to the house and get the ten you took inside."

"And then what?"

"Even if you sell this place," he said, "we still have to do something with the machines."

"Are you going to drive down to Reno?"

"Yes," he said. "Unless something else comes up."

"When you get back, I hope to have sold this place." She said it in such a way that he believed her. She meant it. If she could, she undoubtedly would. But, he thought, it can't be done that quick. It would take some time. And some doing.

"Can I draw fifty bucks for expenses?" he asked her. He had used up all the money he had.

"I think so," she said. She looked into the register and then she gave him twenty-five dollars from her purse and two tens from the register and, to wind it up, a roll of nickels. "Almost fifty," she said.

"It's enough," he said. "I have my credit card to buy gas."

"Did you believe me when I said I'd call your old boss?"

"We'll see," he said. He did not believe that when it came down to it she would jeopardize the sale. They both understood the situation; they could not afford the pleasure of telling anyone about the keyboards. Like Baranowski, they would have to keep it quiet and hope it wouldn't be noticed. Possibly Baranowski hadn't discovered it himself until after he had bought up the four hundred machines . . .

All along the line, he thought. The machines passing from one hand to the next. From one city to the next. Up from Mexico to Seattle, through San Diego and Los Angeles, San Francisco and Portland, maybe even some of the smaller towns in-between.

And now we own a bunch of them.

Now it's up to us to make the wheels turn; to get rid of them, push the things into motion again.

In his mind he believed that she saw it like that, too. It was too serious. What other way was there?

Susan said, "You know, when you called me from up there, and told me about Milt — it worried me. That you could walk off and leave him. I guess you'll walk out of here sometime, like last night. When you calculate in your mind that it's unprofitable to stay with me. When you get to the point that you can't see a living to be made out of this place, or out of being married to me. Maybe I can talk to you in your own terms. I think there is a living to be made out of me. I can probably make a living on my own; I always have. At least, since I was — I started to say, Since I was your age. But actually it was since I was nineteen. Isn't that something for you to consider? A wife who can support herself, and possibly support you as well?"

He said, "You know I've never thought about anything like that."

"Maybe not consciously," she said.

"That damn talk," he said, with loathing.

"Haven't you subconsciously wanted to lean on me? The situation cries out for it. An older woman that you recognize as a figure you used to look up to and depend on for guidance."

"I never depended on you," he said, at the doorway of the office. "I was afraid of you. I lived for the day I could get out of your class."

"You liar," she said. "You needed somebody to guide you. You had to be led around."

"Don't be vindictive," he said, hardly able to stand hearing her tell him such things. Such obviously made-up things for no other purpose than to injure him. She was saying whatever she could think of.

"You were a weak child," she said, her face white but composed. "A dependent child that followed the lead of the other children."

"Not true," he said, having difficulty speaking.

"That's right," she said. "You had an older brother. He's doing medical research, isn't he? He won a lot of scholarships. I remember seeing his school records. He was brilliant; I remember that."

"Having fun?" he said. "Have fun. Have a lot of fun."

"I can understand your wanting to demonstrate to me that you're an adult and capable of taking your place as an equal," she said, with the perverse acuteness that had always shown up in her when she was terribly angry, determined to get back at any cost. "If only you had been able to pull off this deal of yours. For your own sake, as well of course as for ours, I wish you had actually been able to do what you maintained you had the experience to do. I guess I shouldn't be saying things like this to you, should I? You're not psychologically strong enough to hear them. I'm sorry." But even as she apologized her eyes shone with cruelty; she was still searching for something more to say. "Sooner or later you have to learn about yourself," she told him, her voice rising to that sharp, carrying, speech-like tone that had entered into his bones years ago and stuck with him. He winced at the sound. It made him cringe and feel guilt and fright, and the remembered hopeless dislike toward her. Suddenly, with triumph, she waved her finger at him and said, "I think I have your motivations worked out; you deliberately managed to buy these machines, knowing subconsciously that they were defective, to pay me back for the hostility you felt toward me when you were eleven years old. You're still eleven. Emotionally, you're living out the life of a grammar school child." Panting, she stared at him, waiting to hear what he had to say.

There was nothing to say. He left the office without answering. For a time he did not know or care where he went; he wandered around downtown Boise, in a blank.

What meanness, he thought. Anything to score a hit.

Maybe it was true. Maybe — subconsciously — he had noticed that the keyboard was not right. After all, he had had plenty of opportunity to study it. In the same manner that Milt Lumky had arranged to become ill at the proper moment, to pay him and Susan back.

How can anybody ever know? he asked himself.

Maybe it doesn't matter, he thought. Maybe it has no meaning, one way or another. I did buy the machines; Milt did get sick. Motives or secret reasons have no significance in this. I still have to get rid of the sixty Mithrias portable electric typewriters.

And I'll be god damned if I'm going to say anything to anybody about the keyboards. Let them find out for themselves.

* * * * *

HE WAITED UNTIL SUNSET and then he started out on the highway.

I had better cook up a darn good story, he said to himself. Because the first thing he'll want to know is why I'm trying to unload them. The sale will be made or lost there.

As he drove he meditated.

Nothing entered his mind for several hours. And then, out of nowhere, he thought up one of the most sensational lies that he had ever heard of. An absolutely perfect explanation for his purposes.

He had to dump the Mithrias machines because a representative of some major U.S. typewriter — Royal or Underwood or Remington — had gotten wind that he had them and was about to peddle them. The factory representative had shown up and told him that if he sold them over the counter he would never get a U.S. typewriter franchise as long as he lived. And that furthermore he would not even get parts or supplies; they would strangle him on the vine.

On the other hand, if he dumped the Mithrias machines outside of the area, they would see that he got a decent franchise arrangement.

It was the superiority of the Mithrias that had frightened the U.S. typewriter people.

A discount house like C.B.B. would jump at a chance to get the machines, once they had been fed such a story. Assuming they believed it.

As he drove he thought, If they believe it, then I have a sale. If they don't, then I don't. And, he thought, if they buy, they'll buy at a good price. I can probably sell it to them at a good profit. Not for fifty bucks a machine but more like seventy-five. That would mean a clear net profit of fifteen hundred dollars. Fifty percent mark-up, which is good enough for anybody.

Of course, he realized, I'll never be able to set foot in Nevada again.

I wonder if I can pull it off, he asked himself. The idea of it intrigued and excited him. Not merely dumping the machines, but making a good profit. And selling them not just to anybody but to a discount house. One that he had learned the business from.

And to his own former employers . . . it was a challenge.

15

IN THE UPSTAIRS OFFICE overlooking the main floor of the Consumers' Buying Bureau building, Ed von Scharf met him and sat down with him.

"Let's have a look at them," von Scharf said briskly.

Bruce said, "You sound as if you had been expecting me."

"Your wife called," von Scharf said. "She told us the situation. How much did you pay for them?"

Chagrined, he murmured, "Fifty bucks apiece."

"I want to get somebody from the typewriter department in here." Von Scharf excused himself. When he returned he had with him the buyer from the typewriter department and Vince Pareti, one of the Pareti brothers. The three of them huddled together over the Mithrias that Bruce had brought into the building with him.

"We can get a standard keyboard out of it," the typewriter buyer said finally. "With a couple of minor differences. Not enough to matter. All the letters and numbers will be right. That's what does it." He nodded to Pareti and von Scharf and started out.

"How much?" Pareti asked him. "Figure the labor."

"At our cost," the expert said, computing. "Say, at the most five bucks a machine."

After he had left, von Scharf retired to the rear of the office while Pareti conducted the negotiations. "We'll take them off your hands," Pareti said to Bruce. "We'll pay you forty-five dollars apiece, and we want all sixty plus the name of your supplier. How many more does he have, according to your knowledge?"

"About three hundred and forty more," Bruce said.

"And how much would he want?"

"I don't know," he said, feeling the futility of the thing fall onto him. "You can probably haggle him down below fifty bucks apiece. Which is what I paid."

"Yes," Pareti said. "That's what your wife told us. We just wanted to be sure. We don't want you to take a loss, but you can see that it's going to cost us to get them into shape where we can sell them. What do you say to forty-five apiece? That means you take a loss of only three hundred bucks; that's chicken feed."

"To you, maybe," Bruce said.

"I'd just as soon give him the full fifty he paid," von Scharf said.

"Oh no," Pareti answered, with finality.

"He got them down here for us. And he scouted them up in the first place; that ought to be worth something. His wife says he was on the road a week. We're going to be listing them for almost two hundred."

"I'm against it," Pareti said, "but if you want, go ahead and make out a check for three thousand." To Bruce he said, "How does that make you feel? You're out from under them and you didn't lose a nickel."

Feebly, Bruce said, "I think they're worth more than fifty bucks." The two men grinned.

"Flip a coin," von Scharf said. He dug out a fifty-cent piece and spun it up into the air. "Heads you sell, tails you don't." The coin missed his hand and fell to the floor. "Tails," he said. "You don't sell." He picked up the coin and put it back in his pocket.

Bruce said, "Give me an hour or so to decide. Okay?"

They both nodded.

As he left the office, von Scharf clapped him on the back and then walked along with him, to the exit door. "You know," he said, "I'm a little surprised at you. You didn't accept them sight unseen, did you?"

"No," Bruce said. "I looked at them."

"If you'd been working for us, you wouldn't be now."

"I'll see you in an hour," Bruce said. Turning his back he walked outside to the parking lot and his car.

For an hour he drove around and then he stopped at a drive-in ice cream stand and bought a pineapple malt. On long dry trips he found that a pineapple malt tasted least like the countryside; it made him think of girls and beaches and blue water, portable radios and dances, the happiness of his high school days. What there had been of it.

In most of the cars near his he saw teen-agers. Kids with their girls, parked in Mercury coupes, listening to their car radios, eating hamburgers and sipping malts.

I wonder if I ought to sell them the machines, he asked himself. If they can put them in shape for five bucks apiece, so could I. No, he realized. That's their price; they have benches in the back and mechanically-inclined flunkies to do the job.

Yet it occurred to him, as a sort of last-resort possibility, that he might make an attempt to have the work done himself. It would cost at least three hundred dollars. Probably more. But he wouldn't need all sixty machines altered at once; he could start with a few, sell them, and with the money get more changed, and so forth.

Finishing his malt he drove until he saw a typewriter repair shop. He parked and got out and carried a Mithrias inside. Showing it to the repairman he asked him what it would cost to have the keyboard changed.

The man, a short little solemn fellow, neatly-dressed in a white shirt, tie, and pressed sharkskin trousers, poked around inside the machine and then quoted a figure of twenty to twenty-five dollars.

"That much?" Bruce said, with a sinking heart.

The man explained that for some of the changes the type slugs would be unsoldered. Or the typebars could be cut, exchanged, and rewelded in a different sequence. But some of the keys would have to be split, and that was tricky work.

"Is there any chance," Bruce said, "that I could do the work myself?"

The man said, "Depends on how good you are."

"What about tools?"

"Yes, you'd need tools. But for one machine."

"I have sixty of them," he said.

"The man said, "What you ought to do is make an arrangement with some fellow who's in the business. Who has a shop, tools, and knows how to do it. If you try on your own you'll damage a couple of letters, and that'll finish the machine. Because I'll bet you can't get parts for these."

Thanking the man he left the shop.

That was that. Unless, of course, he could make a deal with some repairman. Maybe cut him in.

And who did he know? Nobody. At least, nobody qualified.

They've got me, he told himself. They'll buy the machines from me, make the changes, and roll up a hell of a big profit. All my work and all my driving and planning and farting around . . . and, he thought, the R & J Mimeographing Service or whatever we'd be eventually calling it. We'd have our money back — most of it — but I doubt very much if we'd go on from there. In fact, I know we wouldn't go on from there. How could we? Where would we go?

Here I have the machines, he thought, and I can't do anything with them. I can't fix them and I can't sell them. *All I need is money*. Money. A few hundred dollars. A thousand. Better yet, two thousand. But anyhow something. And where can I get it? We owe the bank fifteen hundred plus interest; I've hit my family, and Milt Lumky, and that does it. Nothing to sell, rent, exchange, put up for security.

What about my car?

His equity wasn't large enough. That was out.

Maybe Susan's house. Borrow against it. Long enough to get these goddamn machines in shape to peddle.

And then he thought, She did phone. She did call them and tell them about the keyboard. So perhaps, he thought, I don't want to go on with it any further. Maybe this is a good place to stop.

What an immoral thing to do, he said to himself. Although of course it wouldn't seem like that to her. In fact, to her it was virtuous.

That was the worst part. She had done it out of moral duty.

But to him it was lousy; it had put him in a terrible spot. *Your wife called us*, Ed von Scharf had said. Your wife told us. She tripped you up, you ridiculous bugger. You clown. In the name of what? To help the C.B.B discount house, which she has never seen and clearly doesn't like?

I will never know, he thought. I don't understand her. So the heck with it.

At a payphone in a drugstore he called her. "They'll take them off our hands," he said.

"Oh thank god," Susan said fervently. "At how much?"

"Forty-five apiece," he said.

"Oh what a relief." She sighed. "Bruce, that's wonderful. That means we get almost all our money back. How much do we lose? Three hundred dollars? I'm too excited to figure it. We could call that Milt's money; part of the five hundred he gave us as a wedding present. I called him, incidently. I got hold of him at Pocatello, at a friend's place. You met her — Cathy Hermes."

"How is he?" he said.

"Much better. He's back on the road again. He asked me if we got the typewriters and I told him —" She hesitated. "I told him we decided not to."

"Why?" he said.

"Because — well, I thought perhaps it would worry him."

"Why should it worry him?"

"I got to thinking about it and I decided that maybe you're right. He might have known subconsciously. And then if he knew we'd gone ahead and bought them he'd have guilt to wrestle with. I think that's why he gave us the five hundred dollars; to appease his conscience. I was wondering about that . . . it's an awful lot of money."

"I just assumed it was for old times' sake," he said. "Because you and he used to be such friends."

"No," she said. "What gave you that idea? I probably don't know him any better then you do."

He said, "Shall I sell the machines to them, then?"

"Yes, yes," she said. "By all means. Before they change their minds."

"They won't change their minds," he said. "They're going to make something like nine thousand dollars out of this, give or take a few man-hours of repairwork."

Susan said, "Did Mr. von Scharf say anything to you about your job?"

"Why?" he said, chilled.

"I wondered if he had. If we're going to close up the office you'll have to give some thought to that. I mean to close it, Bruce. I talked to Fancourt after you left and he said he thought it would be a good idea. Then I can be home with Taffy."

He said, "Did you say anything to von Scharf about it?"

"I — told him that I thought we might be moving down to Reno."

"What did he say?"

"He said your job is open."

"Okay," he said. "I'll see you." He started to hang up.

"You'll be home tomorrow?" she said.

"Yes," he said. He hung up.

By god, he thought, she did talk to them about my job. They probably arranged it among them. Time, salary, duties.

He returned to his car. For a few minutes he sat, and then he started the motor and drove back to the typewriter repair shop where the short little neatly-dressed man had given him the estimate.

"I see you're back," the man said in his severe, quiet manner, as he entered with the Mithrias.

Bruce said, "I want you to go ahead and do the work. Can you do it right now?"

"I suppose I can," the man said. "Set it down here." He took the machine and placed it on his work table. "It's certainly not very heavy," he said.

"I'd like to watch," Bruce said. "It won't make you nervous, will it?" He got out a ball point pen and paper and placed himself nearby.

The man said, "You're going to see how it's done, right?"

"Yes," he said.

"Let's be honest about this. If this is going to help you any, you're going to have to know more about it than you'll get by watching me work." The man considered. "Are you in a hurry? For instance, can you manage to hold your water until tonight?"

"I guess so," he said.

The man said, "Come by here after dinner. Around seven o'clock. I'll go over it step by step for you, show you what tools you'll need. And you can do it here on my bench until I'm satisfied you know what you're doing. Otherwise you'll wreck your sixty typewriters."

"Can I learn, do you think?" he asked.

"Undoubtedly. It'll cost you about thirty bucks for my labor. I'll let you do as much of it as possible. I'll break about even." The man put the Mithrias off to one side. "See you at seven, then."

Feeling a little better, Bruce left the shop. Behind him, at the bench, the unemotional, ordinary-looking man, his necktie dangling out and in his way, resumed his work on an old IBM electric.

A person I never saw before, he thought to himself.

That evening he returned to the shop. The man let him in and then began work on the typewriter. It did not look hard. When he had finished he supervised while Bruce tackled a second machine. By ten o'clock he had learned the soldering part, the cutting and rewelding part, and was on the business of splitting a key in half. After that the man showed him how to align the keys, using special tools that pinched and bent the typebars.

"You'll have to buy the tools," the man said. He methodically wrote out the trade names and sizes for him in an old-fashioned formal hand. "Here's the names of a couple of places you might try; if they don't have them then you can send out to the Coast or back East. You can use them later on for certain other kinds of service. You know, if you're going to be selling typewriters you ought to work out your own service. Get a man, set up a bench. Otherwise it'll cost you too much."

He paid the man, thanked him, and left.

I know I can make the changes myself, he said to himself as he got back into his car. All I need is the tools. He had written everything down, step by step, and then gone over it from the written instructions. A week or a month from now he could pick it up again. According to the man the tools wouldn't set him back more than fifteen dollars, if he could get a good buy on the alcohol torch. And he knew where he could get that: in the hardware department at C.B.B.

That night, with the sixty typewriters still in the car, he started the drive back to Boise.

WHEN SUSAN SAW the cartons still piled up in the car she said, "Why didn't you sell them? Did they renege?"

"No," he said. "I did."

"Why?"

He said, "I'm going to fix them. A fellow down in Reno showed me how."

"But you aren't a typewriter repairman!"

"I'm only doing this one job." He had already picked up the tools he needed, back in Reno. "It won't cost us anything. Unless you want to write the labor down as cost." Getting the hand-truck he began to load it with the cartons.

"It's not up to you to decide," she said.

"I already decided," he said.

"When I talked to them on the phone," she said, "I told them you were bringing the machines in to sell to them."

"We couldn't agree," he said.

"There was nothing to agree to. We made all the arrangements on the phone. Did you try to talk them up to paying more, is that it? Did you try to get a better price, and they wouldn't pay it, so you stormed out of there?" She seemed more bewildered than angry; she did not understand why he had come back with the machines and she knew that there had to be a reason. He had done it deliberately; she seemed to grasp that. Watching him carrying the machines, she could not decide between curiosity and outrage. Meanwhile, she kept on with her harangue. He paid no attention to her.

"I'll do the work down here at the office," he said when she paused. "If I can clear a desk. We don't need them all done at once, just enough to get a few on sale." In the office window he set down the two that had been worked on. "There's two already."

She bent over them, wondering what had been done. So he stopped the unloading and showed her.

"You'll ruin them," she said.

"No," he said.

Now she had gotten better control of herself. Folding her arms she took a deep breath and said in a low, strained voice, "Well, I hired you to make buying decisions."

That could have meant anything, he realized. "That's right," he said. "And when you hire somebody to do something, the most practical business procedure is to leave them alone and let them do their work. Any big business organization will tell you that."

She gazed at him with an expression that he could make nothing of.

"That's how President Eisenhower operated in Europe," he said.

After a time, Susan said, "Maybe you should keep one of these to use as a model."

"It's all written down," he said. He spread out his notes. "See?"

Susan said, "Keep one as a model anyhow."

"We're going to have to figure out some kind of time-payment contract," he said.

"Is that right," she murmured, in a way that might have been sarcastic. But he could not hear her well enough to tell.

While she stood watching him, her arms folded, he finished up the unloading. Neither of them said anything. But as he worked he thought to himself, She has to recognize that this is what she hired me for. This is my job. I'm the one who decides.

THAT EVENING he worked late, by himself, down at the office, altering machines. He finished a couple and then, tired, he shut off the lights and drove across town to the house. Susan of course had already gone to bed. How nice to be back, he thought to himself as he took a shower in the familiar bathroom. He put on a pair of fresh pajamas and got into bed beside her.

The following morning he slept late. When he woke up he found that she had already gotten out of bed, dressed and eaten and gone. For a while he lay in the bed, on his back, enjoying the peace. Then he, too, got up. He ate a leisurely breakfast, shaved, put on a clean striped cotton shirt, tie, slacks, and then, savoring his possession of the house, wandered about into the different rooms.

From the living room window he could see the yard. The grass and rose bushes. The coiled-up garden hose.

Fine sight, he thought. Up high off the street. A milk truck came noisily along; he watched it stop, the driver hop out. The sight of the milkman hurrying up a long flight of cement steps across the street satisfied something in him. Nice to watch somebody else hustle, he decided. The world's work. Every man has his niche, and I must say I'm not too dissatisfied with mine.

End of a long journey, he thought. Hell of a lot of hard driving.

Putting on his coat he left the house, walked down to his car, got in and started up the motor.

Presently he was driving along the street, toward the office.

At the curb, in front of the R & J Mimeographing Service office, a yellow pick-up truck was parked with its tailgate down. As he approached it he thought to himself, That truck's familiar. He entered a parking slot, stopped his car, and shut off the motor. Sitting there, he watched the pick-up truck.

The front door of the office was open, propped back with a brick. After a moment a boy wearing a brown khaki shirt and trousers appeared, tugging a hand-truck. On the hand-truck were cartons. The boy wheeled the hand-truck expertly around, worked it up onto the tailgate of the pick-up, and then slid the cartons up into the bed. Cheerfully hopping down he started back into the office with the empty hand-truck and disappeared.

I know him, Bruce thought.

The son of a bitch, he thought, is from Consumers' Buying Bureau, and that truck belongs to them. He's picking up the typewriters. He's loading them onto the truck while I'm home sleeping.

Throwing open the car door he jumped out and ran down the sidewalk to the pick-up truck. "Hey," he said breathlessly. "What the hell are you doing?"

The boy, once more appearing from the office with his load of cartons, glanced at him and recognized him. "Hi," he said, with some confusion. "Let me see — you used to work down at C.B.B. Wait a minute and I'll think of your name." Tilting the hand-truck back, he pondered, tapping his forehead. He was about seventeen, with short-cropped hair, heavy cheeks and large, muscular arms.

Bruce said, "Is she inside?"

"Mrs. Stevens, you mean?" the boy said. Then he waved his hand and said, "That's who you are. Bruce Stevens."

Bruce went into the office. In the back, Susan sat on the edge of one of the desks, smoking a cigarette. She had on a formal dark-green suit; her hair was made up and she looked somber and controlled. As he entered, she glanced up at him. But she said nothing.

Making his voice sound as natural as possible, he said, "What's all this about?"

Susan said, "I've decided to let you go."

Oh god, he thought.

"What you said was true," she said. "That I hired you to make buying decisions."

"I'll be god damned," he said, and this time his voice shook and was weak. He had to stick his hands in his pockets to keep them from trembling. Meanwhile, behind them, the boy resumed his loading of the cartons; he discreetly wheeled the hand-truck back and forth, saying nothing and being as quiet as possible.

Facing Susan, Bruce said, "Are we still married?"

"Oh yes," she said emphatically, blinking a little as if taken by surprise.

So she had fired him. He no longer had a job; during the night or the early morning she had thought things over and made up her mind. And she had phoned C.B.B. and now the truck was up getting the typewriters. How had it made the trip so fast? Maybe she had called last night, while he was working on the machines. She had already decided before he even got home and into bed. Made the arrangement with them as soon as possible; gone out of the office and directly to a phone. Possibly she had decided as soon as she saw the machines. But she hadn't said a word.

"What's the idea of not telling me?" he said. Bits of his voice returned.

"I was tired of arguing."

To that, he could think of nothing to say.

"It seemed to me," she said, "that it was a waste of time to talk about it any more. I knew that you had your mind made up and there was no way to reason with you."

He said, "I think this is a hell of a thing."

"It's my store," Susan said. "We both have to accept the fact that I'm the owner." Looking up at him steadily, she said, "The machines belong to me. Isn't that right? I hate to be hard about this, but they are mine. They were bought with my money."

"Not all of the money was yours," he said. "What about the money my folks gave us?"

"Half of that is mine," Susan said. "That leaves only five hundred dollars."

"And the money Milt gave us."

"Half of that legally belongs to me."

He said, "Some of the machines are mine."

To that, she nodded. But it did not seem as if that was very important to her.

"I'm going to take mine," he said.

"Suit yourself," she said. She smoked her cigarette rapidly.

He walked outside, to the pick-up truck. There, the boy was putting the tailgate back up. He had tied the cartons down, so that they would not shift around during the trip back down to Reno. "Damn you," Bruce said. "Some of those belong to me."

At the office door, Susan appeared. "That's right," she said to the boy. "Some belong to him." With a pad and pencil she made computations.

"The hell with it," Bruce said. He turned and walked off, away from the pick-up truck and the two of them, back to his parked Merc. Getting inside he slammed the door, started the motor, and at once backed away from the curb and out into traffic. He drove by the pick-up truck and a moment later he had left it behind, still at the curb with its load of cartons, Susan and the boy standing beside it on the sidewalk, deep in discussion.

They can have them, he thought. They can stuff them up their asses.

Shaking, he slowed down, pulled over to the right and turned the corner. On a quiet side street he coasted to a stop. Traffic noises had fallen away behind him. Peacefulness. He shut off the engine. The car rolled a trifle. He put on the hand-brake.

Should I go by the house? he asked himself. And pick up my stuff? No, he thought. I probably will never go back there again. I don't see any reason for it. Too bad, he thought. After all my work. What a thing to have happen. How could she have done that kind of thinking, figuring out exactly what part of the machines belonged to her, and the reasons why. Maybe she called her attorney.

Now, he thought, I might as well get back on the road again. But he did not feel like it. Starting up the engine, he drove along, past the houses. Residential section, he thought. Lawns and driveways. For a time he drove at random.

I never thought it would work out like that, he thought. You never can tell. All those years of knowing her. Back to grammar school. When I knew her in high school and delivered her newspaper to her. That should have tipped me off, that business where I wasn't invited into the house. It's the same thing all over again. I should have been warned.

Maybe the best thing to do, he decided, is to rent a room. I'll rent one here in town somewhere and stay in it for a while until I can get rested up. Then I can think better and know what to do.

Right now he did not feel able to think it out.

Later on I can plan, he decided.

Accordingly, he turned the car in the direction of the rooming house section of town. He came at last to a large white board building with several doorbells and mailboxes. In one of the front windows hung a sign reading: ROOM FOR RENT. So he parked and got out.

Not a bad neighborhood, he thought as he walked up the steps to the porch. On the porch was a carton of empty Coca-Cola bottles. He rang the top bell. Presently the door opened and there stood a fat middle-aged man in trousers and underwear, his huge stomach hanging out over his belt.

"What is it?" the man said, putting his finger into his eye to rub at it.

He explained to the man that he was interested in the room. The man said that he was not the manager, only one of the tenants, a fireman who slept during the day. But he led Bruce up a flight of carpeted stairs, past a potted rubber plant, and showed him the vacant room. It was recently painted and it smelled clean. In one corner was a sofa; in the other a gas circulating heater. The windows had both shades and curtains. The fireman stood in the entrance, still rubbing at his eye.

"This is fine," Bruce said.

"You can move right in," the fireman said, turning his back and starting downstairs again. "The building manager'll be around some-time this evening and you can pay him the rent then. It's twenty bucks as I recall, but you better settle that with him."

In the car Bruce still had enough of his things; he had his clothes, and that was what counted. And he had his toilet articles, his hair brush and aftershave and cuff links and shoes. He carried the suitcase upstairs to the room and put the articles away in the dresser drawers and the cardboard wardrobe closet. Then he shut the door, took off his coat, and lay down on the single bed. It had sheets and blankets on it, and even a pillow. All I need, he thought, lying on his back with his arms at his sides. I'll have to eat out, but I'm used to that.

I'll stay here a few days, he thought. Until I make up my mind.

In his wallet he had twenty or thirty dollars, possibly more. He considered getting up to look into his wallet, but after debating it for a time he decided not to go to the trouble. There's enough there, he decided. I'll make out okay.

The room seemed to him comfortable and quiet. Downstairs, along the street, a car or two passed. He listened to their motor noises. This could be a lot worse, he said to himself. I don't really have it so bad. Hell, he thought. I've got my health and my youth; they say if you have that you've got nothing to worry about. And I learned something. You always profit by experience. And if I want to I can go back and claim the machines that belong to me. But why go to the trouble? Let her have them. If it's so important to her. Make a buck, if she wants to.

He lay there, thinking about that.

16

LYING ON THE BED, he thought back to the first day they had seen her, the young new woman teacher standing at the board. Alone in the rented room he recalled that important day, years ago, when he had come into the classroom and seen the new teacher writing in large clear letters:

MISS REUBEN

Miss Reuben wore a blue suit, not a regular dress. It seemed to all of them as if she were dressed up for some occasion, for church or visiting. The color of her hair amazed them, and there was some whispering about that. It was yellow, not dark gray as was Mrs. Jaffey's. None of them had ever seen a teacher with yellow hair; it was like the hair of one of the girls, not a teacher's hair at all.

When she turned from the board they saw she was smiling at them, at the whole roomful of them, not to any one of them in particular. Some of them were frightened by that and took seats in the far back of the room. Her face had a freckled, reddish roundness, smooth and peculiarly active. Her eyes, too, struck them as alarming; she seemed to be watching everything in the room. She did not focus on anything. Some of the children noticed that she had a cluster of white flowers fastened to her suit, where her coat came together and buttoned. The buttons of her blue suit were white, too; they noticed that.

The final bell rang.

Seating herself at Mrs. Jaffey's desk, Miss Reuben said. "All right, children." The few of them that had been talking now ceased. "I'm going to be your teacher until the end of the semester," Miss Reuben said. "Mrs. Jaffey won't be coming back. She's very ill. Now, I want to take the roll." On the desk was Mrs. Jaffey's attendance book. "I know you're supposed to be seated alphabetically," Miss Reuben said, "but I can see you're not. There's not one of you in your regular seat."

All the boys had gone over to one side, leaving the girls in a group by themselves. And no one was in the front row. So that was how Miss Reuben had known. But they all felt uneasy. How clever she was. Mrs. Jaffey would never have noticed, and yet Miss Reuben had seen that at first glance.

A girl stood up and said, "I'm Mrs. Jaffey's proctor. I always call the roll for her."

This was true. But the new teacher Miss Reuben said, "Thank you, but today I'll take the roll myself. Here's what I want you to do." Again she smiled at all of them together. "When I read a student's name I don't want him or her to answer. Do you understand that?"

Taken aback, they remained silent. They had planned to answer "president," as they had done with the temporary teacher during the last day and a half.

"What I want you to do," Miss Reuben said, sitting with her hands folded in the center of the desk, "is this. When I call a student's name I want all the other children — together! — to point to him or her. And I don't want him to speak a word. Do you all understand that?"

Miss Reuben called a name, then. A few pupils pointed to that boy. Miss Reuben scrutinized the boy and made an entry in the attendance book. Again she called a name. This time more pupils pointed. By the time she had finished calling the roll, the students were enthusiastically pointing one another out to her.

"Good," she said. "Now I think I have you all firmly in mind. I'm going to have you sit alphabetically, the way Mrs. Jaffey did. And if I call on you and I get your name wrong, I want everybody else to tell me right away." She smiled. "So please get to your feet and without any noise seat yourselves in your usual seats."

As they did so she stared intently at them, as if she were watching for something in particular. None of them knew what it was, and even the independent boys from the back of the room had nothing to say as they took their usual seats. "Fine," Miss Reuben said, when it had been done.

All was still. They sat waiting, fearfully.

"You children have had quite a good time the last couple of weeks," Miss Reuben said. "You've had your summer vacation in advance. You've done exactly as you please. I hope you enjoyed it, because in the next month you're going to be looking back to it and thinking to yourselves how lucky you were.

"Do you care to know what the result of your behavior was? You drove an old lady out of this school. An old lady who was one of the original teachers here at Garret A. Hobart Grammar School. Before your parents were born.

"And in another month she was going to retire. You made her last month here impossible. You made it impossible for her to have her last month, which she deserved.

"You made her ill.

"Of course, I know not all of you were equally responsible. I had a long talk with Mrs. Jaffey.

"I asked her who was responsible. Which of you.

"Do you know what she said?

"Mrs. Jaffey wouldn't tell me which of you. 'They're all fine children,' she said. What do you think of that? You hounded her out of this school where she taught forty-one years and you made her ill, and do you think she'd tell on you? No, not a word."

Even the larger, tougher boys had slunk down in their seats. Shame and unhappiness touched them all.

"Do you know what you're going to do?" Miss Reuben said, in a voice that grew gradually louder. "You're going to write to Mrs. Jaffey and tell her how sorry you are.

"I'm going to find out which of you are the smart-alecks. I'll find out. I can tell.

"I've taught children a lot older than you. Back in the East where I come from I taught a high school class.

"Some of you are going to bide your time and then you're going to test me. All right. We'll see. I'm waiting."

From the rear of the room a rude noise sounded.

Miss Reuben arose from her chair. "All right," she said. She walked slowly down the aisle toward the back of the room. Her face was red and her forehead and lips were swollen. As she passed the children they saw that her eyes were bright and sharp and shining, like a bird's eyes.

No one said anything. They cowered.

At the back of the room Miss Reuben stopped by a boy's desk. That boy had not made the noise. Miss Reuben gazed down at him until he slouched with apprehension. They all saw him trembling, and some of them sniggered. At once Miss Reuben spun around and said,

"Be still!"

They were instantly still.

"Stand up," Miss Reuben said to the boy.

The boy got to his feet, shoving his chair back clumsily.

"What's his name?" Miss Reuben asked the class.

Together, they all said, "Skip Stevens, Miss Reuben."

Swallowing with nervousness, Skip Stevens said, "I didn't do it."

"Do what?" Miss Reuben said. "I didn't accuse you of doing anything." She said it in such a manner that all the rest of them knew it was a joke, and they screamed with laughter.

As soon as they were finished, Skip Stevens gathered himself together and said as steadily and clearly as possible, "He did it." He pointed to Joe St. James, who had done it.

Miss Reuben said to him, "Come up front, Skip. You're going to sit in front of the desk." Without glancing back, she started off up the aisle to her desk. Skip Stevens knew that he had to follow. He had done nothing, but he had to go along with her. His head down, conscious of his mortification, he shuffled along after her.

"Get a chair," Miss Reuben ordered him.

He went to find an empty desk-chair from the back. But Miss Reuben said,

"Over here. Right beside me. Where I can watch you."

So he had to drag a chair up and sit directly beside her. He tried to keep his eyes fixed on the floor; he tried to pretend that she was not there, close to him.

Time passed. The class was silent, afraid she would notice them and ask them something or make them do something.

What have I done wrong? he asked himself, his head down, eyes fixed on the floor. Why am I here? How did this ever come about?

There's no reason for her to do something like that, he thought to himself. It's unfair. Hatred of her grew in him, but, far more than that, the sense of guilt, of having made a mistake, maintained itself. The hatred passed away, but the feeling that he had been unable to do the right thing remained. It's my own fault, he thought to himself. I made a mistake and I'm paying for it. She's right. I hate her, he thought, but she's right. Goddamn her.

He put his hands up over his face, covering his eyes.

"Have any of you ever been to New York?" Miss Reuben said presently, again smiling at them in her stern, efficient, impersonal way.

Finally, when no one said anything or dared to stir, a girl raised her hand.

"When was it?" Miss Reuben said.

The girl said, "Three years ago, Miss Reuben."

To Skip Stevens, Miss Reuben said, "Go to the supply closet and get out the ruled paper and pass it around to each pupil." She showed him the size sheet she had in mind. "For the first thing this morning," she said, arising and going to the board, "I want you to write a composition." On the board in huge printed letters she wrote:

MY IDEA OF NEW YORK CITY

"I want you to imagine you're on a trip East, to New York," she said. "I want you to tell me all the things you suppose you'd see there. Write about the subway, if you want. Or Coney Island. Or the stock market. Or the Yankees. How you think a ballgame would be to watch. Or the museums. Whatever you'd like."

Without resistance, each student accepted the piece of paper that was handed out. The students began at once to scratch away. He returned to his seat, directly by Miss Reuben's desk, and picked up his own pencil to write his name at the right-hand top of the paper. The only noise in the room was the handling of the paper, the breathing of the students, the pencils and erasers.

His seat was so close to Miss Reuben that he could smell the flowers that she wore. In the stuffy, closed-up room the smell reminded him of blackberries. Of lying in the garden, in the late afternoons at the end of summer, among the sweet, warm blackberries under the vines.

What the hell do I know about New York, he thought to himself. I've never been there. I've driven all around, but I've never driven that far East. It's just something more to make us suffer. Something to make me feel more shame.

I can't do it, he decided.

Presently Miss Reuben said, "Skip Stevens." Her eyes were fixed on him, directly at him across the desk. "Why aren't you writing?"

He had pushed away his paper and put down his pencil. On the paper was nothing but his name and the title of the composition.

"I can't do it," he told her. He sank down in his seat and avoided looking at her; his voice faded off into a mumble so that he could hardly make it sound. "Is it okay if I don't write it?" he asked.

Miss Reuben said, "Everyone else continue writing." Bringing her chair around she leaned toward him and over him, saying, "Why can't you write about New York?"

"I never have been there," he said. The smell of blackberries became so strong that he held his breath. He did not dare breathe; he felt hot all over, and his skin itched. He thought he might sneeze.

"Couldn't you pretend?" she said in his ear, softly, bending down so that she was speaking only to him, in a whisper that none of the other students were intended to hear. Her voice lost its harshness. His head down, he shut his eyes. Above him, close to him, her voice murmured and rustled. "Just think what it would be like," she said, her lips almost at his ear. "Wouldn't it be very nice?"

"I guess so," he answered, not daring to raise his head or open his eyes. Yes, he thought, it would be nice. But it's too far. Too unreal. There's no point in concerning myself about something that remote. "I'd like to go to New York," he said to her. "I'd like to do a lot of things. But hell — I know my own limitations. I'll never get there. Let's try to be realistic."

She said, "Then what would you like to do your composition on?"

I have no desire to do it on anything, he thought as he lay on his back, his hands over his face. Why should I? Where will it get me? Can't I find anything pleasant? Imagine this or that; an imaginary journey to a peaceful, comfortable land. He picked up the pencil and considered. Anything? he wondered. On any topic at all? Am I free to do that? Pretend anything I wish?

"I think I'll write about what's going to happen," he said. I'll imagine ahead into the future a few months. Even more: several years. How it would have worked out between us. If everything had gone okay. If I could have brought the goddamn typewriters back and go to working on them down at the office, in the evenings, until for almost no money I had transformed them so that they could be sold at a really good price. If she hadn't gone behind my back and dumped them, and then, when I found out — as I was inevitably going to find out — she dumped me, too. And put an end to everything. So all I can do is lie here and put together an imaginary composition.

The title, he said to himself, is:

HOW WE MADE A KILLING WITH THE JAP TYPEWRITERS.

AND WHAT BECAME OF US BECAUSE OF THAT.

When the Mithrias typewriters get sold, he decided, we'll have enough money to interest some major American typewriter company. We can really represent them, once we get the franchise. Maybe they won't want to dole out any more franchises in Boise. But that won't bother us. We can open up a place somewhere else with all the money we've made. We can operate anywhere we want.

He thought, For instance, we could open a store in Montario. I know the town so darn well we'd really have an edge. I'll have to drop down there, some Sunday, by myself. And see what the situation is.

THE LUXOR MOVIE THEATER was open, since it was Sunday, and a few boys in jeans and girls in skirts and blouses had collected around the box office.

At each end of town the drugstores were open and doing business, but except for them and the cafes and the movie theater everything was shut up tight. Most of the parking slots were empty. Dust and a litter of paper lay spread out over the pavement and street. Beyond the railroad tracks the cut-rate gas station was doing a fair business with out-of-state cars. And, in the front of the Roman Columns Motel, on the lawn, a woman in shorts sat reading a magazine.

Getting out of his car he strolled around, gazing into the shop windows. Most of the stores had been there all his life, but he saw them now from a different perspective; he was not a kid or even a customer but a potential business-equal wanting to open up his own place. And it was not a dream but a very real, close possibility.

Down at the corner, in his drugstore, Mr. Hagopian puttered about with a display of insect repellent. There goes the fat old man, Bruce thought. Still glum. If he saw me he'd revert to being sore at me. As long as he lives.

I wonder, he thought, what old man Hagopian would think if I opened up a store next to his.

Will he have a heart attack? Will he chase me around with a broom? Or, he thought, maybe he'll be unable to understand that it's me.

Hands in his pockets he wandered on, across the railroad tracks and then back past the abandoned warehouses. On the bench at the train station an elderly man with a cane sat slapping at the long-winged lake flies that gathered in the afternoon air.

Far off on the highway a truck horn tooted.

IN AUGUST they closed up the store in Boise and moved everything to Montario. They had rented what had formerly been the town's older hardware store. It had been vacant for months, a narrow, dust-begrimed building squeezed in between a Scandinavian bakery and a laundry. But rent was low. And they did not have to buy any of the fixtures; the owner let them simply rip out the ancient counters and lighting and throw everything away.

Early in the morning he and his wife arrived wearing old clothes. First they scoured and then they painted. And then, using basalt blocks and mortar, he built a new front the length of the display window. He put up a sturdy stone window box for shrubs and planted a couple of evergreens and some short-stemmed perennials. And finally he took off the door and mounted in its place a modern glass and copper door with a star-shaped lock.

Business, almost from the start, flowed in satisfactorily. But during the second or third month he became conscious of something that neither he nor Susan had anticipated. Nothing in the town interested him any longer. Even operating his own business there had a monotony to it; the same old Hill Street from his childhood confronting him every day, and the same Idaho farmers, and even with a good steady business he would never be really happy. So he began to cast around, trying to stir up some new opportunity. Now, for the first time, he began to think in terms of a real move; not just down the highway a dozen miles, but a move perhaps to a city he had never seen before, another state entirely.

And, too, this was still Milton Lumky territory.

One afternoon Lumky dropped by with his leather satchel, on his official rounds for the Whalen Paper Company.

"Where's your car?" Susan said. "I don't see it."

"I sold it," Milt said. "Too hard to get service for it out on the road." He pointed out the window at a foreign sedan parked at the curb. "I traded it in on a Swedish car."

"Won't you have trouble getting service on a Swedish car?" Bruce asked. They walked outdoors, to the far side of the street, to view the car.

"It's new," Milt said. "It won't need service."

From where they stood they could see Susan inside the office, at work behind one of the desks.

"How'd you happen to locate yourselves in a dinky out-of-the-way town like Montario?" Milt asked him.

Bruce said, "I was born here. I grew up here."

"That's right. You're an Idaho boy. I keep picturing you as a big-city man. Wasn't that discount place of yours down in Reno?" Pondering, Milt said, "Somebody else lived here for a while. Yes, it was Susan. She told me once she used to teach grammar school here."

"I was in her fifth grade class," Bruce said.

A slow expression appeared on Milt's face, a register of disbelief. "Is that the truth?"

"Yes," he said.

"I never know when to believe you. You get a big boot out of saying things to shock people."

"I don't see what's shocking about that," Bruce said.

They meandered back toward the store, and then Lumky, still battling away inside himself with his emotions, said, "Did you know that when you married her?"

"Sure," he said.

"How about her?"

"Sure," he said. And then a malicious delight seized him; he could not restrain himself. "That's why we got married," he said.

With horrified suspicion, Milt said, "What do you mean?"

"I mean we fulfilled our childhood attachment for each other. At the time it wasn't possible since she was in her twenties and I was only eleven."

"What sort of attachment?" They had by now entered the store. The posture that Milt had taken caused Susan to look up from her work. Milt said to her, "Is it true you were his fifth grade teacher?"

"Oh yes," Susan said. She glanced at Bruce, and they exchanged an irresponsible amusement. Without hesitation she took up where he had left off; she saw the whole situation. "He was my favorite pupil. I don't mean because he was bright. I mean because he was so mature, and by that I mean he was so sexually attractive."

Milt could say nothing.

"I still have a picture of him when he was eleven," Susan said, in her calm, reasonable voice. "When it was possible, I had him sit up at my desk with me while I taught the class. But even so we had to wait. We saw each other secretly over the years. He used to visit me at my house when he was in high school. That was almost old enough; we came very close to consummating it then. But we still had to wait just a little longer. Do you want to see the picture?"

"No," Milt muttered.

"It was worth waiting," Susan said. "The longer you hold off the better it is. Isn't that right, Bruce?" she said.

Milt's discomfort had become so obvious that they stopped. But Milt remained gloomy and taciturn, hanging around the rest of the afternoon, unable to leave but not able to converse any more with them. Finally he said good-bye and went out to his parked Swedish car. Waving, but not looking in their direction, he started up and drove off.

"We shouldn't have teased him," Bruce said. But it had been fun. They had enjoyed doing it, and now they smiled at each other. If we had a chance, he realized, we would do it again.

Later on in the month he got wind of something from a salesman who had driven up from Colorado. In Denver a typewriter shop was up for sale, a small place the owner of which had been killed in an auto accident. The man's relatives had no taste for the business and they hadn't set much of a price on it. According to the salesman, there were several good franchises that came along with it, plus a modern front and fixtures, and not too moldy an inventory. And Denver was expanding every day.

If the place was any kind of buy it might get snapped up by someone else, he realized. So now he did not drive; he took a plane. A relative of the deceased owner met him at the Denver airport and they drove to the store together. It had a neon sign, and the rather new cash register alone was worth four hundred dollars. Most of the inventory was made up of expensive office model machines, but he did not doubt that he could trade them back to the manufacturers for lower priced models. He liked the location; of course he did not know Denver, but the business district seemed active, and he saw plenty of traffic. And the other stores, especially those on the same side of the street, seemed quite modern and well-tended.

He flew back to Boise, picked up his car and drove to Montario, and discussed the Denver store with Susan. With him he had brought back pictures of it; he showed them to her and she agreed that it looked good. And they did need something else. The Montario store was not enough.

"Should I sell my house in Boise?" she asked. They had rented it out, thinking that they might someday decide to go back there.

"Sell it," he said. "We'll sell everything here. It's too far to transport anything from here to Denver. Anyhow, the place has better fixtures than we have here."

"Won't we take a loss if we sell out here?"

"We didn't take a loss when we sold the R & J Mimeographing Service," he said.

She nodded. "Do you want to make an offer on the Denver place, then? I haven't seen it, but if you think it's what we want, and you think we can get rid of our place here —" She smiled at him. "I'll leave it up to you."

"I'll make them an offer," he said. We'll see what comes of it."

Through their attorney Fancourt they offered the Denver people twelve thousand dollars for the inventory, fixtures, franchises, lease, and location. After weeks of quibbling, the Denver people accepted their offer.

Toward the end of the year they completed arrangements to sell the Montario Typewriter Center and take over the Denver place. The whole thing dragged on, since the Denver store — called the Colorado Office Equipment Company — comprised part of an estate divided between a number of heirs. But finally everything had been untangled. He and Susan made a final trip back to Montario, and then they took up the proprietorship in Denver. And that was that.

BUSINESS, in Denver, worked out well and they could see that if they kept at it long enough they would have what they wanted. By degrees Susan retired from the store and he took it over on his own. He bought what he felt he could sell, and the store's policies were his; she did not complain about his handling and each of them was able to take a relaxed position with the other when they were home together at night. They bought a house in Denver; Taffy entered the Denver public school system; they came to realize that they had done the right thing and that probably there would be no basic changes from now on. They would continue in the retail typewriter business in Denver, and they would live in terms of each other as they were doing as long as nothing happened to either of them, or, for that matter, to the country and the society around them. If the world in which they were living managed to maintain itself, they could probably maintain their store and house and family. Their doubts, over the months, diminished and were gone. At no particular time the last anxiety left them. They were not even conscious of it; it occurred naturally, in the course of the regular working day.

The following summer Bruce heard from a roundabout source that Milt Lumky had died.

He still had Cathy Hermes' address in Pocatello, so he and Susan wrote her. A week or so passed and then they got a letter from her, giving them some of the details about his death.

According to Cathy he had died of his Bright's disease. She thought that it could have been avoided if he had taken care of himself. In the letter Bruce read an oblique bitterness directed toward him, but probably directed toward everyone else as well, everything that had to do with Milt, including Milt himself. Several times in the letter she upbraided Milt and herself in retrospect. Milt should have given up traveling around his territory, first of all. He should have taken a desk job somewhere, so he could go to the bathroom when he needed to, and rest when he needed to. Her fixation on those points showed up again and again in her letter. The best thing would have been if she could have gotten a divorce and then Milt and she could have married and settled down in Pocatello. After Bruce and Susan had gotten married, she said, Milt had talked about it, but at last he had stopped talking about it. And it had never come up again.

Other than that the letter was filled with formal phrases. She seemed matter-of-fact about his death.

A day or so later their telephone at home rang, and when Susan answered it he heard her say, "Maybe you better talk to Bruce."

"Who is it?" he said, getting up from his chair.

With an odd expression on her face, Susan said, "It's Cathy Hermes, calling long-distance from Pocatello." As he started into the hall toward the phone she said, "It's something about money."

"What money?" he said.

"You better talk to her," she said.

He picked up the receiver and said hello. "This is Mrs. Hermes," a woman's voice said in his ear. "I wanted to ask you something, Mr. Stevens." After beating around the bush, Cathy at last said that Milt, before his death, had told her about different people who owed him money, and that he had mentioned several times that Bruce owed him five hundred dollars.

"Did he say what for?" he asked, with mixed reactions.

Cathy said, "He told me he loaned it to you to buy something. I don't want to pester you for it, but if you want to do something for him now that he's gone, maybe you could give it to me." She explained to him at great length how close she and Milt had been.

"Let me talk to my wife," Bruce said. "Can I call you in a day or so or write you?"

With the obvious conviction that she would never see the money, Cathy said, "Anything you and Susan do is perfectly satisfactory with me. You understand there's nothing written down about it."

"Yes," he said. He told her he was glad to hear from her, and then he hung up.

"Does she say you borrowed it?" Susan said. "He gave it to you, didn't he?"

"He gave it to both of us," he said. "As a wedding gift."

"Do you suppose he told her it was just a loan? Maybe he forgot he gave it to us, or he changed his mind. You know how he was."

Getting out the bills that had come in during the last week, he sat down and began figuring out their immediate financial obligations. "We can do it," he decided finally. "But it would be a lot easier on us if we could divide it into two portions, a month apart. Two-fifty this month and the rest next month."

"Do what you want," Susan said, with a tremor of uneasiness. "If you feel it won't put us in a bad situation. I'll let you decide."

"I'll write her a check and stick it in the mail right away," he said. That was the only way he could bring himself to hand out any money to anyone; in the last year or so he had picked up a stern habit of keeping a tight control on all expenses.

"She must need it," Susan said, "or she wouldn't have done a thing like that. Calling up and asking for it."

In the end he mailed off a check to Cathy Hermes for the full five hundred dollars. But it brought him no sense of relief.

Death, he thought, has always been remote from me. My parents are both alive. My brother, too. The closest it ever came, in the past, was when Mrs. Jaffey became ill, left the Garret A. Hobart Grammar School, and finally passed on. And then of course we got this store in Denver because a man we never saw died in an auto accident. But it's never had a decisive influence on anything affecting me.

For a moment he thought, Is it possible that Milt went around complaining about money? Complaining because I didn't pay it back?

Anyhow, he thought, now it's only a plain flat sum that somebody I barely know wants and that has to come out of our books, like any other five-hundred-dollar outlay. His reasons for giving it to me — those are gone. Vanished. I never knew; Cathy Hermes doesn't care; and Milt himself is in no position to think about it one way or another.

But it's too bad, he thought, that I'll always have that hanging over me. Never having known what it was that Milt really meant or felt; whether he changed his mind, or whether he simply did not mean what he said. I didn't understand him. There was not enough contact.

It occurred to him, then, that outside of Milton Lumky he had never had any friends at all, and certainly he had none now. Susan and the store made up his entire existence. Was that intentional on his part? Or had he allowed it to drift into that?

As far as I'm concerned, he decided, they're enough. Whether it's right or not. It's what I want.

In the kitchen, washing the dinner dishes, Susan said, "Bruce. I want to ask you something. Don't you miss him?"

"No," he said.

"Are you sure?"

He said, "I've got too much to think about to miss anybody."

"I'll try to make it up to you," she said. "Tying you down while you're so young. It's a dreadful thing when an older woman does that."

He considered that.

"You could have plowed through one state after another, you and Milt in your cars," she said. "Had different women; you know."

"I know," he said.

"And here you are, at twenty-six, with a wife ten years older than you, and a step-daughter, and a house and a business to manage. I woke up the other night and I had to get out of bed and go off by myself; I was shivering all over. I sat up for an hour or so. Did you notice that?"

"No," he said. He had not awakened.

Susan said, "Do you still think you might walk off and leave me someday?" She gazed at him. "I don't think I could stand that. In fact I know I couldn't."

"You mean," he said, "am I going to die of a kidney ailment because I don't go to the bathroom often enough during the working day?"

"When you drove down to Reno to sell the Japanese machines to Mr. von Scharf," she said. "I was positive you wouldn't come back."

"Is that why you called?"

"Maybe," she said.

He laughed.

"I was so glad to see you when you came back," she said. "I didn't care if you had the machines with you or not."

"I see," he said. But he did not believe her. But it wasn't important. He had come back, and he was here now.

"I had my good times," he said. "Before we were married. Or don't you remember Peg Googer?"

Still gazing at him she said, "Are you happy with me?"

"Yes," he said.

At that moment Taffy rushed into the kitchen in her bathrobe and slippers, pleading to be allowed to watch a television program to its end. And after that, she informed them, she would go to bed.

The program had to do with action aboard submarines, and he went in to look at it with her. They sat together on the couch, facing the television set. In the peacefulness of the living room he basked and relaxed and half-dozed. The adventures beneath the water, the submarine fighting for its life against dim sea monsters and Soviet atomic mines, and, later on, the cowboys and spacemen and detectives and all the endless thrilling noisy western adventures, retreated from him. He heard his wife in the kitchen and he was aware of the child beside him, and that brought him his happiness.

The world's greatest novelists now available in
paperback from Grafton Books

Jack Kerouac

Big Sur	£2.50	☐
Visions of Cody	£2.50	☐
Doctor Sax	£1.95	☐
Lonesome Traveller	£2.50	☐
Desolation Angels	£1.95	☐
The Dharma Bums	£2.50	☐
The Subterraneans and Pic	£1.50	☐
Maggie Cassidy	£1.50	☐
Vanity of Duluoz	£1.95	☐

Norman Mailer

Cannibals and Christians (non-fiction)	£1.50	☐
The Presidential Papers	£1.50	☐
Advertisements for Myself	£2.95	☐
The Naked and The Dead	£2.95	☐
The Deer Park	£2.95	☐

Henry Miller

Black Spring	£1.95	☐
Tropic of Cancer	£2.95	☐
Tropic of Capricorn	£2.95	☐
Nexus	£3.50	☐
Sexus	£2.50	☐
Plexus	£2.95	☐
The Air-Conditioned Nightmare	£2.50	☐

Luke Rhinehart

The Dice Man	£2.95	☐
The Long Voyage Back	£1.95	☐

To order direct from the publisher just tick the titles you want
and fill in the order form.   **GF281**

The world's greatest novelists now available in paperback from Grafton Books

Angus Wilson

Such Darling Dodos	£1.50	☐
Late Call	£1.95	☐
The Wrong Set	£1.95	☐
For Whom the Cloche Tolls	£1.25	☐
A Bit Off the Map	£1.50	☐
As If By Magic	£2.50	☐
Hemlock and After	£1.50	☐
No Laughing Matter	£1.95	☐
The Old Men at the Zoo	£1.95	☐
The Middle Age of Mrs Eliot	£1.95	☐
Setting the World on Fire	£1.95	☐
Anglo-Saxon Attitudes	£2.95	☐
The Strange Ride of Rudyard Kipling (non-fiction)	£1.95	☐
The World of Charles Dickens (non-fiction)	£3.95	☐

John Fowles

The Ebony Tower	£2.50	☐
The Collector	£1.95	☐
The French Lieutenant's Woman	£2.50	☐
The Magus	£2.95	☐
Daniel Martin	£3.95	☐
Mantissa	£2.50	☐
The Aristos (non-fiction)	£2.50	☐

Brian Moore

The Lonely Passion of Judith Hearne	£2.50	☐
I am Mary Dunne	£1.50	☐
Catholics	£1.50	☐
Fergus	£1.50	☐
The Temptation of Eileen Hughes	£1.50	☐
The Feast of Lupercal	£1.50	☐
Cold Heaven	£2.50	☐

To order direct from the publisher just tick the titles you want and fill in the order form. **GF581**

The world's greatest novelists now available in paperback from Grafton Books

Kurt Vonnegut

Breakfast of Champions	£2.50	☐
Mother Night	£1.95	☐
Slaughterhouse 5	£2.50	☐
Player Piano	£2.50	☐
Welcome to the Monkey House	£1.95	☐
God Bless You, Mr Rosewater	£2.50	☐
Happy Birthday, Wanda June	£1.95	☐
Slapstick	£2.50	☐
Wampeters Foma & Granfalloons (non-fiction)	£2.50	☐
Between Time and Timbuktu (illustrated)	£2.95	☐
Jailbird	£1.95	☐
Palm Sunday	£1.95	☐
Deadeye Dick	£1.95	☐

John Barth

The Sot-Weed Factor	£3.95	☐
Giles Goat-Boy	£2.95	☐
The Floating Opera	£2.50	☐
Letters	£3.95	☐
Sabbatical	£2.50	☐

Tim O'Brien

If I Die in a Combat Zone	£1.95	☐

To order direct from the publisher just tick the titles you want and fill in the order form. **GF481**

The world's greatest novelists now available in paperback from Grafton Books

Gore Vidal
The American Quartet

Lincoln	£2.50	☐
Washington DC	£2.50	☐
Burr	£2.95	☐
1876	£2.95	☐

Other Titles

A Thirsty Evil	£1.50	☐
The Judgement of Paris	£2.50	☐
Two Sisters	£1.25	☐
Myron	£1.95	☐
Myra Breckinridge	£2.50	☐
Messiah	£2.50	☐
Williwaw	£2.50	☐
Kalki	£2.50	☐
A Search for the King	£1.25	☐
Dark Green, Bright Red	£1.25	☐
In A Yellow Wood	£1.25	☐
On Our Own Now (Collected Essays 1952–1972)	£1.50	☐
Matters of Fact and of Fiction (Essays 1973–1976)	£1.50	☐
Pink Triangle & Yellow Star	£1.95	☐
Creation	£2.95	☐
Duluth	£1.95	☐

To order direct from the publisher just tick the titles you want and fill in the order form.

GF681

The world's greatest novelists now available in paperback from Grafton Books

John Barth
The Sot-Weed Factor	£3.95	☐
Giles Goat-Boy	£2.95	☐
The Floating Opera	£2.50	☐
Letters	£3.95	☐
Sabbatical	£2.50	☐

John Banville
Kepler	£1.95	☐
Dr Copernicus	£2.50	☐
Birchwood	£1.95	☐
The Newton Letter	£1.95	☐

Christopher Hope
Private Parts	£1.95	☐
A Separate Development	£1.95	☐

To order direct from the publisher just tick the titles you want and fill in the order form.　　　GF881

Fiction in Paladin

The Businessman: A Tale of Terror £2.95 ☐
Thomas M. Disch
'Each of the sixty short chapters of THE BUSINESSMAN is a *tour de force* of polished, distanced, sly narrative art . . . always the vision of America stays with us: melancholic, subversive and perfectly put . . . In this vision lies the terror of THE BUSINESSMAN'
Times Literary Supplement

'An entertaining nightmare out of Thomas Berger and Stephen King'
Time

Filthy English £2.95 ☐
Jonathan Meades
'Incest and lily-boys, loose livers and ruched red anal compulsives, rape, murder and literary looting . . . Meades tosses off quips, cracks and crossword clues, stirs up the smut and stuffs in the erudition, pokes you in the ribs and prods you in the kidneys (as in Renal, home of Irene and Albert) . . . a delicious treat (full of fruit and nuts) for the vile and filthy mind to savour'
Time Out

Dancing with Mermaids £2.95 ☐
Miles Gibson
'An excellent, imaginative comic tale . . . an original and wholly entertaining fiction . . . extremely funny and curiously touching'
Cosmopolitan

'The impact of the early Ian McEwan or Martin Amis, electrifying, a dazzler'
Financial Times

'It is as if Milk Wood had burst forth with those obscene-looking blossoms one finds in sweaty tropical palm houses . . . murder and mayhem decked out in fantastic and erotic prose'
The Times

To order direct from the publisher just tick the titles you want and fill in the order form.

Original Fiction in Paladin

Paper Thin £2.95 ☐
Philip First
From the author of THE GREAT PERVADER: a wonderfully original
collection of stories about madness, love, passion, violence, sex and
humour.

Don Quixote £2.95 ☐
Kathy Acker
From the author of BLOOD AND GUTS IN HIGH SCHOOL: a
visionary collage–novel in which Don Quixote is a woman on an
intractable quest; a late twentieth-century LEVIATHAN; a stingingly
powerful and definitely unique novel.

To order direct from the publisher just tick the titles you want
and fill in the order form. **PF2**

Fiction in Paladin

In the Shadow of the Wind £2.95 ☐
Anne Hébert
Winner of the Prix Femina
'A bewitching and savage novel . . . there is constant magic in it'
Le Matin

'Beautifully written with great simplicity and originality . . . an
unusual and haunting novel'
London Standard

Love is a Durable Fire £2.95 ☐
Brian Burland
'Burland has the power to evoke time and place with total authority
. . . compelling . . . the stuff of which real literature is made'
Irish Times

To order direct from the publisher just tick the titles you want
and fill in the order form.

The world's greatest science fiction authors
now available in paperback from Grafton Books

Ray Bradbury

Fahrenheit 451	£2.50	☐
The Small Assassin	£2.50	☐
The October Country	£1.50	☐
The Illustrated Man	£1.95	☐
The Martian Chronicles	£1.95	☐
Dandelion Wine	£1.50	☐
The Golden Apples of the Sun	£1.95	☐
Something Wicked This Way Comes	£2.50	☐
The Machineries of Joy	£1.50	☐
Long After Midnight	£1.95	☐
The Stories of Ray Bradbury (Volume 1)	£3.95	☐
The Stories of Ray Bradbury (Volume 2)	£3.95	☐

Philip K Dick

Flow My Tears, The Policeman Said	£1.95	☐
Blade Runner (Do Androids Dream of Electric Sheep?)	£1.95	☐
Now Wait for Last Year	£1.95	☐
The Zap Gun	£1.95	☐
A Handful of Darkness	£1.50	☐
A Maze of Death	£1.50	☐
Ubik	£1.95	☐
Our Friends from Frolix 8	£1.95	☐
Clans of the Alphane Moon	£1.95	☐
The Transmigration of Timothy Archer	£1.95	☐
A Scanner Darkly	£1.95	☐
The Three Stigmata of Palmer Eldrich	£1.95	☐
The Penultimate Truth	£1.95	☐
We Can Build You	£2.50	☐

To order direct from the publisher just tick the titles you want
and fill in the order form.

SF981

All these books are available at your local bookshop or newsagent, or can be ordered direct from the publisher.

To order direct from the publishers just tick the titles you want and fill in the form below.

Name _____

Address _____

_____

Send to:
Paladin Cash Sales
PO Box 11, Falmouth, Cornwall TR10 9EN.

Please enclose remittance to the value of the cover price plus:

UK 55p for the first book, 22p for the second book plus 14p per copy for each additional book ordered to a maximum charge of £1.75.

BFPO and Eire 55p for the first book, 22p for the second book plus 14p per copy for the next 7 books, thereafter 8p per book.

Overseas £1.25 for the first book and 31p for each additional book.

Paladin Books reserve the right to show new retail prices on covers, which may differ from those previously advertised in the text or elsewhere.